ATUNIS GALAXY ANTHOLOGY – 2022

ANTHOLOGY OF CONTEMPORARY WORLD POETRY
ATUNIS POETRY

Demer Press

Edition: 2022

Copyright: all poets, contributors

Cover: Mordechai Geldman

ISBN: 978-1-304-80391-7

ATUNIS GALAXY ANTHOLOGY – 2022

ANTHOLOGY OF CONTEMPORARY
WORLD POETRY
ATUNIS POETRY

LEADERSHIP STAFF:

Editor in Chief: Agron Shele
https://atunispoetry.com
Deputy Editor in Chief: Hannie Rouweler
　　　　　　　　　　　Alicja Kuberska
　　　　　　　　　　　Sunita Paul
Deputy Editor in Chief : Hasije Selishta Kryeziu
　　　　　　　　　　　Susana Roberts
Editor: Raimonda Moisiu & Dr. Claudia Piccino
Responsible for Literary Information: Merita Paparisto
Responsible for Literary Information: Eden S Trinidad
Consultant: Peter Tase https://petertase.com/
Consultant: Lumo Kolleshi & Leda García Pérez
Literary Editor: Enertin Dheskali
Graphics: Irina Hysi & Mordechai Geldman

Advisory Board: Dr. Maria Miraglia, Caroline Nazareno-Gabis, Juljana Mehmeti, Günsel Djemal, Roula Pollard, Sinan Vaka, Dr. Eftichia Kapardeli, Shefqete Gosalci, Lumo Kolleshi, Luz María López, Rami Kamberi, Leyla Işık, NilavroNill Shoovro, Milica Jeftimijević Lilić.

Every Collaboration: Dr. Aprilia Zank, Irina Hysi, Alicia Minjarez Ramírez, Elvira Kujović, Alisa Velaj, Bilall M. Maliqi, Kujtim Morina, Dr. Tarana Turan Rahimli, Luan Maloku, Anton Gojcaj.

WITH ATUNIS IS WELCOMED
A PUBLICATION OF POETICAL GALAXY ATUNIS

Table of Contents

A
Adolf P. Shvedchikov (Russia)
Ann Christine Tabaka (USA)
Agron Shele (Albania–Belgium)
Alicja Maria Kuberska (Poland)
Alexander Pak (Uzbekistan)
Antje Stehn (Germany)
Alexey Kalakutin (Russia)
Allison Grayhurst (Canada)
Anastasia N. Margeti (Greece)
Ali Al Hazmi (Saudi Arabia)
Agnieszka Herman (Poland)
Dr. Alicia Minjarez Ramírez (Mexico)
Anila Varfi (Albania)
Amy Barry (Ireland)
Abdukakhor Kosim (Tajikistan)
Aviva Golan (Israel)
Ajne Iberhysaj (Kosova)
Alessandra Corbetta (Italy)
Agnieszka Jarzębowska (Poland)
Alexa Prada (Costa Rica)
Anna Maria Sprzęczka-Stępień (Poland)
Andrea Tavares de Sousa (Cape Verde)

B
Borche Panov (North Macedonia)
Basudhara Roy (India)

C
Chen Hsiu-chen 陳秀珍 (Taiwan）
Christopher Okemwa (Kenya)
Caroline Nazareno – Gabis (Philippines)

D
Dinos Koubatis (Greece)
Duška Vrhovac (Serbia)

Dr. Deepti Gupta (India)
Daniela Andonovska Trjakovska (North Macedonia)
Darcie Friesen Hossack (Canada)

E
Ekaterini Vlachopanagiotou Batalia (Greece)
Ekene May (Nigeria)
Evgenia Tagareva (Bulgaria)
Eduard Harents (Armenia)
Eden Soriano Trinidad (Philippines)
Eva Petropoulou Lianoy (Greece)
Emna Copedi (Colombia)
Eltona Lakuriqi (Albania)
Enxhi Drapi (Albania)

F
Florin M. Ciocea (Romania)
Faleeha Hassan (Iraq)
F. Attila Balázs (Hungary)

G
Gopal Lahiri (India)
Gianpaolo G. Mastropzsqua (Italy)
Gloria Sofia (Cape Verde)
Ganu Ganev (Bulgaria)

H
Hannie Rouweler (Netherlands)
Hasije Selishta – Kryeziu (Kosova)
Hassanal Abdullah (Bangladesh–USA)
Halmosi Sándor (Hungary)
Hana Xhihani (Albania–France)
Hussein Habasch (Kurdistan)

I
Isilda Nunes (Portugal)
Irma Kurti (Albania – Italy)
Isabelle Berck (Belgium)
Imen Melliti (Tunisia)

Irina-Roxana Georgescu (Romania)

J
Jose Sarria (Spain)
Juljana Mehmeti (Albania-Italy)
Jose Luis Rubio (Spain)
Jana Orlová (Czech Republic)
John Guzlowski (USA)
Joanna Kalinowska (Poland)
Job Degenaar (Netherlands)
Janaq Jano (Albania)
Jaydeep Sarangi (India)
Jeanette Esmeralda Tiburcio Márquez (Jeanette Eureka)-(Mexico)
José María Zonta (Costa Rica)

K
Krishna Prasai (Nepal)
Katarina Saric (Montenegro)
Kari Krenn (Argentina)
Kazimierz Burnat (Poland)
Kamrul Islam (Bangladesh)

L
Lucia Daramus (Romania-UK)
Lidia Chiarelli (Italy)
Liang Shenling (China)
Ledia Dushi (Albania)
Luca Ariano (Italy)
Linda. S. Goldberg (USA)
Leda García Pérez (Costa Rica)
Laura Garavaglia (Italy)
Leoreta Xhaferi (Albania)
Lyubka Slavova (Bulgaria)
Lali Tsipi Michaeli (Israel)
Lily Swarn (India)
Lilla Latus (Poland)

M
Prof. Dr. Academic Milutin Đuričković (Serbia)

Maram al-Masri (Syria–France)
Mark Meekers (Belgium)
Moaen Shalabia (Palestine)
Maria do Sameiro Barroso (Portugal)
Mahmoud Said Kawash (Palestine)
Michela Zanarella (Italy)
Mordechai Geldman (Israel)
Prof. Masudul Hoq (Bangladesh)
Merita Paparisto (Albania-Canada)
Małgorzata Borzeszkowska (Poland)
Metin Cengiz (Turkey)
Mariela Cordero (Venezuela)
Prof. Migena Arllati (Albania)
Maria Del Castillo Sucerquia (Colombia)
Mbizo Chirasha (Zimbabwe)
Marija Najthefer Popov (Serbia)
Marianella Sáenz Mora (Costa Rica)
Miljana Živanovič (Croatia–Switzerland)
Mario Meléndez (Chile)
Marion de Vos-Hoekstra (Netherlands)
Maria Dayana Fraile (Venezuela)
Majlinda Zeqiri-Shaqiri (Kosova)
Mónika Tóth (Romania)

N
Ngoc Le Ninh (Vietnam)
Nevin Koçoğlu (Turkey)
Nina Lys Affane (Algeria)
Nahid Ensafpour (Iran-Germany)
Nurie Emrullai (North Macedonia)
Nigar Arif (Azerbaijan)

O
Olga Lalić – Krowicka (Serbia-Poland)

P
Panagiota Christopoulou-Zaloni (Greece)
Petraq Risto (Albania–USA)

Padmaja Iyengar-Paddy (India)
Pankhuri Sinha (India)

R
Rudina Çupi (Albania)
Rahman Shaari (Malaysia)
Rozalia Aleksandrova (Bulgaria)
Ricardo Plata (Mexico)
Rajashree Mohapatra (India)

S
Susana Roberts (Argentina)
Stanislav Penev (Bulgaria)
Sunita Paul (India)
Prof. Sungrye Han (South Korea)
Satis Shroff (Germany)
Sophy Chen (China)
Silvana Kühtz (Italy)
Stefania Miola (Italy)
Dr. Salma Naimi (Algeria)
Smaragdi Mitropoulou (Greece)
Sylwia K. Malinowska (Poland)
Sakineh Asadzadeh (Iran)
Senem Gökel (Cyprus)
Slavka Bozovic (Montenegro)
Sirojiddin Sayyid (Uzbekistan)
Sue Zhu (淑文) (New Zealand)
Sofia Doko Arapaj (Albania)
Shikdar Mohammed Kibriah (Bangladesh)
Shanita Vichare (India)
Shoshana Vegh (Israel)
Shurouk Hammod (Syria)
Shodiya Sultonova (Uzbekistan)

T
Teresa Jolanta Podemska – Abt (Australia)
Tadeusz Zawadowski (Poland)
Tatiana Koshkina (Russia)
Tareq al Karmy (Palestine)

Taghrid Fayad (Lebanon)
Tuğçe Tekhanlı (Cyprus)

V
Dr. Verónica Valadez Lopez (Mexico)
Viacheslav Kupriyanov (Russia)
Vesna Mundishevska-Veljanovska (North Macedonia)
Vesna Andrejić Mišković (Croatia)

W
Wang Mengren (China)
Wansoo Kim (South Korea)
Wendy Mary Lister (UK)

X
Xi Ke (China)

Y
Yuleisy Cruz Lezcano (Cuba–Italy)
Yordanka Getsova (Bulgaria)

Z
Dr. Zejnepe Alili – Rexhepi (North Macedonia)

Painters

Jacqueline Ripstein (USA)
Mar Thieriot (Canada)
Paola Iotti (Italy)
Miradije Ramiqi (Kosova)
Emine Tokmakkaya (Turkey)
Irina Hysi. MA (Albania)
Giorgio Fileni (Italy)
Rajashree Mohapatra (India)

Introduction – Editorial Staff of "ATUNIS"

***

Atunis Anthology - 2022 experiences its fifth anniversary and certainly comes as the input and novelty of the whole contemporary spirit of postmodern poetry today.

Why was it considered a calendar publication a year ago?

Therefore are the creators the messengers of what will come tomorrow, the sensibility and the mosaic of another season, the sudden silence and explosion at the extreme limits, the meditations and emotions which overstep the present.
Writing is the same as traveling through the infinity of souls, while reflecting on it is the same as touching and feeling the highest levels of your breath.

Let's imagine for a while the disciples of the written word, looking at the view of today's world through their candle and understand and believe as well that our whole morphosis is just a vision born in the eyes of the brain and hidden sources continuing the everlasting journey of universal's forms and shapes.

Editor in Chief: Agron Shele

Poets and their worldviews

The world of most poets is a microcosm in itself, touching the ends of existence. You even can speak of a microcosm in a grain of sand. The amount of poems written by poets does not play a decisive role, but after years of intensive work many often put together a whole oeuvre. In addition to collections of poetry also novels, stories, essays, which give you a good insight into the content, writing style, and themes of each poet.

We must be extremely grateful to translators, as without translations it would not be possible to become acquainted with the work of a wide variety of poets from various countries, each bringing their own personal and individual aspects, culture and history into their work.

As a publisher, I am very pleased to see that the torch is being passed on from generation to generation and that more and more poems, however different they may be, are linked to other poems from other regions, as well as connections are found with other artistic expressions: painting and sculpture - visual poems -, music, dance, and all other forms. They share something in common: the source.

In these rapidly changing times, really in every area, it is not always easy for publishers to determine what they can and want to edit, especially now that so many digital possibilities, e books, e magazines, exist and paper publications seem less important. Yet there are many people outside poets themselves, including the readers, who hold the book's existence very seriously. I am one of them too. A book is tangible, you can easily browse through a book, a book is a precious asset. Especially when it concerns an anthology of world poetry, it is a gigantic enjoyment to taking notice of all those wonderful poems at your leisure and at a convenient time.

You can put the book in a bag, it travels with you to all conceivable places, a village, a big city, on holidays in a vacation house, on the train, along the beach, in a forest area, on an endless plain with a view of flat landscapes or high mountains.

A poetry book feels at home everywhere.

Deputy Editor in Chief: Hannie Rouweler

Poetry and Atunis

The word Poetry derives from a Greek word poesies, which means in a "making". Poetry is a unique art of literacy, but it doesn't have a clear definition of what it is. It is said that poetry uses a fictional plot, a specialized language, and it is written in a special form (style). When writing poems, authors try to express their thoughts in less space using that "specialized language", not compare to novels and short stories that use much more space.

Poetry is an ancient art of literacy, before people use to carve poetry in the caves, and that is known to exist long before. There are many poets, and uncountable written poems thought the time, but there isn't a clear definition of what poetry is. Although, many poets have their "own" definition of poetry. For example Paul Engle definition of poetry is: "Poetry is boned with ideas, nerved and blooded with emotions, all held together by the delicate, tough skin of words" (Poetry America, 2009) by Paul Engle. Another quote by Aristotle: "Poetry is more philosophical and of higher value than history; for poetry tends to express the universal, history the particular" (Poetry America, 2009).

Even though it is difficult to define poetry, most people are able to recognize it when they see it. It is worth remembering that poetry especially in the form of the song is one of the oldest forms of artistic expression, it is much older than prose and is seems to originate in a human impulse that reached for expression in joy, grief, doubt, hope, loneliness, love, etc. For example, the National Anthems are poems, that are turned into songs or the Anthem that express so much feeling, about joy, victory of being proud of their heroes and their Nation.

Poetry expresses complex meanings & feelings in compact forms. To understand the multiple meanings the poet wanted to express, you should examine all words & phrases in the lines from different aspects.

Atunis collects poetry that have greatly influenced the world. Written by poets and critics from a wide range of historical, cultural, and aesthetic perspectives, the Atunis anthology addresses the purpose of poetry, the possibilities of language, and the role of the poets in the world.

Sunita Paul - Founder of AABS Publishing House
www.aabspublishinghouse.com
www.sunitapaul.in

©Jacqueline Ripstein (USA) "Footprints", 1984

www.Jacquelineripstein.com

Art & Healing Pioneer & World Peace Envoy
United Nations ECOSOC Representative of the International Association of Educators for World Peace. International renowned Fine Art Artist /Author. WorldPeace Envoy
For 39 yrs. she has inspired thousands of people across the world. With more than 380 International shows. Born in Mexico, self-taught, won a national Prismacolor diploma at 12 yrs. old.
A unique creative that has dared cross the boundaries of the traditional Art schools, to create New Invisible Art techniques as: Invisible Art & Light tech. ©(pat.1986). Her deep desire has been to reveal the unseen dimensions and to offer a breath of hope to our humanity. Her art reveals the Light within all of us and the Invisible dimensions that create our everyday lives.

Adolf P. Shvedchikov (Russia)

In 2013 he was nominated for the Nobel Prize for Literature

Adolf P. Shvedchikov is a Russian scientist, poet and translator. Born in 1937 in Russia, he graduated from Moscow State University, Department of Chemistry. He was a Senior researcher at the Institute of Chemical Physics, Russian Academy of Sciences, Moscow. Since 1997 he has been chief chemist at the company Pulsatron Technology Corporation, Los Angeles, California. He is a Doctor of Literature, World Academy of Arts and Letters. He has published more than 150 scientific papers and many of his poems have been published in international poetry magazines in Russia, the USA, Brazil, India, China, Korea, Japan, Italy, Malta, Spain, France, Greece, England and Australia. He has also published 13 books of poetry. His poems have been translated into Italian, Spanish, Portuguese, Greek, Chinese, Japanese, and Hindi. He is a Member of the International Society of Poets, of the World Congress of Poets, of the International Association of Writers and Artists, of the A. L. I. A. S. (Italian-Australian Literary Writers' Association, Melbourne, Australia). He is known for his translations of English poetry: 16th – 19th Century English sonnets and Shakespeare's sonnets, as well as the translation of many modern poets from Brazil, India, Italy, Greece, USA, England, China and Japan.

BEING

My path was hard and long. For many years
I sloshed through the mud under the endless rain.
Being tired I have continued to walk.
I tried to change this dreary world,
I have woven the enchanting wreaths of my imagination.
I thought that only crazy dreams could save the gray life.

A SIMPLE TRUTH

In time of meditation and wandering
I thought how great was our Creator!
My soul dreamed about significant deeds,
But life had become full of monotonies.
The end of life is more sad.
But nevertheless I don't know
Where I may find the proper words to describe
How dear to me is this withered grass.

I AM A PART OF ETERNAL MOVEMENT

I am a part of eternal movement, I keep in my mind
All the events that happened in this world
From the BIG BANG until today.
I remember the axes of stone and the wet caves,
Bronze and iron centuries, ancient Egypt and pyramids.
I remember rivers of blood from all the wars.
I was a witness to those events
When people conquered space
And were launched to the moon.
I remember the last information explosion
When personal computers and cellular telephones
Spread through the world!
What else do I expect in the nearest future?
I am but a tiny piece of matter.
Where is the limit of my memory?

When the burden will be so heavy
And my memory will be overloaded?
Then Universal will perhaps collapse
Transforming into the dot again?
Then maybe, it will initiate a "NEW BIG BANG"!

Ann Christine Tabaka (USA)

Ann Christine Tabaka was nominated for the 2017 Pushcart Prize in Poetry. She is the winner of Spillwords Press 2020 Publication of the Year, her bio is featured in the "Who's Who of Emerging Writers 2020," published by Sweetycat Press. Chris has been internationally published, and won poetry awards from numerous publications. Her work has been translated into Sequoyah-Cherokee Syllabics, and into Spanish. She is the author of 13 poetry books. She has been published micro-fiction anthologies and short story publications. Christine lives in Delaware, USA. She loves gardening and cooking. Chris lives with her husband and four cats. Her most recent credits are: The American Writers Review; The Phoenix; Burningword Literary Journal; Muddy River Poetry Review; The Scribe, The Silver Blade, Silver Birch Press, Pomona Valley Review, Page & Spine, West Texas Literary Review, The Hungry Chimera, Sheila-Na-Gig, Foliate Oak Review, The Stray Branch, The McKinley Review, Fourth & Sycamore.
* (a complete list of publications is available upon request)

Ode to the Wind

Your gentle cool breath sweeps over me
as I lie upon the garden wall.

Trees sway to the sound
of your stirring symphony.

Faces lift to greet your touch,
and hear your murmured sigh.

Your sensuous caress upon my hair,
a thrill that fills all depths.

Element of ancient cultures,
with earth, water, and fire you dwell.

Harmony of grace and movement,
you arouse all with anticipation.

Your forces strong, and songs sweet.
A wild child, tamed by none.

* Published by Stanzaic Stylings, August 2019

Early Spring

A Cold gray day in March,
counting heartbeats until spring.
Dormant trees nod to a cold breeze,
that whispers in return.
Searching fervently for warmth.
Dreaming of rebirth.
Slivers of blue sky
among dense white clouds.
Evening comes too soon.
Sunset wraps around night
like a shawl around cold shoulders,
as April waits her turn.

Published by Apricity Magazine, March 2020

Agron Shele (Albania – Belgium)

President of the International Poetical Galaxy "Atunis"
https://atunispoetry.com/

Agron Shele was born in October 7th, 1972, in the Village of Leskaj, city of Permet, Albania. Is the author of the following literary works: "The Steps of Clara" (Novel), "Beyond a grey curtain" (Novel), "Wrong Image" (Novel), "Innocent Passage" (Poetry), White stones (poetry) RIME SPARSE -Il suono di due voci poetiche del Mediterraneo (Poesie di Agron Shele e Claudia Piccinno), La mia Musa ("Libri di-versi in diversi libri" – Italy, 2020); Murmure d' un autre monde (poetry), "Ese-I and Ese-II)".

Mr. Shele is also the coordinator of International Anthologies: "Open Lane- 1," "Pegasiada, Open Lane-2, ATUNIS magazine (Nr 1, 2, 3, 4, 5, 6, 7, 8)" and Atunis Galaxy Anthology 2018, 2019, 2020, 2021. He is the winner of some international literary prizes. Is a member of the Albanian Association of Writers, member of the World Writers Association, in Ohio, United States, Poetas del Mundo, WPS, Unione world Poetry and the President of the International Poetical Galaxy "Atunis". He is published in many newspapers, national and international magazines, as well as published in many global anthologies: Almanac 2008, 2017; World Poetry Yearbook 2009, 2013, 2015, The Second Genesis-2013, Kibatek 2015-Italy, Metafora (Poland), Keleno-Greece, etc. Currently resides in Belgium and continues to dedicate his time and efforts in publishing literary works with universal values.

The Silent journey

Sailing on a boat, through a stormy sea
we distinguish the gaze following us from the shore
frightened of the fate that pushes us toward the wild waves, swollen with blood
down to the perturbed centuries

to the strange roots holding us in stasis
rotating around the satellite that extinguishes in the air
to the moment of abyss that separate life from death
of the lost illusion.

Again we wonder, trying to understand
the attempt in half dreams
on the wrinkled waves of tomorrow
under the mane of a horse that runs in a gust of wind,
through the nostrils of air
It is halted by the tether that pulls it
the footprints of the half of gallop are left
on the bank where the seafoam sleeps
and the Circes eyes are dissolute.

Run, liberated from this rising like a mirage
breath and shape of this hectic darkness
like an everlasting song of this echo that attracts
our sorrow
the finish line
walking with youthful steps
and the grey aging through snowfall.

My Cypress

Every time that snow starts falling
I don't know why I come to you
might be a promise;
the silent exchange of our stories.

Mine are simpler
there's no noise, no glory that you can listen to.
yours, I don't know,
but I see the prints on your skin
and believe too many hands have touched you
they have prayed and asked for more love
met with a bowing of the head and a Namaste
that you hold deep in your soul.

Here I am again today
you know, when the snowflakes start I will be here
I see the prints of the running wind as well
not those of the wind's reindeer, because they are fare away
but just the pain that we feel, you and me
when wildly winds rock the top of the tree
shaking off the snow to your shoulders
to shelter more birds
As for me…I am shaken by silent memory
of people that I unconditionally love.

My cypress,
there is no end to the odes and songs
that come to me
along with this cold air
which can't ever strip your green joy
as it murmurs in your branches,
as for me, I do not need more than a greeting when I come
always unspeakably understanding each other
you, still in your world of old love reposing
I, again forgotten on my bench.

I need to lit a cigarette and see through the smoke,
the reappearance of what is gone
whereas I am stealing your body
and take it with me, to my very last station.

Conversation with Charles Baudelaire

You always came in the same way
sometimes as a ghost
stuck in the grey matter of the brain
other times as a bad flower's blossom
even as it appears in dark colors
shows the greatness of a painting of a sea
the white sails of a ship that comes and goes away

from the bewildered and confused sight of the eyes
or the lily of the lake shining
on the body of life
body and soul sorrow endeavored
devils and angels
painted centuries ago by masters on the chapels.

I am sure that your sight is fixed at these same church
with different appearances
you were crazy about horses' manes
at the cattle fair
whereas I, get caught amongst the traffic, at the same cross road
at the same cobblestone plaza that look like Cadmus teeth
those letters
what you murmured until the last breath
as the most glorious soul of sorrow
that never got the peace…!

Note: *Today I was at the same church that Charles Baudelaire used to go and lit a remembrance candle for his soul.*

Translated into English by Merita Paparisto

Alicja Maria Kuberska (Poland)

Alicja Maria Kuberska – awarded Polish poetess, novelist, journalist, editor.

She is a member of the Polish Writers Associations in Warsaw, Poland and IWA Bogdani, Albania. She is also a member of directors' board of Soflay Literature Foundation, Our Poetry Archive (India) and Cultural Ambassador for Poland (Inner Child Press, USA).

Her poems have been published in numerous anthologies and magazines in: Poland, Czech Republic, Slovakia, Hungary, Belgium, Bulgaria, Albania, Spain, the UK, Italy, the USA, Canada, the UK, Argentina, Chile, Peru, Israel, Turkey, India, Uzbekistan, South Korea, Taiwan, Australia, South Africa, Zambia, Nigeria.

She received three medals – the Nosside UNESCO Competition in Italy (2015 and 2020) and European Academy of Science Arts and Letters in France (2017). She also received a reward of international literary competition in Italy "Tra le parole e 'elfinito" (2018). She was announced a poet of the 2017 year by Soflay Literature Foundation (2018). She also received: Bolesław Prus Prize Poland (2019), Culture Animator Poland (2019) and first prize Premio Internazionale di Poesia Poseidonia-Paestrum Italy (2019).

My village Borow

I no longer have a nest here
But I come back, like a swallow,
To places of my childhood.

I wander the sandy hedgerows,
To participate in the mystery of lark song.
I arrange bouquets
Of wild poppies and cornflowers –

And raise up to the clouds.

Old trees, to which I confided my secrets,
Still grow,
Tart, wild cherries
And sweet-scented linden
As once –
I divine the world in the mirror of the lake.
I listen to the waves and the wind.

Apparently nothing has changed.
Only the cemetery hill,
Like a diary of life,
Is ever more clear

A Philosopher and a Poet

they met between heaven and earth
at the place where time and matter are irrelevant
at a higher level of abstraction
they overcame the barriers of the real world

he brought a white canvas and philosophical maxims
she brought the paint brushes
and a handful of dreams in words
they painted the picture in many shades of blue
they poured their thoughts and feelings into the ether

he sketched the outlines of life with a bold navy blue line
she filled the background with gentle azure brushes
together they added a few colorful spots of astonishment
his eyes are hazel and hers are green

Alexander Pak (Uzbekistan)

Alexander Pak was born on May 14, 1953 in the village of Khudzhaili, Uzbekistan, in karakalpat. Belongs to the union of writers of Russia. He graduated from the I. E. Repin Academy of Fine Arts in St. Petersburg. He was mainly interested in graphics. He participated in many exhibitions, organized at home and abroad. During the VIII Festival" published in Altai", which was dedicated to the 125th anniversary of the founding of the Regional Scientific public library named after V. J. Shishkov in Altai, the winners of the competition in the category" best poetic collection "received a collection of his poems together with a graphic entitled"Shadow of a butterfly". His works also illustrated national and regional anthologies and collections of poetry by the authors of the Altai country, while the graphic entitled "Adam and Eve" appeared on the cover of the manual for family physicians entitled "fundamentals of clinical education in reproductive health" (1999). Pictures of Alexander Pak appeared in the wall calendar "Kyrgyzstan-2000", which was printed under the auspices of UNESCO. He is the author of the Olympic sign"IV Summer Olympic games of small towns of Altai". In contrast, the monument to St. Peter and Fevronia designed by him is located in front of the civil status office in slavgorod and the village of kosicha, which is located on the territory of the Siberian Altai territory, which is part of Russia. In 2009, in Barnaul, was released the album of Alexander Pak entitled "graphics". His works are in private collections in Russia, Kyrgyzstan, France, Germany, Belgium and Japan.

He is the winner of literary competitions, m.in. international poetry competition "golden stanza 2012", in which he took second place. He published in the" Russian anthology of the White poem", in the Moscow literary magazine" Arion", as well as in the anthology" the word about the mother", which was published in Italy. The author has published a number of books of poetry, including: Russian-German collection "Apple of sin", for which he received the award "Best Book of the year" (2007);

Russian-German collection "hieroglyph of loneliness" (2015); Russian-Korean-German collection "you and I", for which he received the prize of the all-Russian competition "Germany of Russian origin in the vanguard of the future" (2017). For his activities in the field of culture, Alexander Pak was awarded the prize" golden pen of Russia "(2016) and the honorary medal of the Altai Republic" for services to society " (2013).

***

Click. Misfire.
And an unborn shot
Lives on in the flight of a bird.

***

R.S.
Having left my father's house,
I will return all my life
To the doorsteps of my home.

***

T.N.V.
What's Petersburg without my beloved eyes, without you?
Just a grey cloudy day and endless drizzling rain.
Flap the wings of your opening bridges,
So that the "lonely sail" of my belated love
can find the long-sought pier in your heart.

Translated from Russian to English by Andrea Ostertag

Antje Stehn (Germany)

Antje Stehn, born in Germany, resides in Italy. Poet, visual artist, video producer, art curator. Since 1990 she has been showing her work in a number of international exhibitions around Europe and the US. At the moment she is curating the international art-poetry project "Rucksack a Global Poetry Patchwork". She is part of the international Collective "Poetry is my Passion" which is operating in Milan and organizes transcultural events for the promotion of language and cultural diversity. She is editing the international poetry voice "Milano, una città mille lingue" for the poetry magazine TamTamBumBum and is co-editor in the latin-american Blog Los Ablucionistas and the Blog Teerandaz in Bangladesh. She is member of the scientific committee of the Piccolo Museo della Poesia of Piacenza, Italy.

Epiphany on Capitol Hill

It looked like sewing long, loose stitches,
done by hand

the basting together of a film already seen
where aliens and mutants
overthrow The Great Power
like children in a game they are about to lose.

At the capture of the winter palace
a ramshackle mob
sticking all over the monumental whiteness
like window cleaners,
in the Rotonda
baseball caps and bats, madmen smashing glass
and the American buffalo man
Undecided between taking a selfy

or escaping from tear gas.
Terrified congressmen beg the
President for help
but he is too busy
following in live streaming
his tweeds becoming flesh.
L'Epifania a Capitol Hill
Sembrava un'imbastitura provvisoria
eseguita a mano
di un film già visto in cui
alieni e mutanti
rovesciano La Grande Potenza
come bambini un gioco
che stanno per perdere.

Alla presa del palazzo d'inverno
una masnada sgangherata
appiccicati sull'imponente bianchezza
come lavavetri
nella Rotonda
capelli e mazze da baseball,
energumeni trita vetri
e l'uomo bisonte
combattuti tra un selfi e
la fuga dai lacrimogeni.

Deputati terrorizzati supplicano l'aiuto
del Presidente
troppo impegnato a seguire
in streaming i suoi tweed
che si sono fatti carne.

Alexey Kalakutin (Russia)

Alexey Kalakutin (October 30, 1973) lives in Nizhny Novgorod, Russia. He is a Russian writer, a philologist. He studied at the Philological Faculty of Nizhny Novgorod State Pedagogical University. His debut publication is "Khokhloma Pattern & quot; 1990 (fairy-tale novel for children) co-authored with E.V. Kalakutin. He is the author of six novels in verse, as well as of six poems and pieces of poetry.

Alexey is a member of the Professional Writers Union of Russia (PWUR). He was awarded the 1 st degree diploma (PWUR) for high professional skills. International Ambassador for Peace, participant in several international poetic anthologies, awarded with certificates of recognition.

A fragment from the poem: "The Sweet Martyr"

Rumors are flies and the tattles are gadflies
Feeling the high blood and stinging aggressively,
Driving the sting into flesh and the souls
Of the sovereigns and royal successors shamelessly.

The virulent piercers in Russian Empire
Fell to the lady from Alemannia,
That one inspiring love and admiration
Of high-minded Romanov, son of Emperor.

Anna, excuse me, I state things straightforwardly,
Wounding your feelings by tactless pronouncements,
Cannot be secretive, cannot gloss over,
Thoughts seething madly in brain like denouncements.

In former times, you remember, the common herd
Twisted the face with dislike for the empress,
As if for dinner not vodka, but cider
Is served with steak that is coarse and tasteless.

Members of gentry glanced at her askance,
Merchants did not start to dance with excitement.
Gingerbread cookies baked in the Russian lands
Didn't accept Alemannic sweet items.

Old and young, in a jacket and fashions,
Did not compassion the peregrine queen.
The ancestor worship is dear to Russians,
The image of Mother is in the genes!

Father the Tsar, and the queen should be Mother!
But she was born by the Britons and Germans.
To understand Russian world like the others
For stranger's heart is extremely uncommon!

You may the name Alexandra receive,
You may feel alone so much less,
But cannot wear your heart on your sleeve,
Because you are proud Alice of Hesse.

Big Russian soul cannot be bought!
You are a Russian since you were born –
With Pushkin, Yesenin, the noise of birches,
With tear of the Virgin inside your core!

Allison Grayhurst (Canada)

Allison Grayhurst is a member of the League of Canadian Poets. Four of her poems were nominated for "Best of the Net" in 2015/2018, and one eight-part story-poem was nominated for "Best of the Net" in 2017. She has over 1,260 poems published in more than 500 international journals and anthologies. In 2018, her book Sight at Zero, was listed #34 on CBC's "Your Ultimate Canadian Poetry List". In 2020, her work was translated into Chinese and published in "Rendition of International Poetry Quarterly" and in "Poetry Hall". Her book Somewhere Falling was published by Beach Holme Publishers, a Porcepic Book, in Vancouver in 1995. Since then she has published sixteen other books of poetry and six collections with Edge Unlimited Publishing. Prior to the publication of Somewhere Falling she had a poetry book published, Common Dream, and four chapbooks published by The Plowman. Her poetry chapbook The River is Blind was published by Ottawa publisher above/ground press December 2012. In 2014 her chapbook Surrogate Dharma was published by Kind of a Hurricane Press, Barometric Pressures Author Series. In 2015, her book No Raft – No Ocean was published by Scars Publications. Also, her book Make the Wind was published in 2016 by Scars Publications. As well, her book Trial and Witness – selected poems, was published in 2016 by Creative Talents Unleashed (CTU Publishing Group). More recently, her book Tadpoles Find the Sun was published by Cyberwit, August 2020. She is a vegan. She lives in Toronto with her family. She also sculpts, working with clay.
http://www.allisongrayhurst.com

Resolved

Forgetful, in exile,
in the fires of failure,
honouring suffering
like a story told in form,
a totem-working of visual permanence.
I bore my marriage
to the joyous wilderness in one hand,
and sacrilegious duty
in the other.
Today, I join these hands
to create stability, sanctuary,
creativity touching ground and discipline.
I burn the dead wood, releasing
my prisoner-identity and climb out of
the fishnet into deep fulfillment like
into a valley with a lake and untamed
foliage all around.
The pull and tug of two lives is gone,
tension internalized as useful energy,
as something to be incorporated, harnessed,
the generator of a mature dream – a dream
with no division, bound,
and happy to be bound.

Rescue

End of the day, relenting,
easing off the mighty restlessness
that overtook the morning
and most of the afternoon.

I know the deeds of my happiness
and the hot flesh branding of my imprisonment.
I know as I held council with the speakers
in my mind – all of them directing me

to wide open freedom and teamwork
to stave off the forces of death
and unrighteous burial.

They tell me it is time to close fast the wounds
that siphon out our power, be brave
as if we were in a deserted city on a mountain
surrounded by a rising sea and shouting winds
clanking their lock-fast swallowing chains.

Hold out they tell me, on the highest tower,
at the highest point, and never
let our trust become captive to fear.

They tell me, even though we look right,
we look left, seeing nothing but sky and clouds,
even though our ankles and knees are already immersed,
as the smells of fishy salt fill our nostrils,
holding our hands above the pressing doom,
engage with God, they tell me.

All at once, the voices tell me,
stand equal, and in that equality,
the light come.

Let us be one and we will know mercy,
stronger than gravity, than all of our bones combined.
The light will come and it will love us,
conquering, alleviating the final struggle.

Anastasia N. Margeti (Greece)

Anastasia N. Margeti was born and raised in Athens. She studied education, history and literature at the University of Athens. Articles of hers have appeared in pedagogical journals and conference minutes. She teaches in the Athens public school system. She published the poetry collection "The Third from Truth" (AΩ Editions, 2015 & Editions GRIGORIS, 2019). Her verse has been included in group anthologies.

Translated by Robert & Despina Crist

POETICETHICS

...for where we are free to act
we are also free to refrain from acting,
and where we are able to say No
we are also able to say Yes.

Aristotle, Nicomachean Ethics

It aged upon her
the role's
attire.

Now
she sheds it
in silence.

All of her
beholds
her naked image
in the mirror.

Shadows of night
listen secretly
to mid-life hopes
curves of air
and sadness
hollows of anger
at the edge of touch.
Unsmiling
she again tightly dons
the same past.
And turns her gaze
on the unspoken.

THE REPUBLIC

Whatever you fear
you judge
and you condemn it
ceaselessly
to death.

Take heed!
The way you behave
you become
an absolute monarch.

And thereby
your life
depends
on your own justice.

Ali Al Hazmi (Saudi Arabia)

Born in (Damad) – Saudi Arabia (1970).Participated in numerous recitals of poetry inside and outside of Saudi Arabia:
International Poetry Festival Costa Rica 2013-Toledo, Spain 2014–Punta del Este, Uruguay 2015 Madrid. Spain 2016-Havana, Cuba 2016-Medellín, Colombia 2016-Istanbul-Turkey, 2016-Roma,2017-Romania2017. The world Grand prize (for Poetry) International Academy Orient – Occident in Romania 2017. Medalof honor to the poetic and literary merit in the XIV Encuentro Internacional Poetas y Narradores De las Dos Orillas y 4o Congreso de Literatura 2015, Punta del Este Uruguay. The poem (A street through a wall) Grand prize Verbumlandi- international poems – Italy 2017.

He has published the following books of poetry: (Gate of the Body) Jeddah- 1993-(Losing)-Cairo 2000-(The gazelle drinks his image)-Beirut 2004-(Reassuring on the Edge)-Beirut 2009, (Now in past) Arab Cultural Center- Beirut, 2018.

Arab and international critics wrote about his poetic production. Has six printed books translated into different languages:
(Tree of absence), Translated into French-lilDiston – France 2016.
(Reassuring on the Edge), Translated into Spanish published by University of Costa Rica Editorial 2013, House of Poetry Foundation.
(Reassuring on the Edge), Translated into French- larmatan – Paris 2016 (fragmentation of life), Translated into Turkish – Art Shop Istanbul -Turkey 2017 (A definite way in the mist), Translated into English and Romanian language – Academy Orient – Occident – Romania 2017.
(Take Me to My Body), Translated into Serbia – Alma- Belgrade 2019.

Throwing Your Grief as a Rock into the Sea

In your forties,
Wingless,
You urge the meaning to fly once again,

As though you are powerful enough, once more,
To step over the clouds.
Heading towards your own wilderness,
The winds put all sins of the tale upon your shoulders.
Since you stopped at the gates of your past,
With chained legs,
Neither your years returned to the song,
Nor did the gorgeous girls come back
From the trees of childhood jocundly
To your fields.
In your forties,
There, near the springs,
Longing takes you towards the deers,
That no more listen to your songs,
When you feel their approaching foot-steps,
And when the bird of words chirps
On a lonely branch in the heart.
You throw your grief like a rock into the sea
And see your face burning
In the furnace of the lost painful moment.

In your forties,
When you are fastened
To the flutes on the shawl of a ballad,
Find a dove forgotten in your own travelling meaning.
Do not exhaust the tender melody
With sighs of the memory that circle around your soul
Like a bracelet.
In your forties,
The past assumes you are so close to its orchards,
While you are there still stuck in the wilderness of your fantasies.
When you started your voyage
Towards your glittering metaphor,
You paid no attention to the thorny questions
Staring from afar at your feet.
In your forties on the roads,
No more you need to fold your shadows,
As you head towards the pleasures of life,
Trying to reach the lost bank of the river.

Memory asks, "When was it when you went bewildered
In the presence of oblivion?"
What would have hurt your innocent past if you stopped
At its noble gates for greeting,
For dropping off the burdens of rejection
That have watered your eyes with thirst of nothingness?"
In your forties,
A woman from the past visits you;
Don't be rude to her flutes
By asking about her distant love stories.
Save her from the deceptive mills,

Restore her to pure joy,
And to her flowers;
Listen to the bird of her soul
Neglected in the trees of absence;
Be like soft rains for her if she goes astray;
Be a metaphorical chord if she smiles;
And be an existential passion,
If she looks at you.
But, when you approach her extensive fires,
Be nothing but ashes.

Agnieszka Herman (Poland)

Agnieszka Herman – polish poetess, journalist, graphic designer. She published five poetry books: "The Sun Exploded" (Warsaw, 1990), "Written by the light" (Warsaw, 1995) "The hardest thing is walking in the middle of the day during the fall" (Warsaw, 2015), "The crosspoint" poems collected in Bulgarian (2018) and "Background" (Warsaw, 2019).
Her poems have been published in numerous anthologies and magazines in Poland, Bulgaria, India, Turkey, Japan, United Kingdom, Ukraine and USA. The member of international poetry festivals in Bulgaria, Turkey and Ukraine.
She has received many poetry awards. The last one – she is the finalist in Orpheus – Poetry Award K.I. Gałczyński 2020 for the book Tło (Background, Warsaw 2019). She won the voting of readers and participants of the awards gala [Poetry Award K.I. Gałczyński 2020].
She cooperates with large publishing houses in Poland where project book covers.
She is the author of cover designs, some of them are the world bestsellers. She is a memmber of Polish Haiku Association.
Her haiku are regularly published in the Japanese newspaper Kuzu.

https://pl.wikipedia.org/wiki/Agnieszka_Herman
http://www.agnieszkaherman.pl

Translated by Ada Stańczak

The rhythm of the earth

Just hug the tree
especially when the wind is blowing strong

The earth is pulsating in it
my heart wants to keep up
I feel two souls within me
there is me and god
the body has an expiration date
god is immortal
The walk
A deserted town or a film mockup.
Opened gates await the return of the hosts.
There are satiating cats in sunspots
and their narrowed eyes.
According to Epicurus
the happiness is a conversation about philosophy
with a friend in your own garden.
Or maybe happiness is a morning walk,
in which it solidifies like in an amber.
Especially when everywhere is
full of the byzantine splendor. Gold and purple.
So much death this autumn – says M.
Let the poems – like burning linden trees –
stand face to face with the dark.

OVER AGAIN

Autumn is like forbidden love
In the rustling leaves there is
more hope than farewells.
I have never traveled so far
to find myself.
The hourglass can be turned
and you can see grains of sand
pour all over again.

Translated by Ada Stańczak

Alicia Minjarez Ramírez
(Mexico)

She is an internationally renowned Mexican poetess and translator who has won numerous awards including: Honorary Doctorate granted by IFCH Morocco and a thousand minds for Mexico Association 2020. The World Cultural Excellence Award 2020 granted by the government of Peru. The Excellence Prize World Poetry Championship Romania 2019. Literary Prize "Tra le Parole e L'infinito" Italy 2019. Winner of the EASAL medal Award by The European Academy of Sciences and Letters France 2018. Her poems have been translated in several languages and published in more than 200 International Anthologies, magazines and newspapers around the world. She speaks: French, English, Italian and Spanish.

NOCTURNAL SUN

There, where the wind fades away
The sky waves its own branches
Retouching icy mornings
In the shades,
Blackbirds and pigeons flapping
And disturbing the sky.
I aimlessly wander through.

Every corner evokes
Spiral lines of perpetually
Ever written sonnets,
Unveiled brides
Blur the color lines
Upon vacant altars.
I become chrysalis
Under the chaos of progress.
I extend my hands

And find only emptiness.
Where do these streets lead me to?

I try to jump over my shadow,
Gradually move
From green to yellow...
Exorbitant looks
Lacking everything
And nothing at all.
In the swinging mist
Every step reflected upon
Its own reflection,
When the twilight expands
I force myself to take shortcuts
That lead me nowhere.

Broken hearts,
Moon's usurped glow,
Yielding ghosts
To the impregnable shine
Of window cars.
Stillness moves,
Static seconds,
Silence declines,
I emigrate with no belongings;
Brittle and gloomy spectrum
De-kernelling good-byes.

My mind is on hold,
Stars cry about
Humidity's shortage
And eclectic rains,
My voice drowns.
Blink away
The ethereal fire of my eyes,
I release myself from prejudice.

I release myself
From body and soul

As nocturnal sun
Amidst the desert.

MUNDANE

Among sweet and bleak
A perfect intersection;
Between desire and darkness.
Between magic and the divine
Spiritual mundane I am.

Uncertain contrasts
Break blueprints
In the desert,
Replacing emotions
At every corner.
Dresses up with dreams,
Carrying nothing more.

A single name directs my life,
Dancing naked in the dark;
Amongst alchemy and agony.
Mundane I am in your own reality.

Translated by Alaric Gutiérrez

Anila Varfi (Albania)

Anila Varfi was born in Albania in 1970. She is known as a professional with decades of experience in radio, television and cinema. She graduated summa cum laude in drama from the Academy of Fine Arts in Albania. Anila is also known for her work as the creative director of Durres International Film Festival. A talented director, producer, writer and professor who is very skilled in any artistic undertaking. She is a member of the European Film Academy. She has also published 3 books in poetry and prose.

THE DREAM CHASER

HE wanted to quit all and leave...
But not with the charred soul of his
Tangled in the tentacles of nothingness.
It's day-nights burnt to bits
As the lightning of pain stroke in the mad storm.

He wanted to quit the hours, weeks and beyond lives
Which hideously, drip, drip poisoning his tomorrow.
He wanted
Nothing

But to see the day's joy and shine
In the eyes of every child.

He was not asking for the Moon
He was after the basic thing on earth
He was chasing the dream.
When the golden birds of these dreams
Nested under his eyes.

Then he would feel beyond eternity.
The dreaming child of liberty.

AS IN THE LAST DAY

If Lady Death calls for me tonight…
Spare your tears for me
Cherish tomorrow as we did yesterday,
Play as we used to.
And follow your dreams
With no sorrow
I will keep my vows
I'll be there.
When you walk the streets every morning
And your face strangely is frozen by the breeze,
that very moment, my gentle caress you'll feel

Have a glass of wine on me in the evening
And share your joy with the stars.
Meet me at the mad ball dancing
Don't look for me in your dreams,
No pleas to join them, I know
When you will be overwhelmed
And I need to come.

Cheers to the freedom of love,
And all its virtue-made jewellery.
Be happy and live like it was my last day.

Translated into English by Gezim Guri

Amy Barry (Ireland)

Amy Barry lives in Athlone, Ireland. She writes poems and short stories. She gets her inspiration from a wide range where she colourfully covers universal themes and she explores love, family, nature, death, current issues. Her work has been published in anthologies, journals and e-zines, in Ireland and abroad. Her poems have been translated into many languages including Turkish, Malay, Azerbaijani, Persian, Spanish, French and Italian. She loves traveling and trips to India, Nepal, China, Bali, Paris, Berlin, Falkerberg- have all inspired her work. Her poems have been shared on the radio in Australia, Canada and Ireland. Amy regularly organises Poetry events in her hometown - Athlone where she promotes poets and musicians. These events featured local and international poets. She has read at festivals and literary events in Ireland and abroad.
She is a nominee for the Pushcart 2021 Poetry Prize.

Divine parallelism

What I want is to hear
my heart beats like lusty fire
and see my fingers reach out
to touch your breath.

What I want is to embrace you,
and my feverish lips
to kiss you with urgency
like the desire of a storm —

where
beauty and passion erupt
like the rising sun.

Kaleidoscope

Maybe it is the calm
the change of pace
that brings us here,
the sense of isolation
far from the crowd —
enticing
lovers.

Maybe the scents of the place,
the fragrance of pines and
candied wild angelicas,
the feel of dry grasses,
a bed of comfort —
the crunch,
so springy
so earthy.

Maybe where rabbits pirouette,
and daisies sing
but nettles sting
in sunny buttercup fields
and musical insistence of
burbling water
spilling
over rocks.

Maybe the swirl of fresh breeze
clearing our minds,
and copper bells tinkling
weaving silken tunes.
And Robins singing
a paean
to summer.

Abdukakhor Kosim (Tajikistan)

Poet, translator, singer-writer, publicist, journalist "Excellence in Education and Science of the Tajikistan" (Excellence in Culture of the Republic of Tajikistan), higher pedagogical education, author of more than 100 songs in the Tajik and Russian languages, 12 books, participated in the Anthology of modern Eurasian writers and more than 20 collections. His works have been translated into English, Spanish, Chinese, French, German, Serbian, Portuguese, Turkish, Azerbaijani, Persian and other languages. Chief editor of the newspaper "Khidoyat" of the People's Democratic Party of Tajikistan. Co-chairman of the literary council of the International Union of Writers of the Eurasian Peoples' Assembly, member of the International Union of Writers, member of the International Confederation of Journalists, coordinator of the International Council of the International Union of Writers. Member of the Eurasian Creative Guild. Silver medalist of the elevator festival, St. Winner of the Grand Prix (Outstanding Winners) of the 1st World Satellite Television Poetry Competition 2020, Beijing, "Sergei Yesenin Medal-2020", "Order of the Mahatma-2020".
Grand Prix of the International Festival named after de Richelieu "The Brilliant Duke", etc.

MISSION OF POET

In the poems draw the pearl of meaning one after another,
Poet, extract zam-zam water of the depth of meaning.
As a cable transmit the sparkle of suffering,
Honesty, you are taking the load of whole world.
Sometimes as an artist in the castle of dreams,
In beauty draw face of you-beloved as a dew.
Next time in the dessert of sorrow and mysteries,
Pull the caravan of grieves with the bowed head.

To the God Almighty you sometimes tell you mysteries,
Pull the love parting with the full of tears eyes.

HEART OF THE POET

You know, there isn't the place of sorrow in my heart,
No place for the darkness of dense forest.
No place for today's and tomorrow's grieve,
No place for light on my self-burning candle.
My heart breaks to hundred parts,
My heart breaks to hundred parts.
Love sound doesn't come to my ears,
No more tear come to my eyes.
Romantic look went through my calm eyes.
Love moments are pleasing of colorful world.
My heart breaks to hundred parts,
My heart breaks to hundred parts.
Why? Maybe you ask me,
Isn't more extented of perishable world of poets heart?
If breaks to hundred parts, it isn't the end of love world?
I say-let the poet's heart be as your heart,
But more sensitive, as it is the mission from God.
Greatness of poet's heart is that embraces the pain of the world,
If separate to hundred parts, but never don't die.
Even cries whole life, but bring jolly,
Burns fall in my hearts and bring spring.
To heart of each man brings kindness and peace,
Brings spring in the spring,
Brings flower scattering spring.

Translated into English by Tajik Khaibatullo Shodieva

Aviva Golan (Israel)

A poet. Born in Israel. Her songs are published in respectable anthologies in Israel and around the world.

Her "Homeland Song" won the first place in a production exhibition by the Hebrew Writers Association and The Bible House, Won the Manfred Winkler Prize on behalf of the President of Bukovina for her participation in the bilingual anthology "The Motherland of the Poet" in 2015. Some poems are used for psychological treatments.

A selection of her poems have been translated to English, Romanian and Esperanto, Composed and performed by singers and choirs in Israel and abroad, And also folk dances.

Waves of Happiness

Oh Wind,
Scatter the gunpowder
and on your cloud lined wing,
carry the peace bearing messenger dove
To friendly shores

Into the singing silence
Spread waves of light
and essence of blossoming citrus with,
a heart warming gust of compassion.
Ripe is our Earth, quench our thirst
Bring a rain, rain of salvation, salvation seed's passion.

Oh Wind,
Scatter the gunpowder
and on your cloud lined wing,

carry the snow white messenger dove
To friendly shores

Oh Wind,
Scatter the gunpowder
and on your cloud lined wing,
carry the peace bearing messenger dove
To friendly shores

English translated by Ernest Samuel Llime

The peace's language/ Aviva Golan

Words, melting frozen walls
Poetry, awakening dormant tones.
I have opened my salty tearful eyes
I promised my soldier, no more wars.
The soil is thirsty for water, the heart for love's oxygen
The hope will break through like the rain in the desert.
The world's center, in human life's Holiness
We are all one family, blood relation.
To the time's rhythm and the comfort's light
Our feet will pace in brotherhood's trails and peace.
Dear son, may we be granted in our days,
a time of Heavenly mercy
In her the language's peace will be carried in multitude.

Translated by Eitan Medini

Ajne Iberhysaj (Kosova)

Ajne Ibërhysaj was born on November 17, 1973 in Deçan. She studied at the University "Aleksandër Xhuvani" in Elbasan-Albania, branch General Bio-Chemistry.

In the "Victory" college, in Prishtina she studied the bachelor and master study programme "International Politics and Diplomacy" where she received the Master of Arts degree for International Politics and Diplomacy. In the municipality of Deçan she works in the position of Inspector for Environmental Protection.

Works:

"Chestnut Day", PH "Lena Graphic-design", Prishtina 2020,
"I will come with the shadow of the wind". "Lena Graphic-design", Prishtina 2020

YOU, MY LIFE....

The days as they are fisting
the earth
Boundaries of love are
within us
The kisses do warm up also
the evil abyss
One day this fear expedition
will run away
In every breathe
I take your air
Even to the smile
I give a color

Among books I burn myself
and I find also the hope
I am there at the edge of darkness
and I am your light
With patience catching the days
I highlight them with
Fingers
Like a soldier of an endless
Army
One goal keeps me up
There is a sun where love
rests
One day this fear expedition
will run away
I am the destination
You are the boundary
I am the dream
You are the light
What the entire world has
Inside
There is a drop of tear and of
hope
Me and You
We are only a
Breathing
My life
I kiss you up to
Eternity.....

Alessandra Corbetta (Italy)
http://www.alessandracorbetta.net

Alessandra Corbetta has a research doctorate in Sociology of Communication and Media and works as Adjunct Professor and Teaching Assistant at the LIUC – Carlo Cattaneo University. She has taken her masters in Digital Communication and in Storytelling. She is founder and manager of the blog Alma Poesia (http://www.almapoesia.it), a project which is entirely dedicated to Italian and international poetical language. She cooperates with Vuela Palabra, a literary journal which is committed to spreading poetry in Spanish. She writes for the online newspapers Gli Stati Generali and Progressonline. Her latest publication in verse is Corpo della gioventù (Puntoacapo Editrice 2019).

Translated by Barbara Herzog

POST SCRIPTUM

The bodies await low cost salvations.
The shutters closed in order not to say there's too much light
cast a shadow on the overlapping voices
and separate before from after.
Nodding at advice one different from the other
for a little, keep them silent.
Making an agreement only with the steps of the staircase.
A week. A month, a year. Waiting for
the pain at the exit with its
pale face, terror's shadows under the eyes.
Every finger. Every bone, every bad mood
will be where it had to be.
To survive –someone will be told – one changes
even name

UNDERGROUND RAILWAY

Time is in search of bodies to reveal itself.
Four hours have already passed the yellow line
is due in 2,5 minutes. Love is in search of souls
it will arrive from the right heading Central*. Passages
need to be opened, hoping no nog is missing
in the roman arch used as comparison
to explain the absence of a molar.

(I have dug with my hands to reduce the space
but our past belongs to somebody else)

Another six steps five four
and the fingers will be on the half-warm bars
saving presence, so almost-true will be again
the day I gave you who I was, the day
where leaving was only recognizing oneself by the name

(*Central is referring to the railway station Milano Centrale)

FIRST FLOOR
(For Riccardo & Debbie)

With fury they move from floor to floor,
the craving for reaching
the room, doing those grown-up
things – us too, remember?
we were at twenty up
and down, a continuous opening
of doors mirrors passings
yet she has that punk cut
crooked glasses in the picture where
you were still you, and the game
we believed it easy – stop the elevator,
intertwine hands, enough one for another

Agnieszka Jarzębowska (Poland)
Agnieszka Jarzębowska (b. Sieradz, Poland), graduate of Łódź University, member of „Anima" Literary Club, „Poets after hours" Informal Group, honorary member of Janów Literary Club.
Her works were translated to English, Serbian, German, Lithuanian, Slovak, Bulgarian, Dutch, Italian, Russian, Telugu, Hungarian, French, Spanish, Ukrainian and Swedish. Published four books of epigrams and four books of poems. Guest of the 14th International Day of Poetry and 2nd European Poetic Dialogues (London 2014), 22nd International Poetry Festival "Maj nad Wilią (Vilnius 2016), 4th, 5th and 6th International Poetry Festival "Słowiańska Brosza" (Lodon, 2016, 2017 and 2018), 1st and 2nd International Poetry Festival "Duchowość bez granic" (Plovdiv 2017 and 2018) and "Słowiańska Brosza" (Czechowice-Dziedzice, 2018, 2019) 12th Guntur International Poetry Festival (Guntur, Hyderabad) 2019. She has been recognized in various literary contests, including 2nd award in National Satirical Contest in Zebrzydowice (2017), special recognition for a regional-themed poem in National Contest "Mój list do świata" (2010), 1st place in TJW VIII Mława Poet's Night (2015). Received the award of the Municipal Council of Sieradz for achievements in literature (2012). She presented her works in magazines, radio, TV, Internet. Published anthologies and almanacs in Poland, USA, Great Britain, Serbia, Slovakia, Bulgaria, India and many other, book of 200 epigrams "Fraszki i uśmiechy" (Regiony, Sieradz 2010), Polish-German book of poetry "Miejsce po przecinku/Die stele nach dem komma" (Regiony, Sieradz 2012), book of epigrams "Fraszkomat" (Regiony, Sieradz 2012), Polish-Serbian book of poetry "Układam siebie/Slažem sebe" (Krosno 2012), Polish-English book of epigrams "Nic-Nothing" (Bez Erraty, Lublin 2014), Polish-Lithuanian book of poems "Przekładaniec" (Fundacja Jana Kochanowskiego, Sosnowiec 2014), "Bez żartów" (Bezerraty, Lublin 2017)," Polish-English book of poems "Piąta pora roku" (MK, 2017).

Three days of happiness

I saw three days of happiness
blue-pink.
They tasted like always and never
they were wearing
a quiet coat made from smile.

On that day

You waited out my dream
you had to tell me something important yourself.
I opened my eyes
I heard the most important for you on that day:
– Good morning.

Where you have been

Far,
far away,
where you have been,
reached all my thoughts.

Enough

You can't ask too much
but I don't expect
that much.
Your presence is enough for me
a cheap bouquet of flowers
and some season of the year
let's say spring.

Translated into English by Marta Jarzębowska

Alexa Prada (Costa Rica)

Alexa Prada is a young Costa Rican artist. She is a 22-year-old singer-songwriter and poet. Some of her texts can be found in magazines and anthologies such as Y2K" (2018), "Desacuerdos" (2020), fanzine of Otro Taller Literario (2020), "Nueva Poesía Costarricense" (2020), Revista Atunis Galaxy Poetry (2021) and Liberoamérica (2020).

Bipolar love

You know, when you treat me like that
distant,
freezing, as if we met last week.
And when you love me like that
when we're alone
so warm
so us.

And i know
that if i tell you this
you'll have an explanation
a theory,
a counterargument
because you always have an answer
and a perfect way to make everything about me
nothing about you
It is never about you.

And always having answers
it's just a way of hiding.
Because you need to feel safe
more than you need to feel.
You are just playing chess
and hiding and seek,

disclaiming the reality that you actually feel.

So here you are
pulling myself away
planning your next answer
Because this
this is real, you know?
And that's why you are so afraid of
so if you can't embrace that
if you can't accept that
i don't know about you
but me, i have just one life to love
One.
And maybe we'll be dead by tomorrow
and i'm so tired unvoicing that i love you
so here were are
again
but this time
i swear
is the last time
i try to convince you
of what
you
already
know.

Anna Maria Sprzęczka-Stępień (Poland)

Born in 1980 in Tarnobrzeg (Poland, present Podkarpackie Region). An economist and an English philologist. In 2020, she graduated from the Jagiellonian University in Kraków, where she studied specialized translation, postgradually. For over 17 years, a teacher of English and also a translator; she loves her profession. Once, an accountant working for an international company. Now, an editor and an editorial secretary in World Taifas Literary Magazine (Romania), and also an editor and a Polish representative in Anirban International Literary Magazine (Bangladesh). Anna Maria writes poems, short stories and anecdotes (so far around 53 English poems composed, and 80 Polish ones). Acclaimed worldwide in artistic circles; her poems have been translated into other languages and published in more International Anthologys. Her first book (poetic chronicles*) will be released next year, and her ambition is undertaking doctoral studies in literature translation and linguistics.

Prescription

You will find nobody on the Earth, I guess
Whose paths are smooth, summer and winter.
Since time immemorial it's always been like that...
Worries and fears, or something we mull over
No matter small or big we are...
A life test awaits us day in day out.

And there is no one on this Earth
Who is about everything glad
That fate brings them as a gift.
Ups and downs, endless adventures
– the good and bad ones...
And in addition, it will sometimes add

A sack like a rainbow multicoloured
Full of beautiful, of happiness, dreams.

When you realize this fact
Then a prescription for your ills you've found:
How to cope, even when
Things don't want to go your way,
When for you all things go wrong,
Seeing what's happening around.

So, lift up your heart, your chest ahead,
Sitting or standing, roll your sleeves up,
To work harness your hands and mind.
And don't think you're alone, though, probably …
It's better as a duo, when the second pair of hands,
When two heads,
To work for a brighter tomorrow
Will get with enthusiasm straight away…

In your dreams' magic power believe,
For you yourself know it best
What dances in your soul, what plays in it!
Or, maybe, you prefer when I tell you this?

Andrea Tavares de Sousa
(Cape Verde)

Andrea Tavares de Sousa was born in Cape Verde, Santa Catarina (Santiago) in april 06 1987. She moved to France since 2005. She is a writer and a poet. Andrea wrote four books (Poet of the year 2019, Women and their destinations, Words of pandemic, the cyclone will end and poetic universe). She writes poem in many languages such as Portuguese, French, Spanish and Cape Verde an Creole. She is mentioned in several anthology books, and she is currently preparing a poetry book in Cape Verdean Creole, as well as a children's book with traditional songs. She is also learning classical music and how to play guitare.

The art of Poetry

Walking in the mysterious mist
My wandering poet life
Is a light of a sad lost soul
Covered by unmeasured verses.

Diving into the rough sea
In the waves of writings
Painted with delicate secrets,
Bluish from the dawn of my being

I will sing about love, sweetly,
I will make the insensible hearts to feel it
My humble verses – The art of Poetry!
My song and my and sweet melody.

The calmness of my poems
In a dream full of petals
The joy of my heart
And the perfume of poet that I am.

Africa

Heart of wonder,
Lap of our islands,
Mother of joy,
Womb of magic.

Oh dear mother,
extend your arms
and receive this love petal,
painted with warmth

Blown with calmness,
friendship and hope.
Greeted by the rain.
And such a friend of the moon!

This affection is for you,
Gifted with medal of honor ,
as the best mother in the world.
You are "Morabeza" of Deep seas!

Oh woman with thigh of clay!
Your fragile look,
is the mirror of pain.
The guilty is the color of my skin!
Please, carry your cross,
Even if it's in the desert of suffering
Let me sing to you my love,
You are the water of my thought.

©Mar Thieriot (Canada) Blue Print (oil on canvas); (20 x30)

Maria Thieriot is a specialist on connecting emotions, philosophy and art, and believe that those connections are helpful to understand and solve human conflicts peacefully. Painting and poetry can express human suffering in a peaceful manner and may help people to deal with emotional conflicts in a creative manner.

http://www.marianathieriot.com

Borche Panov
(North Macedonia)

Borche Panov was born on September 27, 1961 in Radovish, The Republic of North Macedonia. He graduated from the "Sts. Cyril and Methodius" University of Skopje in Macedonian and South Slavic Languages (1986). He has been a member of the "Macedonian Writers' Association" since 1998. He has published: a) poetry: "What did Charlie Ch. See from the Back Side of the Screen" (1991), "The Cyclone Eye" (1995), "Stop, Charlie" (2002), "The Tact" (2006), "The Riddle of Glass" (2008), "The Basilica of Writing" (2010), "Mystical Supper" (2012), "Vdah (The Breathe of Life)" (2014), "The Human Silences" (2016), "Uhania" (2017), "Shell" (2018); and several essays and plays: "The Fifth Season of the Year" (2000), "The Doppelgänger Town" (2011), "A Dead-end in the Middle of an Alley" (2002), "Homo Soapiens" (2004), "Catch the Sleep-walker" (2005), "Split from the Nose Down" (2006), and "The Summertime Cinema" (2007). He has also poetry books published in other languages: "Particles of Hematite" (2016 – in Macedonian and Bulgarian), "Vdah" (2017 – in Slovenian), "Balloon Shaving" (2018 – Serbian), and "Fotostiheza" ("Photopoesis, 2019 – Bulgarian). His poetry was published in a number of anthologies, literary magazines, journals and his works is translated in more languages.

Translated by Daniela Andonovska-Trajkovska

THE ARTIST OF DEATH

He has been making up death for his whole life
he has been filing her nails,
shaving her beard,
trimming her moustaches,
putting mascara on her eyelashes,
cutting her hair, making pedicure, nail polishing, and
applying liquid and powder foundation,
he has been making her up with a smile – a discrete one
like Mona Lisa's smile,
he was doing her makeover like a nice memory, just for a moment –
to be beautiful before the earth covers her appearance,
before she becomes bodiless – a memory only!

– In my dreams, the dead are coming to me,
they are angry with me
because I have forgotten their golden watches,
or because I have tied their shoes with one knot only,
she wanted white instead of yellow rose
that reminds us on the betrayal,
that I have drawn grimace too severe and cold,
in spite of the fact that she was righteous judge,
that she wasn't as much as pretty while she was alive
as she is now as dead,
and now all people will have memories of her prettier death,
that she has never wanted me to cover her wrinkles
under her eyes
with which she was happy,
that she has never worn bow tie,
nor a shirt with little snob wings –
death is miserable among the rich,
she is neither a man nor a woman, he would say.
When my father passed,
we put cardboard shoes on his feet,
and he didn't complain – but we had grief over his death.

And that is how my life was,
and I am thinking to outwit her with me –
I will turn myself into ash,
so the wind will be my grave,
and when the wind starts to blow from the East,
someone will remember that I was shepherd
before I went to America,
and will drink hot Rakia in my name…

Basudhara Roy (India)

Basudhara Roy is Assistant Professor of English at Karim City College, Jamshedpur, Jharkhand, India. An alumnus of Banaras Hindu University, she holds a Ph.D. in diaspora women's writing from Kolhan University, Chaibasa. Her areas of academic interest are diaspora writing, cultural studies, gender studies and postmodern criticism. As a poet and reviewer, her work is featured/upcoming in anthologies and magazines like The Helter Skelter Anthology of New Writing in English, The Aleph Review, The Poetry Society of India, Mad in Asia Pacific, Teesta, Borderless, Muse India, Shabdadguchha, Cerebration, Rupkatha, Triveni, and Setu among others. She has authored two books, Migrations of Hope (Criticism; New Delhi: Atlantic Publishers, 2019) and Moon in My Teacup (Poetry; Kolkata: Writer's Workshop, 2019). Her second poetry collection, Stitching a Home, is forthcoming in 2021.

Across

But how, across
this hungry blackness of time,
will you find your way
back to me?
The syllables of promise
run awry,
like a jigsaw fashioned
wrong;
Your treasure of words
has been spent elsewhere,
and dry winds have blown away
the footprints of faith.
Lest the return
should shatter you,
retrace not in Love's name
these once-abandoned shores.

Forever beyond, though,
the combs of my longing,
it soothes the heart to know that
somewhere, at least, you are whole.

Sun-bound

To thee, wayfarer of light,
that chase the brilliance
of a thousand suns,
darkness is but a rare hour
in the relentless succession of days
as success-studded, glory-borne,
you claim the hopeful wealth of brightness.
If perchance, however, ominous clouds
should choose to gather upon your ways;
if promises should be dimmed, and
the dancing rays shred to dust;
do not then hesitate, to call on me
for I haven't changed my address.

An inhabitant still of these
faithful plains of darknesses,
my refuge shall be yours.
And together once more, we shall read
those unlearned hieroglyphs of waiting,
till your hope strikes roots
and your sun, rises again.

Chen Hsiu-chen 陳秀珍
（Taiwan）

Chen Hsiu-chen, her publications include essay "A Diary About My Son, 2009", poetry "String Echo in Forest, 2010", "Mask, 2018", "Uncertain Landscape, 2017", "Tamsui poetry, 2018" and "Bone Fracture, 2018" , Mandarin-English-Spanish trilingual "Promise, 2017" as well as Mandarin-English "My Beloved Neruda, 2020".

Her poems have been selected into Mandarin-English-Spanish trilingual anthologies "Poetry Road Between Two-Hemispheres, 2015" and "Voices from Taiwan, 2017", Spanish "Opus Testimoni, 2017", Italian "Dialoghi, 2017" and "Quaderni di traduzione, 2018", as well as English "Whispers of Soflay, Vol. 2, 2018" and "Amaravati Poetic Prism, 2018". Her poems have been also translated into Bengali, Albanian, Turkish and the like.

2019. She was awarded with estrella matutina by Festival of Capulí Vallejo y su Tierra in Peru, 2018. Lebanon Naji Naaman Literary Prizes 2020.

Waiting

I have waited for you
on the bridge
for another whole day
without finding you.

The bridge has waited for me
on the water
for another whole night
with holding me.

I have waited for you
on the bridge for years,

the bridge has waited for me
on the water for centuries.

The bridge sighs with an autumn wind,
I bleed out of my heart.

People and God

The people on both sides of the war
believe the same God.
The left side insists——the truth is ours,
The right side insists——the justice is ours.
Both sides face toward the same God at same time
to pray for the victory on the same battlefield.
The God is separated into two halves
and caught in a dilemma.

The people on both sides of the war
believe different Gods.
Both sides face toward own God to pray
for the victory on the same battlefield.
The left side insists own to be victory,
The right side insists opposite to be defeated.
The war between people to people
becomes an innocent war
between God to God.
The people utilizes missiles to decide
whose God
is a real one.

Translated by Lee Kuei-shien

Christopher Okemwa (Kenya)

Christopher Okemwa is a literature lecturer at Kisii University, Kenya. He has a Ph.D. in performance poetry from Moi University, Kenya. He is the founder and current director of Kistrech International Poetry festival in Kenya (www.kistrechpoetry.org). His novella, Sabina and the Mystery of the Ogre won the Canadian Burt Award for African Literature in 2015. Its sequel, Sabina the Rain Girl (Nsemia Inc., 2019) was selected for the UN SDG 2 Zero Hunger reading list and is fast becoming a popular novella among young people in Africa. Okemwa is the editor of Musings during a Time of Pandemic: A World Anthology of poems on COVID-19 & I Can't Breathe: A Poetic Anthology of Social Justice. He has written eight books of poetry and been translated to Armenian, Chinese, Greek, Norwegian, Finnish, Hungarian, Arabic, Polish, Chinese, Nepalese, Turkish, Russian, Spanish, Catalan, Dutch and Serbian. He has also translated four literary works of international poets from English to Swahili. He is the author of ten folktales of the Abagusii people of Kenya, three children's storybooks, one play, two novels and four oral literature textbooks. *Website: www.okemwa.co.ke*

Translated by Alice-Catherine Carls

Africa

Consider Africa, she as virgin
Savour in its sprawling grassland
Its mountains where many rivers begin
Its beautiful game that adorn the land.
Picture Africa, see it as a home
Of comely fair people and great culture
A haven where white tourists come
To seek sunlight, beauty and rapture.
Consider Africa, see it as a goldmine

Nations scramble over her to have share
Of its moon and its sun, both that shine
To bring life and beauty everywhere
To make Africa home to all races
To make her a symbol of all faces

Consider Africa, mould it as a pillar
That holds up stable the world's nations
It cures continents, a true healer
Of the universe and all God's creations
Picture Africa, as a source of life
Nations scramble over its raw resources
Nations scramble over what she can give:
Thistles, cactus, bamboo, thorns and roses
Elephants, lions, giraffes and baboons
Warm rains, quiet nights and crisp days
Soft grass to sit on by the lagoons
Rocks to sit on to watch the sun rays
Africa, you are a land of wonder
Africa, the world's beauty and grandeur.

The Amazing Night

Sometimes I get so amazed when I watch the night
The way stars drop in on the dark bowl of the sky
And the moon clad in its burnished silver-streaked white
Peeps and hides behind sheep of clouds like a spy

I look at this one sheet of black—a mass of darkness
I find it a mystery that suffuses me with fear and horror
From its dark hollow space, its endless sea of emptiness
Could easily spring out a demon, an imp or a giant ogre

Or something simply wicked, malevolent and evil
That could devour me, consume or take away my soul
So I always peep thru the window to be sure no such devil
Spills into the room in its formidable amorphous prowl

I find it hard to imagine how the night comes to be:

The ominous silence that keeps vigil in every mini space
The opaque black that blinds eyes so that they don't see
Its black furs and grey paints that make an intricate maze

The night is like a churning sea, an agitating ocean
I always see it spilling through the window on the wall
Submerging me in my bedroom in its furious motion
Suffocating and choking me up, leaving dead my soul

I get scared to imagine that someone, out of ill intention
Might one night get access to the giant clock of the universe
Then hold the gadget from moving, against Deity's creation
Shall we live in darkness forever?--what hell shall be for us!

Let Me

Let me make you my obokano
To pluck for a melody

Let me make you my bumpkin
To piece you for lunch

May I turn you into a honey-pot
To spoon you every morning

Maybe I should make you a peremende
To suck and lick

Let me turn you into everything
And be my entire life.

Caroline Nazareno – Gabis
(Philippines)

Caroline 'Ceri Naz' Nazareno-Gabis, World Poetry Canada International Director to Philippines is known as a 'poet of peace and friendship', a multi-awarded poet, journalist, polyglot, educator, peace and women's advocate. She believes that learning other's language and culture is a doorway to wisdom. She is Yali's mom. Among her poetic belts include 7 th Prize Winner in the 19 th, 20 th and 21st Italian Award of Literary Festival; Writers International Network-Canada "Amazing Poet 2015", The Frang Bardhi Literary Prize 2014 (Albania), the sair-gazeteci or Poet Journalist Award 2014 (Tuzla, Istanbul, Turkey) and World Poetry Empowered Poet 2013 (Vancouver, Canada). She's a featured member of Association of Women's Rights and Development (AWID), The Poetry Posse, Galaktika Poetike, Asia Pacific Writers and Translators (APWT), Axlepino and Anacbanua. Her poetry and children's stories have been featured in different anthologies and magazines worldwide. Links to her works:
http://panitikan.ph/2018/03/30/caroline-nazareno-gabis/
https://apwriters.org/author/ceri_naz/
http://www.aveviajera.org/nacionesunidasdelasletras/id1181.html

Ikigai

What is life these days?
Isolated and quarantined.
Where is life as to the moment?
Having no time to repent.
Which way you'll going to take?
When all roads seem so bleak and weary,
What does your heart beat?
When everything seem to fleet
Why will you stay late

Overtime, in hurry of things
You own a life to bear,
How will you create a self-care pledge
When you have stolen all the time
To love and be loved
To care and be cared of.
That you never know,
Selfless vs. selfishness,
There is one thing my heart desires
Seeing everything in place
As we smile heartily together
Living un-imprisoned
From worldly splendour.

My Summer Rain

Summers are born many days and nights
Scourging heat, that brought pain and sweat
Drenching, draining mind's well
As it cries numbness.

Where's the cold breeze from the veranda
Where's the roving droplets to the rocking chair
Have you ever touched the mist
As you blow your nose,
And wipe the heavenly dews
From your eyes,
When you miss the rain,
And shared cold shower
When we're still together.

Will you be the same
Story of our last petrichor,
In a summer rain?

Dinos Koubatis (Greece)

Dinos Koubatis was born in Athens. He studied Theater, French Philology and Journalism. As an actor and director he has worked in various parts of the world, such as Greece, France, Belgium, Canada, Albania and has won many international awards, such as the "Ionesco International Award" for all his directing work. He has founded the International Theater Festival "Art without Borders", the International Festival of Inter-Balkan Theater, the Experimental Theater Center, and other theatrical organizations. In the field of Letters he has distinguished himself as a writer, essayist, poet and novelist. One of his essays and three historical novels have become bestsellers and have been nominated for the State Prize for Literature. He has been named Professor of Byzantine Studies at the University of Valencia, is an honorary member of international intellectual institutions and has won many international distinctions and gold medals for his work. His works are the subject of university dissertations at the Universities of Warsaw, Tirana and Zurich. It has been translated in many countries of the world. 32 of his books have been published in Greece, France, Canada, Poland, Kosovo and Albania, while thirty of his plays have been staged. He has collaborated in newspapers, radio and television.

THE NEW WORLD

I kept the hopes all, in my soul,
and their hearts beat I recruited
in the submission of my spirit.
History's root alive me
and the continuation of the human race
that I fell madly in love with life,
I entered the fight and fought.

For the good of the Manhood I have suffered,
for the soul the indestructible continuity,
for the mind the eternal evolution,
I was in pain as if I saw all the ruins around me.
I rose through the ashes,
with faith and strength I was armed
and I set out for new conquests,
to resurrect what was left dead,
to give back the first form
in Life, in Man, in Hope.
At the light of Dawn, the beginning is born
for a new, better world,
full of harmony and consensus.

THE MYTH OF OLIVE ...

Glaucopian, with blue eyes, daughter,
down from Olympus * the palaces,
Goddess, in the name of Athena *, daughter of Zeus *
Poseidon * to fight
for the city's name.
And he, the ruler, the defiant of the sea,
the trident tapped on the rock of the Acropolis *
and salty water sprang,
where the people admired the miracle,
however, water from the sea,
how to serve them and what?
She, God of War and Wisdom,
the spear hit the rock
and the tree of the olive emerged.
At that time, the citizens thought and saw
the difference, and appreciated it,
and cutting branches of olive, from its tree,
they were crowning her divine face
and "Polyada" * have proclaimed it,
protector of their city
which they named, for her sake, "Athens".
And this, for their love

and their appreciation,
with the branches of her tree
the Olympians * hoped to crown
and of the fruit of the oil to drain,
gift of life, gold in color
like the sun the light that life
to Man gives.

THE SONG OF BIRDS
to Ilirian Zhupa

I find your country's birds in my country.
In the courtyard of my house with colorful feasts,
thousands of birds sing in Spring
and weeping sadly in Winter ...

Throughout the world, birds are hiding in the trees.
Only their thoughts leave for other countries,
In all countries the birds sing an Spring
she never tells her to reach ...

Duška Vrhovac (Serbia)

Duška Vrhovac, a poet, writer, journalist and translator was born in Banja Luka, now the state of Serbian Republic of Bosnia and Herzegovina, in 1947. She graduated Comparative Literature (Department of World Literature) at the Faculty of Philology , University of Belgrade. She used to work for the Television Belgrade (Radio Television of Serbia) for many years and simultaneously for a number of major newspapers and magazines. Duška Vrhovac has published 25 books of poetry, some of which have been translated in part or in full into more than 20 languages (English, Spanish, Italian, French, German, Russian, Arabic, Chinese, Polish, Turkish, Greek, Hungarian, Dutch, Bulgarian, Macedonian, Albanian, Jewish...) and is among the most significant contemporary authors of Serbia and beyond. Represented in newspapers, literary journals and anthologies of prime value, she has participated in numerous literary festivals, meetings and events in Serbia and abroad. Duška Vrhovac has received important awards and recognitions for her poetry as are: Majska nagrada za poeziju [May Award for Poetry], 1966 – Yugoslavia; Pesničko uspenije [Poetic Ascension] – 2007, Serbia; Premio Gensini – Gensini Prize-Poetry Section – 2011, Italy; Naji Naaman's International Literary Prize for Complete Works -2015, Lebanon, Beirut; Plaque and medal with image of Sima Matavulj, founder and first president of the Association of Writers of Serbia – the award for significant work and contribution to literature – 2016, Serbia and Golden Badge awarded by the Institute for Culture and Education of the Republic of Serbia – 1992. Duška Vrhovac is a member of the Association of Writers of Serbia, Association of Literary Translators of Serbia, of the International Fderation of Journalists and other literary organisations; she is the Ambassador of the movement Poets of the World for Serbia and their Vice-President for Europe. Duška Vrhovac works as a writer and a freelance journalist and lives in Belgrade. She is mother, grandmother and great-grandmother and she is not a member of any political party.

A CHIPPED PATH

The machine that you made, while you were still a human being
and used to earn money with your own work, is entering your chamber,
waving with its metal hands and ordering you to move aside,
it's telling you not to bother it while it's sorting out your space, your life
and your head.
You're clutching your head, trying to talk,
but there is neither your voice nor anyone to hear it.

The machine is doing its job, everything is well organized,
You are calm and your only emotional click happens
when your identification chip coalesces with flesh
you turn to the reader to sign in or sign out.
You don't even remember that is not something you actually wanted,
that you didn't want to erase yourself, but to become a master.

Memory is frozen and you only have to find a way
How to transmit the self-destructing information
to those who will just come and marvel at the fragility of your bones,
the depth of your eye sockets, and study the composition of the fluid
which used to be called blood,
while they would be replacing the oil for the lubrication of their artificial
joints.
Someone wise would conclude that the beginning of the new era is
happening.

*(Tanslator's note: *Burich, Vladimir – Russian poet,
author of "Lead pillow")*

A BREAK IN LJUBLJANA

Evening completely entered into the room
and closed the door.
Rain is loudly sliding down the window
and smells of the cold north.
Hotel Tourist, room 525.
On one pillow my sleepy eyes
and melancholic thoughts

on another one, Burich* and you.
Slowly, I am putting together, masks of life
and images of the meeting with you
on the white lead pillow.
A break in Ljubljana
a break from life
fear of a return.
Evening completely entered into the room
and closed the door.
Rain is loudly sliding down the window
and smells of the cold north.
I don't suspect anything.
The night is weakened
and the morning delayed.
Slowly, I am putting together, masks of life
and images of the meeting with you
on the white lead pillow.

*(Tanslator's note: *Burich, Vladimir – Russian poet, author of "Lead pillow")*

Translated from Serbian: Aleksandar Malesevic

Dr. Deepti Gupta (India)

Former Professor & Educational Advisor, Ministry of H.R.D., New Delhi, India. Served in the Hindi Depts of three top Indian universities:
Ruhilkhand University, Bareilly; Jamia Millia Islamia, New Delhi: Pune University, Pune (Oxford of India). The President of India deputed her against the post of Educational Advisor in the Dept. of Education, Ministry of Human Resource & Development, New Delhi for a period of 3 years (1989 – 1992) Published Books:

Fiction : Shesh Prasang; Sarhad se Ghar Tak; Hashiye Par Ugate Hue Suraj

Collection of Poems : Antaryatra; Ocean In the Eyes; Dularte Shabd
Tulsi Ke Birave Tale

Research Books :
Amrilal Nagar – Human Values & Ideals; Amrilal Nagar – Historical & Social Aspect; Amrilal Nagar – Vision and Philosophy; Amrilal Nagar – Social & Cultural Aspect; Collection of Reviews

Edited Books : Payame Zindagi Aur Suna – Edited (Collection of Nazm); Waqt ke Aiyene mai – Edited (Collection of Nazm); Lekhak Ke Aiyene mai Lekhak (Collection of Memoirs); Timeless Stories by Munshi Premchand

Silent Bonding

Bonding with heart
Between two passionate persons
never comes to an end
No storm, no squall can ever uproot them
Neither harsh feelings can ever swallow them
Nor the gush of anger Can ever wipe them away
Can ever eliminate them up
Because......!
they have been interwoven
Strand by strand for years with smiles & tears
Pure heart bondings grow up
strongly in the cradle of joy & grief
They are close knitted
With the invisible dainty emotional fibrils
When there is something Offensive between
Two Such intensely close persons
they refrain from talking to each other
In those moments their Silence speaks
Silent bonding is always deep and divine
It is so sublime that two persons don't need
mundane words to transmit
their feelings to each other
Every throb of their heart
conveys those subtle feelings
miles away swiftly on their own
When between them
Silence begins to communicate
This means, they have developed
a soul bonding And bonding with soul is
over 'n above everything
And for ever....!!!

Daniela Andonovska Trajkovska
(North Macedonia)

Daniela Andonovska-Trajkovska (born February 3, 1979, Bitola, North Macedonia) is poetess, scientist, editor, literary critic, doctor of pedagogy, university professor. She works at the Faculty of Education-Bitola, St. "Kliment Ohridski" University-Bitola, Republic of North Macedonia and teaches the courses: Methodology of Teaching Language Arts, Creative Writing, Critical Literacy, Methodology of Teaching Early Reading and Writing, ect. She is co-founder of the University Literary Club "Denicija PFBT UKLO" and also of the Center for Literature, Art, Culture, Rhetoric and Language at the Faculty of Education-Bitola. She is member of the Macedonian Writers' Association, and The Bitola Literary Circle, and was president of the Macedonian Science Society Editorial Council (for two mandates). She is editor in chief of the literary journal "Rast"/ "Growth" issued by the Bitola Literary Circle, and also – editor in chief of the International Journal "Contemporary Dialogues" (Macedonian Science Society), and "Literary Elements" Journal (Perun Artis), several poetry and prose books. Besides her scientific work published in many international scientific journals (over 100 articles), and one university book "Critical Literacy", she writes poetry, prose and literary critics. She has published one prose book: "Coffee, Tea and the Red Sky" (2019), and 8 poetry books: "Word for the Word" (2014), "Poems for the Margins" (2015), "Black Dot" (2017), Footprints" (2017), "Three" (2019), "House of Contrasts" (2019), "Electronic Blood" (2019), and "Math Poetry" (2020). She has won special mention at the Nosside World Poetry Prize (UNESCO, 2011), the award for the best unpublished poem at the Macedonia Writers' Association Festival (2018), "Krste Chachanski" prize for prose (2019), National "Karamanov" Poetry Prize for poetry 2019, Macedonian Literary Avant-garde (2020), "Abduvali Qutbiddin" (third, 2020, Uzbekistan). Her poetry was published in a number of anthologies, literary magazines and journals both at home and abroad, and her works are translated into more International Languages. She has translated many literary works from English, Serbian and Bulgarian language.

PYTHAGOREAN THEOREM

I love the hypotenuse
over which you build our dream house
with the pebbles of all our blind passing by each other
and all our meetings by chance through the centuries
and all our mutual lives
that were born and had been dying
on the line that intersects all of the times at once

I love all of your 90 degrees
and your legs with open palms and separated time
and the naughty looks on my naked body
I love

Me myself – one quarter of a rectangle
– diametric sky of sighs I am dreaming

I love that hypotenuse
over which you build the square
pebble by pebble

PERPENDICULAR LINES

the crystal cells are moving unnoticeably
on the life line
the planes perpendicularly cut my body
in infinite number of points
and I got stomach pain

I have friends that lurk in the shadows
and crucify me on two perpendicular lines
so I could be what I already am
– the best version of myself

Darcie Friesen Hossack (Canada)

Darcie Friesen Hossack is a graduate of the Humber School for Writers in Toronto, Canada. Her short story collection, Mennonites Don't Dance, was shortlisted for the Commonwealth Writers Prize and others. She is the managing editor of WordCity Monthly and is currently finishing a novel.

river

we walked along the riverbed
turned over the bleached bones of
washed down trees

ideas we had when
I thought I knew you

seed heads of anemones
picked up with wind-
swept sand that

scours our eyes until
scales fall away

we used to talk
on the swing on your porch
while hummingbirds perched to
sit and
sip nectar from a jar

we are the hands and the feet
you said, and picked up a stone
to throw in the river,

where it rippled the surface
and sank

you offered me dates from the bank of
another place, where
people have been replaced by trees

skin

they say the pandemic is causing us to dream
and last night I dreamed of you
your still-fatted skin spread out on my floor
where I could touch you one last time
I stripped, got down on my knees and crawled
until we were hands to hands,
thighs to thighs,
face to face.
before I woke, I zipped you up behind me

© Paola Iotti (Italy) "Half Sky" (40 x30), 2021
Pencils on paper

**Ekaterini Vlachopanagiotou Batalia
(Greece)**

President of International Society of Greek Writers and Artists

She was born in Litochoro, Pieria, where she received her first letters. She finished Secondary Education in Thessaloniki. In 1974 she graduated from the Panteion School of Political Science and in 1990 from the Pedagogical Department of the National and Kapodistrian University of Athens. She works as a Classroom Economist, a member of the UN, Ph.D. D. E. T. in Byzantine Humanism. She served also from the position of General Secretary of Letters, Arts, Culture through the great work of the two organizations from 1993 to November 2019, when she was elected President of the International Society of Greek Writers. She contributed greatly, with the president Chrysoula Varveri – Varra, in the organization and with full success of the 1st International Literature and Painting Competition, proposing the registered name of "MELINEIA TROPAIA" 1996.

Her published works are:

– "Critique of existing regional development incentives in Greece and the provincial industry"
– "The concept of classical works"
– "The story of the number"
– "The epic of Digenes Akritas. Folk poetry"
– "Historical background of music" –
– "The Carnival and its customs in Greece"
– "Searching for peaceful coexistence with ourselves"
– "The contribution of the fairy tale to the ethno plastic education of the child"
– "The struggle with ourselves"
– "Become a hero" etc.

From now on, from the position of President of the International Society of Greek Writers (and Artists), she has been working hard to promote the exchange between different cultures of the world, so as to further the cause of world peace and the development of humanity.

THE EARTH

Passenger of the earth
I travel the universe
and I go back in circles
Chartered ship
from to time the earth revolves
and fare, people,
on the ground where do they go?
recipient the death ...
and the fare is dead.
Loaded ship is the round earth
and it turns
and the pilot invisible
does it keep going
but where is it going?
with unknown laws
in astral corridors he rules
and from the sun the road
for light every day passes.
Servant of the earth
on the blanket
I turn and time I fear
and count cycles,
until fare dead to take me.
Loaded ship
is the round earth
and the ballasts are full
by masses of people,
Sarcophagi of death
and life secrets.

Ekene May (Nigeria)

Ekene May is an Award-Winning Poet, Visual Artist and Model. She earned a Bachelor's Degree in English Language from Ahmadu Bello University. Upon graduation, she honed her skills and ventured into Radio production, and would later quit to be a full-time Poet and Visual Artist. She has written and performed on stages for Action-Aid, PLAN, SustyVibes, Nile University, ECWA, Christ Embassy, OkangaLive, Agogo Music Festival, to mention a few. Her poems, Hall of Fame, got rewarded for Best Content by NYPF, Hair Regimen, was placed among the top 20 poems of the Eriata Orhibabor Poetry Prize in 2018, The Butcher, won her the International Castello di Diuno Poetry Prize, from Italy. She recently launched her NGO, The Ekene May Arts Foundation, with an aim to take arts, to public places, for free, working with donations and grants. She writes and paints from Abuja, Nigeria.

my journey to self realization,

is not as easy as some motivational speakers make it seem,
they say I have to remember where I am coming from,
to know where I am going,
what if I do not remember where to start?
what if I don't know to climb the bridge of my mother's nose,
but almost slide off when I try,
so to stay steady, I loop my feet into her nostrils,
hold on to her lower eye lids,
hands and feet apart,
hands and head raised,
I want to see her eyes,
I do not want to fall into her mouth,
and be silent forever,
I do not want to die behind her lips,
trapped by walls of teeth, brown and golden,
or lose my breath beneath her tongue,

when I regain composure,
I crawl to her cheek,
her ear seem a bit far-off, on the right,
I follow the fourth wrinkle instead, at the corners of her face,
away from her temple, it leads straight into her right eye,
fall into it,
and find home.

web

It is a beauty pageant and I am collating bodies
'57 feared dead'
'numbers', Nnamdi mutters under his breath, but his leg has a bullet hole in it
'hmmmp, that's a lot', Ahmad replies, and he walks away, with men who have rods
the men in my dream shoot at sight, outside a mall while a women's football match goes on inside its pitch
and I am collecting stories, bones, nightmares
collating blood on our flag and broken chords of the anthem
I am collating dust, slumped soldiers shoulders and heads
hung in despair
collecting fear and bullet holes in the necks of bodies so peaceful, you'd think Oke were asleep
I am collating votes, that did not count, that will not count, that will not be cast
collecting palm fronds from women whose husbands mourned for
in silence
I am collecting empty spaces
collating nothing, spinning, twirling
whirling history and more dust
no one is beautiful, no one is whole.

Evgenia Tagareva (Bulgaria)

Evgenia Tagareva is a poet, translator of poetry, pianist and music pedagogue, author of songs and piano works. She works from an early age, her first appearances were during the school years – in literary competitions, in periodicals, on radio and television.

She is the author of the poetry collections "House in the Sky" (1993), "Right to Return" (1995), "Music from the Temple" (2013), as well as a collection of original music for piano "Sounds of Infinity" (2019). Her poems have been translated and published in German and Polish. She presents her work at original musical and poetic recitals in different cities in Bulgaria and Europe. She takes an active part in all publications and performances of the International Poetry Festival "Spirituality without Borders" since its establishment in 2015. Member of the Society of Plovdiv Writers. Founder and President of the Foundation for Art, Culture and Young Talents "Fire of Orpheus", which implements a number of national and international projects. Evgenia Tagareva's poetry reveals the spiritual quests and the rich inner world of man – a cosmic being with creative power and a desire to know his original divine essence.

***

I believe in the heavenly magic
And so I call on you
Come, Worlds
Come over here
Transform everything
Oh, Worlds of heaven
Open up to the earthly human
Reveal your deepness, appear to him
May your magic bring light
To the seeming hopelessness of our lives

May the Earth be free
From despair and darkness
                    Let it shine
The soul of the World

The apocalypse
is inside us!

TRIPTYCH

I
Where can the light of the heart be found?
We always question and search, and desire...
Let us ourselves be the light of life
before the darkness makes us blind!

II
May we suffer!
With the patience of an ant,
with the dignity of a flower,
with the fervour in our wings!

Shall we suffer?
Yes, But only if the wailings
leave diamond traces
in our souls!

III
A bloody drop is falling into my earthly eye
A pearl is shining inside the heavenly light eye
A blow! Then pain, and flesh, and darkness in the heart!
The aspiration flows into the soul
                                  and once more
I'm Love!

Eduard Harents (Armenia)

Eduard Harents, born in 1981, is a famous poet. He live in Yerevan, Armenia. He has graduated from Yerevan State University, the faculty of Oriental Studies and Cairo University Center of Arabic Language and Culture. Harents is an author of 10 poem collections. He has been published in numerous Armenian and foreign periodicals and anthologies. He is a quintuple prize winner: in 2007, 2009, 2011 and 2013 he was awarded in Best Poetical Series and Best Translation nominations. Young poets first prize by the name of Irina Gyulnazaryan («The best poetry book of the year») for the book «Lethargic Vigilance», Yerevan, 2013. The International literary prize «Pjeter Bogdani» (2015, Kosovo),- prize for Poetry-2015. The International literary prize «Dardanica» (2019, Belgium). Panorama Global Award («Panorama International Literature Award 2020», Insus Scrolls Press/Writers Capital International Foundation, India-Italy). Eduard Harents poems were translated into more than 50 languages. Eduard Harents is the most translated Armenian writer of all times. In 2016, his book «The life lives me» was published in Belgium («Jeta jeton më mua»; Bruxelles, "Bogdani" publishing house), and in 2017, his book «Lethargic Vigilance» was published in Spain («Vigilia letárgica»; Barcelona, "Emboscall" publishing house). In 2014 he participated in the Festivalul de Internaţionale "Nopţile de Poezie de la Curtea de Argeş" (Romania) and in the Festival Internazionale di Poesia di Genova (Italy).

Translated from Armenian by Herminée Arshakyan & Harout Vartanian

I am plucking now
the eyelashes of silence one by one
to mend my prayer,
which has been torn by nuances of word…
Now the nuance is more than the voice…
And now I enter

the church of Hope barefooted,
so that my steps will not paint voices on my fortune.
How many footprints have been split apart by whispers...
While my footprint
is my prayer of love,
which never ends,
as it never colors itself in words...
And now
the main color is the truth,
that love is the poem of the feeling...
That muses don't turn into women...

Yearning

The shadow of color
is scaling
the scars of day;
walking the serenity
of an encountered dream...

The flower is the secret
of pain;
an introspective smile.
The scion names the sin.

Beyond personal bandages
of prayer,
the self-denial of a tree
is as much bright
as warm are the hands
of night.

I am freezing... your name.

Eden Soriano Trinidad (Philippines)

Eden writes poetry in English, Filipino and Sambal her native dialect. She is labeled as a global iconic personality and a World Leader Ambassador for Peace. Some of her literary works and books are published by the University of the Philippines (UP) Institute for Creative Writing Freelipiniana Online (FOL) Panitikan.ph. Her poems translated in the Chinese Language by Tian Yu have been published in the National newspaper "Science Herald" in China, and she is being featured in the cover of a legendary magazine "Chinese Poetry Influence" now an International magazine, M.S.Jiebao.com, M.P. Weixin. QQ. Com. One of her poems about COVID 19 is a Finalist and published in the First World Daily Poetry Competition in the World daily in Macao. She won first place in the 2020 1st World Daily Poetry Competition in China. Her poetry book collections/series Eden Blooms are translated in Telugu, Hindi, Serbian and Chinese and some of her poems are translated in different major languages in the world. She translated in Filipino the books "The Casket of Vermillion" by Dr. Lanka Siva Rama Prasad, "Sun Shower" by Krishna Prasai, "How the Twin Grew Up" by Dr. Milutin Djurickovic, "The Era of Junk "by Mai Van Phan & the Poetry book of Narsing Bongu Rao "Another Face of Sky". Selected poems of her are published in KELAINO in Greece, Serbian Anthology book, Inner Child Press Anthologies, Azahar Revista, Amaravati Poetic Prism, short story pubished in Soflay magazine, and numerous printed and online international book anthologies, literary magazines, websites, and newspapers. She is the founder of UNITY WORLD PEACE POETS (UNWPP) duly registered in the Philippines. Appointed President of Chinese Spring Poetry Festival - Philippine Branch ,Vice- President of Silk Road Poetry in China & International Vice-President of Jara Foundation Nepal.

Taking the Journey like

In the soaring majestic mountains of life
Black death lurking in hidden canyons,
valleys and plains.
Kept us on long holidays longer than expected,
Regretful, still, we stayed inside our cell.

You came to enshroud me during the twilight of this century
Every day in the sixth hour,
you appeared before me and asked, how's my best friend?
Verily said unto me,
"I want to see you bloom like the Alpine of the Alps."

There were moments my sparkless eyes would glisten,
and you made it twinkle like the million stars in the dark heaven
There were nights that babbling brooks
trespassed from my tired eyes
while you whirled and cuddled me with your grins and jokes.

You've been there for me.
So many miles away, and yet so near
as you waved the bunch of violets and tulips
enliven every moment,
"It's time to celebrate, my dear friend."
Moods changed as you sat beside me
keeping one's eyes on our monitors,
while you nudged me to listen to your favorite songs.

How are you, my friend?
It's now my turn to ring the bell,
Whether we celebrate on these holidays in our season
Taking the journey like swallows and Avian,
Or, live for this moment and pray that God grants us a boon.

Eva Petropoulou Lianoy (Greece)
Blog: http://evalianou.blogspot.gr

Eva was born in Xylokastro where she completed her basics studies. In 1994 she worked as a journalist in French newspaper "Le LIBRE JOURNAL," but her love for Greece won and returned to her sunny home. Since 2002, she lives and works in Athens. She works as a web radio producer reading fairy tales at radio logotexniko vima every sunday. Recently she become responsible for the children literary section in Vivlio anazitiseis publications in Cuprys. She published books and ebooks: " I and my other avenger, my Skia publications Saita." "Zeraldin and The elf of the lake" in Italian and in French as well as "The daughter of the Moon" in 2 languages English and Greek. The Moon Daughter published by Ocelotos 4 times, received best reviews for author's writing and writing style. She is a member of the Unesco Logos and Art Group, of the writers of Corinth, of Panhellenic Writers Association. Also her work is mentioned in the Known Greek awarded encyclopedia for Poets and authors, Harry Patsi, page 300.

Her books have been cleared by the Ministry of Education of Cyprus.

Eva's recent work includes: "The water Amazon fairy called Myrtia" ,illustrated by Vivi Markatos, dedicated to a girl that become handicap after a sexual assault and the translation of stories of Lafcadio Hearn, "Fairytravel with stories from Far East", an idea that she worked more than 6 months illustrated by Ms Ntina Anastasiadoy, very known sculptor and sumi e painter in Greece.

To the unknown man
Long distance relationship

Days you smile
Nights I cry
Days u become silent
I become so communicative
Birds are coming from far lands

Back to their nest
Wondering will you come to our nest
Long distance relationship
My why become so long
Your words are a rainbow
In my rainy moments

Hope the heaven hear my prayers
Soon you are free from unknown chains

Hear my heart beat
Hear my heart voice

More and more
Every day
Every night
Singing for you
My precious man...

***

Wishes become prayers
Prayers become words in the God ears
Wispers coming from Angels
My poetry is a bridge between earth and heaven
One request i have
One word i cry out
... Peace...
... Peace...
... Peace....

Emna Copedi (Colombia)

Poet, writer, declaimer and plastic artist from Colombia, author of several unpublished books and participant in more than one hundred anthologies from fifty countries and her poems have been translated into several languages obtaining important awards and recognitions for her artistic and poetic work. She has participated in multiple art exhibitions and literary meetings. She is a founding member of the Fundación Crea Cultura de Ciénaga Magdalena and a member of the Ambassador of Peace for the (Cercle Universal des Ambassadeurs de la Paix France-Switzerland) and of the Hispanomundial Union of Writers of Peru.

Main motto is "To create lasting works of art, worthy of admiration generation after generation, is to be able to live after death".

RAIN OF WORDS ..

I want to see fall
heavy rain of words
that expands in its drops
A single language,
a single sun, a single you.

ECHOES OF CARNIVAL

Auscultating the tinkling
of drums and bagpipes,
my environment currency
musical colors
when melting real images
in fantastic worlds,
folkloric.
"Carnival" … Your name
Impact walls
of Caribbean hearts,
who enjoy the sound of litanies
and they dance incessantly
discarding any sorrow
anxiety, weakness and sleepiness.
Just mention you
my veins turn
crimson
sand, tricolor and mother jungle.
Brushstrokes
whisper in my ear
an ecstasy of orgasms frenzy
feeling the color
mixed with your laughter,
the bustle crowds
in our minds
without deciphering clearly
the pictures of long-awaited carnival.
Ending your days of revelry
nuance echo
shake my brain,
evoking return to your feasts.

Eltona Lakuriqi (Albania)

Eltona Lakuriqi (born in Tirana in 1984) has published books of poetry such as : "Walking", "The Masks" "Blue glasses", "Within the art without rings", "Spiritual Chaos" and "Poetry". She runs the periodical "Alternativa". She is the editor of the magazine "Mirdita". In 2014 she graduated with a bachelor of "International Relations" in "Political Science". During the period October-November 2016 she was the moderator of the radio talk show "Catch the moment" (Kap Momentin) broadcasted by radio " Voice of Mitrovica" (Zeri I Mitrovices). In February 2017 she collaborated with the newspaper "The covenant of Gore" (Beselidhja Gorare). In March 2017 she was a Jury member of the Poetry Contest organized by the youth center "Anza" on the World Book Day. In August 2017 she was the coordinator of the Poetry Contest organized by the Writers' club "Drita" (The Light). In September 2017 she was the moderator of the artistic Contest "Word carves the stone" organized by the Municipality of Kamez. In August 2018 she was the organizer of the promotion of the volume "Antologjia 5" (Antology 5), published by the writers' club "Drita" (The Light). She lives in Italy.

No title

A time tangled in a web of dark threads,
strives in between anti-values and sufferings.
I wish, I daydream
how what is left behind
by the tireless voyagers
can be healed.

The sun warms and burns
the skin of the earth.
Our existence

Will water the damaged roots.

The seas greatly cracked
at the feet of depth
which rocks us
as a leaf.

This era with
Ugly masks
Is making fun of us.

Remember,
Wake up.
The joy of birds
will return one day
from distant lands
of the unknown.

Strongly
I scream and pray:
Era,
Please change
The tomorrow
between us.

The night of my sky

My sky is changed
in the spaces between the tops of the trees
bird shadows exchange their paths.

My sky is changed
thousands of small clouds.

Enxhi Drapi (Albania)

Enxhi Drapi, born and raised in Tirana, Albania, on August 26, 1999. Since childhood passionate about poetry and acting. Student at the Faculty of Law, University of Tirana. Author of the novel "Diku ku dielli nuk perëndon", which is being positively evaluated by literary critics as well as by readers, due to the special style and authenticity it carries.

Muse with vices

Somewhere i read a miserable philosopher
"the ego"- he said, in shackles will lead the man!
We seeking so much in the cup of coffee,
with great difficulty, we managed to find a mortality in the sack!

I dream of having a muse with vices next to me!
one of those, which confuse my mornings...
I want to love someone stricly prohibited
the one, who shakes the handcuffs on her hands!

I think incessantly,
and fantasy always leads me to you...
With eyes closed
with a dark handkerchief ,try to get there...
I traipse the streets full of blood,
and i can't see the rose with eyes...

I dream of having a muse with vices next to me!
Her irritated face wears the yashmak to the sun...
To admire when she disobeys and becomes angry,
and after a while in the chest ask me to take shelter...

I want it to be full of life and firey ego...
and the peace be stick after the firey victory
I love you forbidden curse!
I also accept death if i am infected!
I hurt you and look forward to the victory of your revenge
I rejoice more than you in that dream victoy!
I rejoice more than you in that dream vict
I dream of having a muse with vices next to me
to destroy everyone in parks and squares...
Fantasize to have the one I hurt and destroyed,
to win, and tell that i changed for her!

I want to have that being with me every day,
and leaves in her hands heavens and the planets.
I realise that somewhere deep i had throw you,
the ecpedition group in the spirit had found you.

I want to have that being with me every day
to see her face as she sleeps
and the sun strikes her with ray...
I contemplate it awaking every cell as at the birth,
with longing i touch her lightly,
wakes up and starts moving...
Whose daughter that swore to me with enemy
to strut.. and ask "who is the winner?"

I love the one who has vices!
I can smell her also on the other side of the continent!
I will recall her when to fall into the armed hand of the enemy...
I will tell them that they are scrabies goats
that have fallen from fig!

Florin M. Ciocea (Romania)

He born 11.06.1957, Fetești city, Ialomitza country, Romania. Poet, prose writer, journalist, published 15 books.

***

Bury your palms in my soul
And bring in light my love for you;
If you don"t
The stars will shine less,
And the clear vacuum will fill
With that despair of matter,
Which puts fear in the face of women.

Hide in the deep well of my eyes
To see how much i love the grass,
Forests, mountains and people,
And may,
Sometime,
You will love me so much.

If you meet me... do not bypass me;
May be season that heals you from sadness
Or the first snow shivering your cheeks in december.

***

Wherever you look can only see the shadows of the people in the sky
And the shadow of the sky coloring their souls,
So, paradise exists in traveling shadows,
We feel it,
But we will never live in it,
Because the matter of your steps
Draws an impenetrable wall
Between the soul imprisoned in the ephemeral shell
And his reflection on the transparent wings of clouds.

***

Because it"s dark and cold in the universe,
Ignite the light in your heart
And leave it there;
A beacon for the saddened,
For lonely wanderers waiting
A little hope to shatter
The cold darkness of their soul.

Faleeha Hassan (Iraq)

She is a poet, teacher, editor, writer, playwriter born in Najaf, Iraq, in 1967, who now lives in the United States. Faleeha is the first woman to wrote poetry for children in Iraq. She received her master's degree in Arabic literature, and has now published 25 books. Her poems have been translated into English, Turkmen, Bosevih, Indian, French, Italian, German, Kurdish, Spain, Korean, Greek, Serbia, Albanian, Pakistani, Romanian, Malayalam and ODIA language. Ms. Hassan has received many awards in Iraq and throughout the Middle East for her poetry and short stories. Her poems and short stories are published in a variety of more magazines and International Anthologies.

Pulitzer Prize Nomination 2018
PushCaret Prize 2019
IWAWiner of the Moonstone Chapbook Contest 2019
Winer of the Moonstone Chapbook Contest 2019.
Cultural Ambassador – Iraq, USA

About war I'm talking

What if I slept all that time
Or
I had hibernated from 1980 to 1988?
To be a safe bear
Or wood frog with full body parts
Is much better than being locked in a damaged soul
Your meaning of existence is peeling harshly
Whenever the storm of war is blowing,
Yes,
I remember

In the time of war
The soldiers' mothers
Are unable to pass their hands through the thickness of
the walls of absence,
To gently smooth the hair of their boys
Or wipe their dusty faces,
Time after time
Disappointment hits them non-stop
like a squash ball in the hand of a beginner player
While hope keeps escaping from their hearts as nimble as a cat
In the end
They will not cry
But their eyes are melting
Drop by drop
Now
Invisibles like us,
They wish they could heal
From the brain perforating
Siren
And not wake up
Everyday
Shouting in the ears of the house
I am here
I am here
Like someone reading a unmemorized manuscript
invisibles like us
Afraid
One day the lips of the bombs
Will drown them with hot kisses
....

1980 to 1988 , the duration of the Iran – Iraqi war
wood frog, this frog dies in the winter time and comes back
to life in summer

F. Attila Balázs (Hungary)

Born in Transylvania on January 15th, 1954. He graduated in Library science and Literary translation in Bucharest. In 1990, he moved to Slovakia. In 1994, he founded AB-ART Publishing, of which he is the director since then. He is a member of the Hungarian Writers' Union, of the European Academy of Sciences, Arts and letters, Paris, of the Writers' Union of Romania, of the Hungarian PEN Club, of the Writers' Association of Slovakia. honorary member of the Academy of Sciences, Arts and letters, Chisinau, Moldova, As the author of more than a dozen collections of poetry and the translator of more than twenty books of poetry and fiction, Attila F. Balázs has received numerous awards and prizes in acknowledgement of his various literary activities (Opera Omnia Arghezi Prize (2014), Dardanica Prize, Brussels-Prishtina , Lucian Blaga Prize (2011), EASAL Prize, Paris, 2020, Madách Prize (Slovakia, 1992), World English Writer's Union award, India, 2019,Lukijan Mušicki Award, Belgrad, 2019. His works have been translated in 22 languages. As an invited poet, he is a regular participant of diverse literary festivals all around the world.

PUZZLE

sit down here on the bed
I gaze at you in silence
I discover you anew
stay next to me

don't rush off, sit down
the swallows are wintering already
not even the clouds rest
on the top of the hill
stay next to me

until I collect myself
with trembling hands
this is a puzzle with ghosts

I'm not afraid of myself
the days are scattered cards
I search for you on the map of your face
hold my hand until I die!

VIPER

you're watching when you're not even
looking what could you see with coins
on your eyes?
what do blind eyes see?

words lose their weight
objects their forms
gestures their meaning
lips their shine
birds their voices
poems their meaning

only you
keep the lifelike moving pictures
who I once was

you look at me inside
in a stiff yoga position
a viper hisses in your lap

Gopal Lahiri (India)

Gopal Lahiri is a Kolkata- based bilingual poet, critic, editor, writer and translator with 22 books published mostly (13) in English and a few (8) in Bengali, including three jointly edited books.
His poetry is also published across various anthologies as well as in eminent journals of India and abroad.
He has been invited in various poetry festivals including World Congress of Poets recently held in India.
He is published in 12 countries and his poems are translated in 12 languages.

Little Light

Someday little light gets into rooms
measure the buoyancy.

The soft voice of the wind wipes the dust
of unforgivable desert inside,

Those ripped out notes, keep it tuned
listening to the walls braces whine,

Morning rays give birth to freedom and hope
meet outline of the dusk's glow,

Why ever people want to go move out?
windows chase butterflies in tow

Aging unsettles into streams of memoir
ebbs and flows, unravels the pristine landscape

Relief

Night misshapen and maimed, stars cease to knock,
dark shadows and the veils of cobwebs
swing on the high ceiling,

Lights on the edges, muffle its curses, look like half a light,
silence follows the footsteps,
the strong wind returns soft words,

Unknown voices dip slowly, a flush comes from behind,
dews of innocence,
night birds flapping their wings over the em

A stretch of black sky pulls down the eyes,
silence wraps all around,
palms storing whispered sentences,

The rains never hurt, never scar the painted walls,
the tiny drops now turn into secret notes,

Grey hairs memorise all those absurd moments.

Gianpaolo G. Mastropzsqua (Italy)

Gianpaolo G. MASTROPASQUA was born in Bari in November 1979. After completing part of his studies in Seville, he graduated from the University of Bari with a thesis in Psychiatry.

He has also completed a Post Graduate Course, at the same University, in Bioethics with a thesis on the relationship betweenpsychiatry and art therapy. Psychiatrist and received a master's degree in Criminology.

He works in Lecce as a psychiatrist in the "Santa Maria Novella" Hospital (ASL – DSM).

He also graduated from the Conservatory of Brescia «Luca Marenzio«, after musical studies at the Conservatory «Egidio Duni» of Matera. He has published "Silence with variations", by Lietocolle, 2005 (finalist for the Prix Festival of the Arts in Bologna in 2006 and winner of the 2007 New International Prize for Literature, the Italian Institute of Culture in Naples), which later became «PoesiaConcerto» of original music by A. Ciavarella for «The Great Narratives.» In 2008, again by Lietocolle editions, he has published "Andante of the lost fragments", "Match for silence and orchestra" in 2015, "Danzas de Amor y Duende" (Ed. Enkuadres, Valencia, bilingual edition, 2016); "Dansuri de Dragoste sin Duende" (Ed. Anamarol, Bucharest, 2017 bilingual edition), Lifesaving Journey (2018, foreword by Giuseppe Conte, among the 10 finalist books at the International Award Gradiva graded 2019 University of New York), "Hologram in A minor" (ed. Caosfera, 2019, foreword By Tomaso Kemeny and Valentina Colonna).

In 2018 he won the Nabokov international Literary Prize.

His lyrics are present in journals, anthologies,newspapers and literary blogs. He edited the anthology "If / say / year" and the Anthology "tag and portray" (Ed. Lietocolle) on poetry in the time of Facebook.With new texts, in 2011, he won the International award Alda Merini.

Mediterranean

When we were gods and we walked with trees
And the robes were souls and live animals
And still we celebrated the birthdays of the clouds
And at the time we danced on the water like anemones
And we called Israel the snow of the desert
And the archangel child faced over the abyss
And the sources sang from the seas to the spring
And the leaves were sailing ships and languages in unison
And the braches transcendental bridges of the light
And the impossible monster was free to love
And each step a flavour and a pedantic name
And the caves were eyes barely open on the unknown
And the stones dialogued in the concentric day
Now that we walk with no legs crawling back
Among the crowd trampled by the killing silence
And the nuclear feasts are expecting us at the gate
And we dream in shreds among the breath of the bombs
And we call the embrace of lead heroic life
And the stones are masses that stone at pasture
And the leaves and the trees ran out/ ended the spring
And the sea with petroleum tongue does not speak anymore
And the fireflies are black and the seagull becoming crow
And the slow blade bill that vibrates and that penetrates
And drains fauna that crowds in stiff thoughts
And the impossible monster is in the cage by now
And the punches are fighting each other in the bloody air
And the caves have the smell of mass graves
And each step is a swamp from which getting out alive
Move forward we are nobody knows why we sleep.

NOTA * impossible monster: human brain (Neurology, Walter)

Gloria Sofia (Cape Verde)

Glória Sofia, is a dreamer as most poets. Born in in the city of Praia in Cape Verde, Gloria shares her dreams with her two children. She graduated in Engineering and Environmental Management in the Azores, another place that she cherishes for allowing her to continue to be an islander.

Gloria is currently pursuing her masters in Management and Nature Conservation in Holland where she lives. She is also active in other cultural arenas, attending several poetry festivals and sharing her work in numerous websites and magazines (youngpoets.eu, Azahar, Miombo Publishing Lepan Africa etc…).

Her poetry has been translated into more than 10 languages and she is published in more International Anthologies. She is the Author of the books: Poetry of Tears (2013); Ties of Poetry (Brial Publishing, 2014); Abriel (2018)– Children's Book – Brial Publishing House 2018 (Bilingual English- Portuguese); Little Bear – Children's Book – United-pc publishing, 2019.

(Bilingual Portuguese – Nederland). Translate book: Rubans de Poesie (Versão Francesa 2015); Intricci di Poesia (Versão Italiana Editora Brial 2016); Lazos de Poesìas (Versão Espanola Editora Brial 2017) Anthologies: "Without Fear of Infamy" poetry anthology by Scurfpea Publishing; Anthology "Our Voices Our Stories": (2019) Advancing, Celebrating, Embracing and Empowering Girls and Women of Color, SS Rotterdam Story Promotion (2019); Universal Oneness: An Anthology of Magnum Opus Poems from around the World' (360 poems by 360 poets from 60 Countries) 2019 published by Authorspress, New Delhi, India Anthology on the theme "Being a Woman" (2019) Cabo Verde Antologia Mundial De Poesia: "La papa, seguridad alimentaria – Bolivia 2018, etc.

She was nominated to apply for R. M. and P.A.I

Translated by Anita Carapinheiro
It wasn't meant for me

They weren't meant for me
The unfaithful kiss of the wind
Not the seductive smile of the sun.
It wasn't meant for me
The perfume of the clay
For the tears of the clouds.
No they weren't meant for me
The smell of freshly washed clothes
The waves of the field grasses
Not the scent of sunrise.
They were only meant for me
Confusing poetry in this labyrinth soul.

Cape Verde Sea

Water of life,
Water of hope,
Water of dreams,
Way that leaves the soul,
Meeting of all the tears.
Sea,
Cradle of fishermen,
Prayer of the fresqueras,
Joy of children,
Lightness of melancholy.
Sea,
Eternal path that separates the bodies,
Eternal path that unites the continents.
Sea,
Dreams of the islanders,
Shattering of hearts.

Ganu Ganev (Bulgaria)

Ganu Ganev was born on June 10, 1958 in the village of Belozem, Bulgaria. In 1989, he founded his own Vollard Gallery, as well he was tightly involved with publishing and producing a variety of music albums. He is a very well-known organizer of festivals related to Bulgarian and European culture. G. Ganev also has a fine talent in poetry, literature, architectural design and composition.

Day seven – Sunday

Time – tick,
Vanity – tack,
Time – tick –
as the hastle vanishes from veins – sic!
And the gong – ding
crunch and dong
a staring lunch interfered.
And the device – click
and voice –calm .
In the afternoon – soon.
Fresh evening knocked "bing- bang" – stubborn gong.
A
day, day-dreaming – calm and dumb,
gained some force – confusing bug.
Inhaling time, the burden rose to – tick
taming the daily fuss

Hannie Rouweler (Netherlands)

Hannie Rouweler (Netherlands, Goor, 13 June 1951), poet and translator, has been living in Leusden, The Netherlands, since the end of 2012. Her sources of inspiration are nature, love, loss, childhood memories and travel. In 1988 she debuted with Raindrops on the water. Since then about 40 poetry volumes have been published, including translations in foreign languages (Polish, Romanian, Spanish, French, Norwegian, English). Poems have been translated in about 35 languages. She followed several commercial and language trainings (Arnhem, Amsterdam, Hasselt BE) and attended five years evening classes in painting and art history, art academy (Belgium). Hannie writes about a variety of diverse topics. 'Poetry is on the street, for the taking', is an adage for her. She mixes observations from reality with imagination and gives a pointe to her feelings and findings. Unrestrained imagination plays a major part in her works. She published a few stories (e.g. short thrillers); is editor of various poetry collections.

About love

I picked up the fallen letters from the floor
love has many faces and vistas
the a joined x y z
sometimes vowels were already together
on the square cards
with the child's play I could use the mini clothespins
attach to a rope

where do I hang this clothesline?
outside the wind blows in my early spring garden
inside it is overflowing with piled up books
paintings in a frame

drawings with adhesive tape on a wall
a red racing car that attracts attention
more than subtle words

the black iron display case as an altar
for candles and special days
is filled with tea lights there too
no room for anything else
than the memory, memorable objects
which I took with me as leftovers.

Little room is left for love
than singing about all that was lost
and just one more trail can be guessed
in the colored glass of window time.

International Poetry Day

For the common people who spend their days
with ordinary things from everyone: pay attention!
If you come across a poet: greet him or her
with respect
take off your hat or bow: that's not too much
asked once a year on this day

for someone who walks half the time
with his head in the clouds and therefore thoughts
constantly encountering impossible phenomena,
for someone who never did the dishes in a normal way
rinse plates and cutlery, constantly makes mistakes
and puts everything in the wrong places
a self-chosen torture, quest, maze.
He's like that man I saw this morning passing on the sidewalk
with a cell phone in his hand, busy talking to one completely
unknown for me, then suddenly disappears behind a hedge
transparent branches and in pieces will accomplish his day.

For ordinary people: pour a cup of coffee
if you see a quenched and overworked face drenched
in nocturnal labor, or someone who has his own angels
and demons constantly to fight, chases them to flight.
Be kind to poets. It's only once a year
that you get the chance to pamper them
who rarely find their labor rewarded and … awarded!

Death and the rose

The evening is like the empty bus driving through the night,
it drives forward without passengers
behind the lifeless windows in the freezing cold
and streets and parks covered with snow;
above this the gathering of silent stars
which throw their lights on earth among cloud covers.
A stray light at the loss
of the most precious. There is still snow
white as white lilies in the fields. They leave
deep traces in the desolate mind
and the landscape following its own laws
between life and death. Frozen in our own memories
your youth is framed with voices, the growth
and progress of the days. The child in you
that goes on its way now parentless, dead end
in the first hours.
The snowbreak soon sets in and feelings follow
slowly across the swamp of new days,
a spring that is as reciprocal as words
reinventing themselves. The rose bushes
that will unfold stubbornly in another morning.

Hasije Selishta – Kryeziu (Kosova)

Member of Board of International Poetical Galaxy ATUNIS and Publication Executive ATUNIS

Hasije Selishta – Kryeziu was born in April 13 of the year 1960 in Kamenica, Kosovo. She sattended the elementary and high education at her birthplace and latter on, she attended the University of Prishtina for Jurisprudence in Prishtina. Hasija has 8 volumes of poetry published and 2 novels. For her creations in prose and poetry she has won with some prizes locally and worldwide. Her poems are included in the Anthology, where many other international authors are presented translated in a few languages. She is member of WPS, IWA and member of Board "ATUNIS".

When the rose was broken

When the rose
Was broken
The girl cried
She did not find again
The dream lost

When the pink rose
Was broken
The girl did not smile again
She took the world in her eyes
The apple's bough dried up

When the white rose
Broke
The girl fell into the fire.

The extinguished light

In the threshold I hold my steps
Along with the wild rose
I think
What room should I enter?
In any of them as to my wish
To go in the hallway
By all means I have to pass in

The extinguished light
From outside is reflected
A light in the wall
Silence
Entering inside
A shadow slipped
In front of me
The wild rose fell from the hand.

The Shiny crown

Long past silhouette
In the rails it enchains
Absorbs grandiosity

At sunset
The crown shines
Until rebirth

In the crown
Beautiful flowers
How beautiful is the day today

Translated by Dritan Kardhashi
Hassanal Abdullah (Bangladesh – USA)

Hassanal Abdullah, author of 46 books including 16 collections of poetry, is a Bangladeshi-American poet and the editor of Shabdaguchha, an International Bilingual Poetry Magazine. His poetry has been translated into ten languages and published in many countries throughout the world. Mr. Abdullah has introduced a new sonnet form, "Swatantra Sonnets," for which he received the Labu Bhai Foundation Award (2013). He has also written a 304-page epic, Nakhatra O Manusar Prochhad (Anyana, 2007), where, based on several scientific theories, he illustrated relations between human beings and the universe.

In 2016, at the International Silk Route Poetry Festival in the Szechuan Province, China, he was awarded the Homer European Medal of Poetry & Art. He also attended international poetry festivals in Greece and Poland. His recent book is the Chinese version of his book, Under the Thin Layers of Light, published in Taiwan. Mr. Abdullah is a NYC high school math teacher.

MY BONES WILL TRAVEL FAR

Whichever way I walk, I walk alone
and every view is of millenniums
of despair, I am just a rattling
skeleton; dry sticks that the worms had
fried, and what once were living veins
are now for insects to tunnel.

My breath now is smoking pollution!
What I write on is parchment torn;
and my own shadow has left my company—
which is why I am no friend of remorse.

My two eyes hanker for sleep, but
sleep has fled those nest. The wild
open wholes no dread for me, nor
has my own house any charm,
its rafters anyway are shaking,
creaky the walls.

What or where then is my home?
Why do I blunder so in the dark?
Maybe the kicks I receive rattling
along the road, are each a flower
in the wreath around my neck.

I was once the owner of my own grave
but was dispossessed by a new comer.
Now that I lack any house or land
where will my seeking bones go
to spread the odor thousand
and thousand years old.

Translated from the Bengali by Jyotirmoy Datta

Halmosi Sándor (Hungary)

Halmosi Sandor (1971), Hungarian poet, literary translator and publisher. Besides all his literary activities he gives presentations on tradition, poetry, the prehistory of the language, symbols, and on how to solve the spriritual crisis both on individual and communal levels.

DON'T YOU EVER FORGET
(És ne feledd soha)

Don't you ever forget, that you are a woman, kin
to the amazons, to Ariadne, Europe, Penelope, kin
to nuns, and courtesans, kin to the Venus of Willendorff,
kin to Frida and the Virgin Mother, don't you ever forget
that you are a woman, you are a muse, you can be a mother,
and joyous lover, but don't forget it either that you are
a twin, a difficult character, you are both Flora and Beatrice,
and the man, with whom you melt into one in love's embrace,
and don't forget, don't you ever forget, that the sky is worth
nothing, your femininity, masculinity, pride and humbleness,
your good intentions and all your efforts are worth nothing
unless you share and offer them, don't you forget.

WHAT WOULD HAPPEN IF
(Mi lenne, ha)

What would happen if I wrote a poem for myself
for once, not to be fashionable, nor as an attitude,
nor for another, to make them happy or heal them,
nor to heal myself, nor for those antediluvian
modern theories, nor for the dead author,
that is, for me,
but for someone I am connected to,
not from nostalgia, love, want, passion
or for the camera as a chronicler,
for the retinue,
nor as an imbecilic medium, nor for the kicks,
but as a man speaks with an angel
about his sweety and his sins,
in the name of humanity,
why would I recite a poem for myself,
after so many years,
knowing that they will read this too,
those whose words were framed,
who loved his words, as he drew from the language,
and those who didn't love how he spoke the language,
for he dared say, that it is the wonder of the world,
at once age-old and modern,
and independent, not raggle-taggle,
what could I say to myself, in this silence,
perhaps, there is nothing but this silence,
and what is between is not speech, but longing
for silence, after speech,
after saying the important things,
which made life worth living,
or how long would this fast last,
or whether it is we who are really doing
this whole thing,
you are a human being,
thus you do even the bad things well,
beautifully,
and gratis,

so throw the account into the rubbish bin,
you have grown up or you will,
when they've cut up the last piano,
and set fire to the last poem,
then it will be come to an end,
women understand this immediately,
but in vain,
for it is they who don't make this easier,
truly I am not saying this to myself,
we speak to someone, who is three, five dear people,
and they play the piano, while the Titanic sinks,
or you can still feel the touch that week,
or you are an adolescent, and it hurts bad,
and it hurts that it can't hurt so much any more,
and it hurts that you don't accept
that this is the wise thing,
no way!
it isn't József Attila's lap that is missing,
neither is the obligation,
but it is the fucking indifference of maturity that hurts,
or the indifference's fucking adulthood in us,
sorry, cheated, conned, irritating, #metoo,
he who says nothing today is a coward,
he who says nothing today is crazy,
he who speaks up, should learn to be silent first,
I love you

Hana Xhihani
(Albania – France)

Hana Xhihani was born in Kavaja City Albania. There, she grew up, got a degree, and worked until she immigrated. She now lives with her family and works in France. There she got a certificate from AFPA (in administration), as well from the French Academy "FORMUL' A" (in colorimetry). She got a degree from Academy de Lion ((in aesthetics), and from CIEP (diploma of French language C2). She has a passion for theatre, but her strongest interest lies in poetry. Through the art of poetry Hana, phrase a vital and human message like a transparency and meditativeness of the soul. This comes freely, sometimes through metric verses and sometimes through free verses. It harmonises and intertwine tradition with postmodernism and creates a special style that uniquely identifies the author. Hana is the author of five published poetry books: "The Season Of Life"; "When I Am Longing"; "The Dreams Do Not Care What I Say"; "The Eyes Of Longing"; "Behind The Glass There Is Life". Hana has been writing poetry for a long time with her works being published in magazines both in Albania and in France such as: NACIONAL, TELEGRAF, MAPO, OBELISK, ZOG MËNGJESI (Kosovo), MËRGATA, in Albanian and in France TRIBUNE, PROGRES, etc. Her poetry could be found as well at: "Arbëria News," "Sofra e poezisë Shqiptare", "Drita TV-Kavajë", "Fokusi", "Tekste Shqip". Besides being an editor for "Radio Lyra", "Radio Vlera" and "Radio Liria". She is the translator of many French poetries.

Monologue in midnight...

...Light and soft
like April breeze
my midnight is coming
Lovely and full of momentum
like a woman's kiss

on the midnight's dreams

Nightmarish and scary,
my midnight comes
like a teenager's shudder

It is dark, voiceless, horrendous, but I love it.
I'm profoundly in love with it

I hug it
It brings to me what I am missing
My world...
My dream...
my mirror image with which I converse
like with no one else.
My midnight.
I get lost in its mystery
Everything else, I let go
I become one with it.
I do not think of anything else.
I become free.

Welcome my midnight
thou starry sky welcome
impatiently I wait like a lover
arguing with myself like a raging storm...

You, my midnight, hated by so many
You are my light.
You are more than the light of day.
You are the star of my desire.
You are the magic of my emotions
You are the secrecy of my thought
The gift of my kisses.
You, like a flaming meteor that shines in the elegant curve,
fill my soul
Shake my heart.
And like that, in love with you I run toward my fragile verses

My midnight. The imagination of my images. Let them be without a logical connection.
I find myself in the memory of a place…
I feel the scent of perfume.
I still hear a trembling voice.
Even if all this does not exist, even if it is too far away for me,
It's real…
I feel it…
You my midnight, bring me many dreams. Does not matter if I do not understand them.
Let them intertwine somewhere between my mind and my heart.

I want my midnight to never end. The day seems too long to me. Extremely long
Almost unbelievably long for other minds.
That makes me afraid
I fear I am losing it.

So every midnight I think that it is the last one.
I live it to the maximum.
For me, tomorrow is something voiceless…
Dawn or the midnight dark?

Suppression, gray hair, darkness, sunset, the yellow leafs, weathering, deserts, lamentations,
cries, deaths, graves, disappointments, tears, pains, my dreamy life scatters love
for all humanity.

Translated into English by Merita Paparisto

Hussein Habasch (Kurdistan)

Hussein Habasch is a poet from Afrin, Kurdistan. He currently lives in Bonn, Germany.

His poems have been translated into English, German, Spanish, French, Chinese, Turkish, Persian, Albanian, Uzbek, Russian, Italian, Bulgarian, Lithuanian, Hungarian, Macedonian, Serbian, Polish and Romanian, and has had his poetry published in a large number of international anthologies.

His books include: Drowning in Roses, Fugitives across Evros River, Higher than Desire and more Delicious than the Gazelle's Flank, Delusions to Salim Barakat, A Flying Angel, No pasarán (in Spanish), Copaci Cu Chef (in Romanian), Dos Árboles and Tiempos de Guerra (in Spanish), Fever of Quince (in Kurdish), Peace for Afrin, peace for Kurdistan (in English and Spanish), The Red Snow (in Chinese), Dead arguing in the corridors (in Arabic) and Drunken trees (in Kurdish).

He participated in many international festivals of poetry including: Colombia, Nicaragua, France, Puerto Rico, Mexico, Germany, Romania, Lithuania, Morocco, Ecuador, El Salvador, Kosovo, Macedonia, Costa Rica, Slovenia, China, Taiwan and New York City.

O love, O war

O war
O an endless filth
Leave here, go to hell
We want to write
Love poems
Without your unpleasant odor penetrating through them.
We want to kiss our wives, sweethearts, and mistresses
Without hearing your noise around us.
We want to die from love, from love alone!

I am in exile, and the war at its height
Oh God, how much I missed your small wars my love,
Your wars which me and my heart are the happy victims.

Go on, be a little crazy, have a little fun
Or if you want, ruin my mood with your huge dosage of grouchiness.
I don't want to think about this nasty war which is taking place in my homeland.

This war is a machine, grinding the meat of love
And crushing its bones with no mercy!
With love we will grind war's bones and eliminate it!

It seems this war has no end
Come, let us plant trees and sleep cuddling up next to it,
until it grow.

Don't say you have no time
This war will drag for long time
I don't want for our love to be defeated.

The lover was saying to his sweetheart
I will kiss you until dawn.
Now he says
I will kiss you until this war explode from rage.

Put your hand on my forehead
Distract this war that almost break my head.
With love we will break its head!

War doesn't like to pause
Doesn't like holidays nor laziness.

It likes work, and does it with the utmost devotion and dedication
And the more its work payoff
The more it grows passionate, energetic, and moving forward
With love we will stop it in its place, yes we will stop it…

War doesn't listen, doesn't obey nor answer to anybody.

It goes to its goal as a fatal bullet goes directly
to the heart of life.
We will return back the favor twice as hard.

In war
We won't build a house, we won't put any stone over stone.
We will write poems and sing lyrics.
Nothing enrages war more than poems and lyrics.

I will go to war.
And what will you do there?
I will kill war!

What you do in wartime?
I write love poems
What else?
I hold on more to love!

Translated by Muna Zinati

Isilda Nunes (Portugal)

Isilda Nunes is a Portuguese award-winning writer and artist. Recently she won the Intercontinental World Poetry Prize "Kairat Dusseinov Parman", the World Prize "Cesar Vallejo 2020" for Literary Excellence, the "Grito de Mujer Lisbon 2021 Award" and the "Aguila de Oro" for Literary and Artistic Excellence. She has poems translated into English, Spanish, Hindi, Serbian, Polish, Bengali and Mandarin and edited in India, Bangladesh, Poland, Serbia, Brazil, Peru, Croatia, Greece, Republic of Seychelles, United States and China. She is co-author of about forty national and international anthologies and solo books of poetry and prose, such as novels, short stories and manuals. She took part in Radio and Television programmes, book fairs and literary festivals. She is: World Executive President Collegiate of the Hispanoworld Writers Union (UHE), an organization with more than 125000 members and delegations in around 150 countries, on all continents; UHE World Ambassador; President and Founder of the HPP-Portugal delegatio; World Administrator of the Official Pages of the UH; Honorary Ambassador of the "World Poets Federation" (WPF); Member of "World Nations Writers Union" (WNWU); Member of the Organizing Committee of "World Festival of Poetry" (WFP) in Portugal; Delegate of the Minho region of the Solidarity Project "Being Woman"; Secretary of the Supervisory Board of GRETP (Recreational and Ethnographic Group Tricanas Poveiras); Member of the Patripove Advisory Board.

She is an Honorary Member of: CEMD (Circle of Mozambican Writers in the Diaspora); UHE-MOZAMBIQUE (Unión Hispanomundial de Escritores, Mozambique); MIL- MOÇAMBIQUE (Portuguese International Movement); ALDCI (Lusophone Association for Development, Culture and Integration) –NGOD; MLA Mor Lírio (International Culture) in the "Lírio Azul" Movement.

The roses withered

The roses withered in the dryness of your gaze!
I no longer dream of them, my dear! I no longer cry for them!
Our bodies, which were once just one,
Today are wrecked in the solitude of the words unsaid.
I get involved in a feeling of longing and lethargy,
Fixing the old clock still, at a time that was once ours...
At a time when we loved each other like the sea and the sky.
And I petrify myself on that horizon,
Where my body made anchorage as a boat.

Reality deranges me!
Maddened by the echo of your tread on bare walls,
That implicit farewell in the disquiet of your hands
And in the sagging of your will!
The slow arrival of winter disturbs me!

The roses you gave me have already withered!
The wet kisses of the older days, are now sinfully dried!
All embrace has expired!
And the grooves on my face exude tired memories,
Loose pieces of a plot that is no longer ours.
The mouth dried up in the refusal of the farewell,
In this delayed death, suspended in the solitude of unsaid words!
I no longer dream of them, dear! I no longer cry!
The roses withered in the dryness of your gaze!

Mother, I don't want to be born!

Mother, you know, I've got your anguish on my inked skin
my body carved by the pain that is in you whipping
and my soul battered by the wind they imposed upon you.
Mother, you know, I drank all the tears that from your eyes
didn't flow
your sobs,
your mourning,
your outcry,
your fear

and that hunger for love, for real.
I hid within your bowels when those big hands
violated your dignity.
Mother, they humiliated you. They humiliated me, too!
Mother, I'm so afraid of the world you live in
Mother, I don't want to be part of that world.
You know, Mother... I'm a wee girl.

IN THE DEAD CITY

in the dead city,
to the cross of indifference,
flow dreams into liquid crematoriums.
the madness decreed ride
shipwrecked desires,
on common walkways.
in the dead city,
hunger, thirst, invades hospices.
ghosts play at children
and old people get childhood.
emigrated the hugs.
there are no bridges to cross the night.
there are sales in this river,
pain on this ship.
Charon smokes a cigarette in the main ditch.
simply blackout.
simply silence.
only tomb
in the dead city.
and me?
and you?
and we?

Irma Kurti (Albania – Italy)

Irma Kurti is an Albanian poetess, writer, lyricist, journalist, and translator naturalized Italian.

She has been writing since she was a child. In 1980, she was honored with the first national prize on the 35th anniversary of the Pionieri magazine for her poem "To my homeland". In 1989, she won the second prize in the National Competition organized by Radio Tirana on the 45th anniversary of the Liberation of Albania.

All her books are dedicated to the memory of her beloved parents Hasan Kurti and Sherife Mezini, who supported and encouraged every step of her literary path.

Kurti has won numerous literary prizes and awards in Italy and Italian Switzerland. She was awarded the "Universum Donna" International Prize IX Edition 2013 for Literature and the lifetime nomination of "Ambassador of Peace" by the University of Peace of Italian Switzerland. In 2020, she received the title of Honorary President of WikiPoesia, the Encyclopedia of Poetry.

In 2021, she was awarded the title "Liria" (Freedom) by the Arbëreshë Community in Italy.

Irma Kurti has published 22 books in Albanian and 15 in Italian. Her books have been translated into English, Spanish, French, Rumanian and Serbian. She has written about 150 lyrics for adults and children, including in Italian and English. She lives in Bergamo, Italy.

A jewel

It's the time of the fading of values,
of the loss of friends one by one,
just like the trees lose their leaves
as the season of autumn arrives.

This is the time of the angry people,
no one knows: with the moon or sun,
of the ones who cannot remain silent,
of those who speak, but say nothing.

Friends are so rare. You find one,
you are suspicious, it seems unreal,
you hold and squeeze it in your palm
as a revelation, just like a rare jewel.

You keep it with anguish and interest,
careful not to drop it from your hands,
but when you slowly open your fingers,
you discover that it is no longer there.

The regret, the affliction invades you,
you realize that you've held it tightly,
you condemn yourself, it's your fault,
unintentionally you have suffocated it.

Perhaps that's why you lost it,
because you adored that jewel …

This house is not sold

This house cannot be sold, there sleep
and wake up thousands of memories,
like colorless crumbs flicker in the air
the words that we left, all our dreams.

The corridor narrowed from solitude
with the steps of my mother was filled,
the comings and goings of my parents
resonate there as a divine symphony.

In the living room the sofas are rotten,
this one – old and decaying may seem,

but my father often leaned on it,
it keeps his presence even now vivid.

It still felt of the smell of hot coffee
two steps away, in a very small annex,
I don't compare it with the best aromas
vended everywhere in the shops today.

The huge picture hanging on the wall
representing a big home on an island,
portrays my desire to live somewhere
with all my family, in a better world.

The memoirs give it a great value,
make it dear, not regarding the price,
but for my heart and for my feelings.
It's not sold, it's not bought – the house!

Isabelle Berck (Belgium)

Isabelle Berck born in Belgium.
She studied at the Catholique University of Leuven and she is graduated in sociology.
She was the organizer of the Franco-German Cultural Center, Karlsruhe, Germany, March 2008 - June 2008; Librarian: Franco-German Cultural Center, Karlsruhe, Germany, January 2010 - March 2010; Librarian: Community Library, Villers-la-Ville, Belgium, November 2012 - July 2013.
She speaks French, German, English and Dutch.
Her poems have been translated in several languages and published in International Anthologies.
She currently lives and works in Nivelles, Belgium.

A good recipe for writing

To write on needs
A pencil to describe you thought
Some papers to express the feeling
A person to inspire
And others to listen to you.

Love

Love for ever
Love every day
And every night
Love whole heartedly
Love as long as you exist

Love
Let it shine and glow
Let this feeling from the bottom of your heart
Lighten up thousand lights...

Nostalgia:

All alone in an empty street
My feet on the wet pavement
Heading towards an uncertain horizon
My youth: my favorite part of life
Ended very quickly
As the sand washed away by the pouring rain.
Alone under the open sky
A gentle breeze around me
I recollect my dreams
Which are embedded deep in my heart.

The Lake

Here, in the woods
I am drowning, in the middle of the lake
The birds seemed are frightened
Seeing me wriggle like a new born
Good bye mother earth.
I am going towards the heaven
Meet again my beloved ones
Near them, I ll look for the pious paradise dwellers.

Imen Melliti (Tunisia)

Imen Melliti a Tunisian writer, qualified in international relations, PhD from the British college, certified in bilingual translation, published a book in 2017 "Master your english", participated in a collective book, translated a novel of the Tunisian writer and professor Béchir Jeljli. She translated several scientific articles in Ecos Russian magazine, published also short stories for teens.

What would you say ?

If you could see me now
Would you recognize my hidden pain

Would you follow my dropping tears
Would you see the greif behind my fake smile
You May see a cold stone
But not a burning fire deep inside
You May notice my crazy laughter
But not a bleeding soule moaing silently
You May get impressed by my artificial beauty
But you can never reach my depth
And touch my lost broken pieces
You May look at My face
But it can't tell you what i faced
You May see me struggle
But never see me quit
I stumble but i get Back up
Im strong now because i've been too fragile
Im fearless because i've known hardship's bitter taste
I keep remembering harsh lesson
To be what im today
I can't forget the day

I begged you to stay
But you have never say
What i need to hear from you guy
Please go away
I stil Wonder what would you say
Im not for you today

Weeping Heart

It rains in my Heart
As it Rains on the city walls
Watering the dry ground
Witnessing the deep sorrow
Empty spaces scared my soul
It rains for no reason
Unjustified greif torturing my fragile Heart
It is by far the pain
Which IS not easy to explain
When tears fall inside
I look for you in my Heart to find your shadaw
I reallize then ..how deep the injury is
Only Time Can heal

Irina-Roxana Georgescu
(Romania)

Irina-Roxana Georgescu got her PhD in Philology (2016) at the University of Bucharest, with a thesis on the influence of Western criticism on Romanian literary criticism (1960-1980). She worked as a French-language editor at the Euresis – Literary and Cultural Studies Magazine (2009-2013).
 She publishes poetry and literary studies in various magazines in Romania and abroad.
Translations of her poems appeared in Serbian, French, and Spanish.
Her books are Intervalle ouvert (L'Harmattan, Paris, 2017), Elementary Notions (Cartea Românească, Bucharest, 2018.)

The Silk Belt

tectonic reshapings on the floor
the soles do not touch the sky outside the ring
only turtles can fly

an apocalypse prepared in the eyes of the one
who weighs more
I will be yokozuma

I will be the supreme obese
worshiped
by my whole body

a 230 kilo Slim Shady
for whom days string
as a mawashi necklace around the waist

I am a rikishi, master,

I don't complain
I make art in the ring

Green Golf

To play like a pro.
To dream of Tiger Woods while jerking off.
To look for the best trajectory.
The best angle.
To spoil yourself on a course rented with your teacher's monthly wages.
To own everything, yet everything
To not be enough.
To have 1000 years ahead to decompose.

Boxing – A Sort of Item Repsonse Theory

Float like a butterfly, sting like a bee.
Muhammad Ali

Training is the most appropriate
response
to pain

Translated by Clara Burghelea

© Miradije Ramiqi Kosova) ("Peizazh imagjinativ", "Imagine Landscaip", Akril ne karton, acryl in carton Dim.70 X 50 / 2003"

Miradije Ramiqi, Pozharan, 1953, Kosova.
She is a poet and painter, is an already well-known artist. Apart from her participation in numerous fine arts individual and collective exhibitions, she has published the following books of poetry: "Shivering Colors" (1981), "Rain in the Mirror" (1990) and "Kingdom Whisper" (1990), "The return of the broken silence" 2008.

Jose Sarria (Spain)

Poet, essayist and literary critic. Correspondent Academician of the Royal Academy of Córdoba. He is secretary general of the Association of Writers of Andalusia, a permanent member of the Jury of the Andalusian Prize of Criticism and general secretary of the International Association for Solidarity Humanism. Author of twenty-three books of poetry, narrative and essays. He has been translated into Arabic, Italian, French, English, Sephardic and Romanian. His work appears in more than forty anthologies and magazines. He has specialized in the research of the Spanish neoliterature in the Maghreb, being a speaker in seminars at the Universities of Spain, Morocco and Tunisia, as well as the Cervantes Institutes of Morocco and Tunisia and the summer courses of the International University of Andalusia (UNIA). He holds numerous national literary prizes. It is included in the General Encyclopedia of Andalusia.

GARDEN OF HEAVEN
(mother's house)

To my mother, always.
My memories are of an arabesque patio adorned with pots of bright red geraniums and a garden that generously bestowed the hospitable shade of the lemon trees, despite the passing of time and their neglect. The song of birds, perched on the tops of the few still standing trees, accompanied the sun's rays passing through their branches. Only their chirping flouted the solitude and silence of this sanctuary, and their sonorous trill transformed the decadence of the house into the gate of paradise.

There, every afternoon, the angels descended the golden stairs of Jacob to listen to the song of the birds, caress my mother's hair and pronounce my name.

That house is the South, garden of heaven, home of the heart and gives birth to the origins of the water.

(JOSÉ SARRIA, from "El Libro de las aguas"
Translation by Charles Olsen)

THE COUNTRY OF WORDS

I have no other country than the word
and the crimson colour of the geraniums:
the last vestige of my southern origin
where there is a white house
that treasures the sound of the wheel
carried by water,
a kingdom of quinces and pomegranates
with its leafy orchards,
a haven of peace on the edge of oblivion:
the place where my submerged hours live.

I always treasured the certainty
that in the end we would have kept
the murmur of water in the ditches,
sustenance of the geraniums
and the common homeland of the word.

(JOSÉ SARRIA, from "El Libro de las aguas"
Translation by Maria Miraglia)

Juljana Mehmeti (Albania- Italy)

Juljana Mehmeti was born in the city of Durres, in Albania. Since she was a child she became fond about literature and writing, especially poetry, a genre that in the following years will turn into a real life motive, a way to better express her ideas, her thoughts, her visions and metaphysics, her point of view according to her consciousness but also improving the awareness of the same suggestion that surrounds the human world. The first book "Soft – Poems" published in Italian language attracted the attention of publishers and Italian literary criticism, not only for its particular style, but also for new words, the language used, the philosophical message and the currents present in her poems that go from Hermetism to Surrealism. The second book comes from the field of translation entitled "Vramendje" – (Rimugino) of the Italian author Alessandro Ferrucci Marcucci Pinoli, which will constitute the first experience in this field, but will also strengthen his long-standing conviction, to know and translate in his language, many popular Italian authors. The collection of poems "Oltrepassare" is her new book, which presents itself with the new tendencies of Albanian literature, postmodernism and universal consciousness, from experimental currents to absurdity. She published in English language "In his light" (Demer Press, 2019, Netherlands in Italian language "Namasté" (Libri di – Versi in Diversi Libri- 2020, Italy) and "Nel dilemma dell'esistenza" in Italian & English Language (Libri di – Versi in Diversi Libri- 202, Italy).
She currently lives and works in Ancona, Italy.

Identity

The leaves turn green and I wake up in thousands of buds
as I observe this confection of the soul
that is generated
in endless fragrances
Resuming of a new journey

accross the spring garden
that opens a gate
and sends me to collect daisies
you make a garland
to my dreams
and to transform intho the hairdresser of troubled desires
there in the lawn of my passages.

I was before
Perhaps at the roots of the earth
at the extreme ends of the age
perhaps in a star collapsing to the lake
to be extinguished, dead and reborn,
empty frames
the eclipse of genesis that raised us
to walk
sitting on the carved platform
castles that murmur inside.

I look beyond the reflex in the mirror
I ask for more courage
To conquer the daily displayed image
and shine the emeralds in the eyes,
not memories of silent fantasies
neither bodies turned into ashes
but the flourishing of the graces of nature
to learn the identity of the soul.

Moire

Wake up!
The times are burned down
The legends as well
with the lost phoenixes.
Dust has covered the ages
The new winds are blowing nowhere.
Some old relics have remained tokens
of the intrigues of consciousness

brawling of thoughts
in a fatigued sleep
of dreams without awakening.

Wake up!
The Gods are replaced by three stubborn Moire
and you can no longer be;
Klote, neither Akesi or nor Atopo
that stretches the fate of human in threads and cuts it with scissors
to sew the bottom gray shapes
of the greyish garment in death.

Wake up
with the strength of Zeus
to direct the balance of the world.

***

I wander to the train of pain ...
rails that go far
abandoned stations of longing
the expectation that knows no return.
Forgotten somewhere ...
To the universe lost in the clouds
Refracted like a weeping willow
Of my most secret desire.

Translated by Arben Hoti

Jose Luis Rubio (Spain)

I was born in Cádiz in 1951. I currently live in Conil de la Frontera
Founder and Coordinator of the Azahar Poetic Magazine since 1989. At present, this magazine has more than 600 collaborators in each issue.
Director and scriptwriter of the program Vientos Flamencos, broadcast by Radio Juventud de Conil, since 1989.
I have published 11 solo books, Mijagas Ardientes, Bubbles, Memory, Unborn, Between lights and shadows, The mirage of kisses, Speaking clearly, Flamenco, The sound of Nature, Imperfect mathematics, Those who dance with color, 1 in collaboration with my niece María José Berbeira, Growing between verses and in various anthologies.
In 1991 I won the local prize of the I Conil Poetry to the Sea Contest, the second prize in 1993, 1994 and 1995 of the Conil Torre de Guzmán Contest, Second Prize in the VII National Poetry Contest of the Fina Palma Poets Group of Horta, from Barcelona in 2003, second prize in the V International Contest of Letters of Love, prose category, in Miami, in 2004, and in 2006 I obtained the Second Prize of the XV Conil Torre de Guzmán Contest.

MY FLAG

What flag is yours?
Mine is not red, nor green, nor white,
not blue, not purple, not yellow.
My flag has the color of freedom,
of equality, of truth, of love.
My flag does not fly on any flagpole.
I wear it under my skin and nobody sees it.
It is a flag that does not carry behind
no army because you don't need weapons

to defend its fundamental principles.
It is a flag that many betray
because they don't know how to love, because they run from the truth, because they don't feel the same, because they don't understand freedom.

MESSAGES

I have written clearly
on the white wall
an old thought
that I read a long time ago
in a holy book:
Love if you want to be loved.

I have noted with red letter
on an immaculate sheet
an unforgettable phrase
that I heard a vate
in a theater recite:
Never give up on freedom.

Read the messages.
Write them everywhere.
Recite them in the streets.
Throw them to the four winds.
Prevent them from getting lost in time.

Jana Orlová (Czech Republic)

http://www.janaorlova.cz.

Jana Orlová (1986) is a Czech poet and a performer.
She published "Čichat oheň" („Sniff the Fire") with her own illustrations at Pavel Mervart publishing house in 2012 and "Újedě" her second book of poetry at Větrné Mlýny publishing house in 2017.
Her works appeared in "Nejlepší české básně" (Best Czech Poems) at Host publishing house. Her poems were translated into Romanian, Ukrainian, Belarusian, Polish, Bulgarian, Hungarian, Hindi, Spanish, English and Arabic. She published poetry book in Ukrainian and Romanian in 2019.
She treats performance art as living poetry.
She gained the "Objev roku 2017" Breakthrough Act Award 2017 at Next Wave Festival for "crossing the boundaries of literature, fine art and theatre naturally and with ease".
She gained the Dardanica Prize in 2020. Her work is to be seen at http://www.janaorlova.cz.
She is the chief editor of art and culture column of Polipet.cz.

***

Solitude is still with me
beautiful, painful
I can caress solitude
in the motionless air
I sense its contures
It is smooth
an empty chair that says:
a moment ago you were alive

***

The ancient gods are still online
I would like to lie with hops
overgrown in the woods like my fur
in the strained fascia of a clerk

I will measure out my desire for you with steps
torture for the advanced
and I know there's still time because
the ancient gods are still online

***

Borderline above me
Lines of sorcery in me
There is my voice on the other side, saying:
"Can you hear me?"
I can hear you, mother?
I can hear you, Death
I can hear you well
I am falling to lift off
My soul is willing
Ceiling is shaking
You are still smoldering inside me

John Guzlowski (USA)

John Guzlowski's writing appears in Garrison Keillor's Writer's Almanac, North American Review, Rattle, Ontario Review, Salon.Com, and many other journals. His poems and personal essays about his Polish parents' experiences as slave laborers in Nazi Germany and refugees making a life for themselves in Chicago appear in his award-winning memoir Echoes of Tattered Tongues (Aquila Polonica Press). He is also a columnist for the Dziennik Zwiazkowy (the oldest Polish language daily in America) and the author of Suitcase Charlie and Little Altar Boy, noir mystery novels set in Chicago.

Our Silence

My silence and your silence
speak a language
we learned long ago
in a world where silence
moved the waves
and every sparrow
flew on wings of silence
into our eyes

And every word
we learned to speak
is part of a prayer
connecting us
to all the words
spoken by all people
everywhere
ever
This silence and these words
invented love

Taught us to whisper
Hello
Taught us
To open our eyes

Taught us
To enter the woods
And fields
And learn the meaning
Of everything

Love

Find a man or a woman
and tell this person
who you truly are
and have this person
tell you truly
from the gray essence
of his or her heart
who he or she
truly is

And that –
if you survive it –
will be love

What I talk about here
is nothing more
then smudges
on a page

Joanna Kalinowska (Poland)

Joanna Kalinowska, says about herself, that she was born under a wandering star. She, as a child (a daughter of an officer), often moved from one place to another. These constant changes taught her the openness and the willingness to meet new people and places. She spent many years in Poland. Twenty years ago she moved to Italy. She has always been writing but she publishes now. Her book "Ascoltando Azzurro – Wsłuchana w błękit" was written so that people who speak different languages can express the same feelings. Three volumes of her poetry were edited and her poems were printed in various anthologies and magazines. She writes and publishes in two languages, both Polish and Italian. She loves these two countries. They are her homelands. She arranged "The Amici Italia-Polonia Association". Its headquarters there is in Taranto — the city where she lives and works. She is a teacher, but she actually works as a translator and an activist of the Polish community. She is a member of the Warsaw Association of Literature's Translators. Joanna works for the Italian literary-cultural group "La Vallisa", too. She also cooperates with magazine of this group. She is the initiator and organizer of many cultural and social events.

Carrier Of Mystery

carrier of mystery
smiles to herself
she sees the universe enclosed in a droplet
she is a priestess
guarding the gates between the worlds
and she is the gate herself
chosen by a soul
what's going to come back to her?

It is in her but it is not her
it feeds on her blood
but it gives her pure light
from which love will flow
the purest in the world

Without The Last Kiss

sometimes you wake up
and it seems like there was nothing there
just an empty sight
as if with every day
life just got away
pride is the virtue of stupid
above every road
some rain may fall
but you loved
and let your love go away
without a single day in luck
and everything went without warning
watch out for the siren song
drifting by the sea
lonely ship without a sail
breakdown like a stone
sinking into despair
and now you are here, on the sea shore
what is it going to be will be
you cannot make a break for it
you cannot escape destiny

Translated into English by Alicja Maria Kuberska

Job Degenaar (Netherlands)

Job Degenaar taught the Dutch language, especially for higher educated foreign students and published poetry, prose and essays about literature and culture in many national and international magazines, anthologies and newspapers. He translated lyrics from Paul McCartney, the German poet Reiner Kunze and persecuted writers, and edited various anthologies. But above all he is a poet. His poetry is characterized as 'clear, with a hint of mystery'. More than a dozen collections of his poems were published in the Netherlands, as well as an anthology of his work in Poland and a trilingual edition (German-English-Dutch) in Germany. His latest poetry collection is Hertenblues (Deer Blues), second edition 2018.

He was a board member of PEN Netherlands for 10 years and since 2017 he is the president of PEN Emergency Fund, a worldwide operating fund for writers in direct need.
Website: http://www.jobdegenaar.nl

High view on this life

There was stacked wood glowing
sun faded behind the mountains
we drank nostalgic for happiness

remained seated, slightly drunk
evening naturally turned into night
Above us developed slowly

a disruptive decor of stars
strumming on our retina, sometimes
crossed by silent satellites

the light arrows of heavenly stones
and the nearby flashing

of softly whirring planes

Then it has been for us, mortals
nice enough again
ground fog surrounded us

one became connected with Facebook
another rolled a cigarette
and blew question marks into space

In the distance, out of darkness
the roaring of deer
their old blues

Translation: Hannie Rouweler

The Art of Writing Poetry

I believe in the dandelion plume
which is quite a strain to catch

and that in one sigh you can blow away
as soon as you're bored

That leaves one so much room
it almost isn't there when it is

but that with delicate barbs
still binds the earth to itself

Translation: Willem Groenewegen

Janaq Jano (Albania)

Janaq Jano was born in 1962, in city of Permet, Albania. He graduated from the Faculty of Agronomy, Tirana. Is the author of the following literary works: "Broken peace" (novel), Tirana 2003; "You have waited for me" (Poetry); "Dancing with the stars" (Poetry, In the process of editing): "Cranes in the snow", (Fable, In the process of editing); "Neither alive or dead" (Poem.). Is a member of the Albanian Association of Writers & Chief Editor of the Newspape "Rreza Prolog". He is published in many newspapers, national and international magazines, as well as published in many global anthologies: Almanac 2008, Keleno- Greece, "Tirana Observer", "Thema", literary newspaper "Light", edition of Albanian writers' Association, etc. Currently resides in Permet, Albania.

OK...

The animals of the forest
together made a deal.
To set a table,
to drink raki.

All would come,
causing no damage,
he – cats, mice,
rabbits, dogs...

The most prudent animals
would all talk by turns,
chatting all around,
freely in a mirth.
The row filled up on spot

according to their sort:
the Donkey, the Pig,
the Tortoise and the Flea.

THE PARTY

The cook fox
set the table with tact.
Meat for dogs and cats,
for rabbits the salad.

While he had prepared
fodder for the Donkey,
he was very worried
for the plate of the flea.

Snorting with rage,
he sad to himself:
" It's the most ignoble trade
I have ever had.

Managing them all,
lion, wolf, jackal,
while for a flea,
I put myself in trouble!…"

Therefore came near,
cringely he said:
" I have heard of you, sir,
that you scarcely eat.

For that reason my surprise
a glass of raki…"
" OK, - said the flea, -
tonight I will drink."

Translated by Mirela Dudi
Jaydeep Sarangi (India)

Jaydeep Sarangi, often tagged as the "Bard on the banks of Dulung", is a widely anthologized and reviewed bilingual poet with eight collections in English, the latest being Heart Raining the Light (2020) released in Rome. Sarangi has read his poems in different shores of the globe. He conducted workshops on poetry writing in different universities in Australia, India, Italy and Poland. With Rob Harle, he has edited six anthologies of poems from India and Australia. He is the President, Guild of Indian English Writers Editors and Critics (Kerala) and Vice President, Executive Council, IPPL, ICCR, Kolkata. He is the Principal of New Alipore College, Kolkata, India and involved in poetry movement for social change.

A Sense of Rainy Days

Rain disappears
dancing joyously on long wires like a rope – dancer.
whichever weather rolls on
gives all cloudy juices
creating a land of poetic romance
where coy fairies descend to dance.

The ship sets off on her maiden voyage.
The voyagers carry their memory luggage.
Everything that takes place in the dark theatre.
foreshadows the mysteries of nature,
night's normal acts

My ill-timed sleep
breaks, secret doors
howl through

the night , looking
for its mother.

Rain in My House of Poems

After a good spell of rain
I want my ideas to change.
Like clothes, to take them off
and the poem, I shall get her back.

I begin to speak in my tongue
eye to eye, page after page, faithfully.

All for a Name

All living thinking heads
All beings that breathe,
Everything our senses perceive,
Even those which lie outside
Where our consciousness reside
Are given a name and rightly so.

The webs move.
An appellation or a pseudonym
Works wonders. A tag.
A right name is worth, dignity and character,
A wrong one deprives us of hues.

Even a bard needs a proper name
To run wild among the trees. To see a
Place far within this deep piercing night.

Jeanette Esmeralda Tiburcio Márquez (Jeanette Eureka) - (Mexico)

Jeanette is a leader of transformation in education, culture and arts. She is a big promotor of values in the unfolding of innovation and the design of new schemes, is an international speaker, audiovisual producer and teacher. Doctorate Honoris Causa by the IFCH in Morocco, she owns eight Doctorates Honoris Causa in Morocco, Nigeria, Switzerland, India, Peru, Haiti, Mexico and the Caribbean. She is Global Director of International Relations of the IFCH of the Kingdom of Morocco and of the OACG Organization of Art Creativity and Goodwill, Morocco. She is President and Founder of Cabina 11 Cadena Global Satelital Television from Mexico and Digital TV with others alliance. She is Presidente and Founder of the delivery of different Awards and Recognitions worldwide, highly respected in the cultural and social field. She collaborates with different organizations in the world to develop Congresses, Seminars, Workshops and lines of connection to underpin the growth of childhood and youth in the world.

Guadalupana I am to death

Mother, here I am
grateful, fragile, vulnerable
loving you every day and blessing
to have had the happiness of being your daughter
your faithful apprentice ... little am I in front of your shine
darkness next to your light ... I just want
that my father allow me to be close to you
enough in this life and in so many deaths
to be able to wake up in a little of your light.
Mother, my brunette, I know that these days
they have not been easy
and that you suffer for your children, for those who are,
those who have left,

for those who do not know you and do not know my Father.
Mother full of roses, of unparalleled fragrance
of celestial light,
my mother of Guadalupe,
thank you, because with my total imperfection
you have allowed me to be born in you.
Let my body have the strength
let my mind have clarity
my heart the innocence,
endow me with allies in love and unity
to be able to return to the world in humanity from
This land of bronze you've chosen to stay
My mother of Guadalupe, inspiration of my life
thank you for your protection and for giving us life …
Guadalupana I am to death

Rhapsody Tequila

Blue Heart,
Macerated, fermented
Heart of light,
At rest and in ritual.
From your field to my mouth,
From your center,
A ray of force
Distilled heat in my landscapes,
Sweet nectar of transformation,
Gifted miracle,
Irreverence that burns,
Steam, Grinding,
Slow dance, Liberty…
We drink in fullness,
Beyond the senses

José María Zonta
(Costa Rica)

Among others, he has received: The International Award Gabriel Celaya in Spain, with the book Los Elefantes Estorban; The Latin American Award Educa with the book Tres Noviembres; Poetry Award City of Irún, Spain with the book Casarsa; Spanish-AmericanPoetry Award Sor Juana Inés de La Cruz, in Mexico, with the book De La Decadencia. He received the Honorable Mention in the PrizePablo Neruda, Temuco, Chile, with the book La Gramática de Anna O. The XXIV International Poetry Award Antonio Oliver Belmás, Cartagena, Spain, with the book La casa de la condescendencia. Andthe 12° Literary Prize LUIS GARCÍA BERLANGA, Alicante, Spain, with the essay "Zapatos descalzos". He has received in Costa Rica the Young Creation Award with his first book La Noche Irreparable, and the National Award three times for the books: "Tres noviembres", "Lobos en la brisa" y el Libro de la Dinastía de Bambú. Winner of the Ibero-American Floral Games Award of Tegucigalpa with the book EL LIBRO DE LOS FLAMINGOS.

His Book DE LA DINASTÍA DE BAMBÚobtained the Iberoamerican Award Entreversos, Caracas Venezuela. Winner with the Book ANTOLOGÍA DE LA DINASTÍA DEL OTOÑO, International Award Miguel Acuña de Poesía, México.

2019 – IV Poetry International Award Gabriel Celaya, Diputación de Gipuskoa, with the Book AL ESTE DE LA MARIPOSA. ANTOLOGÍA DE POESÍA RUMANA.

TOURIST

Not entering as a tourist in the heart of a woman
taking pictures
leaving beer cans
looking for only immense cathedrals
and transparent statues

with the backpack full of maps
and making quick meals

because there's a country
seven cities
a mountain range and a winter
in the heart of a woman
don't just drink a glass of sea there

don't get into a plane
take the crescent train
don't reveal your photos there in an hour

if it's not too cold
get there naked
don't carry an umbrella

and above all don´t cut down trees
in a woman's heart
They don't usually grow back

From the Book "Los elefantes estorban"
International Award Gabriel Celaya, España

THE FAVOR

I'm going to do me the favor to love you

me
that I never tried me with kindness
that I did not complain when the boots pressed me
and not protested for the millions of cold breakfasts

from now I'll give me the sweet gift of kiss you
maybe that does not mean that the words that hurt
be less painful

or stop of cut me when shave my soul

no matter
with my favors I reached me
I put a hand on my shoulder
a coat if it rains and so I offer me to others

without government support but with the applause of the flowers

I'm going to do me the favor to getting off the train
kindle the fire and love you.

From the book "Tres noviembre"- International Award Educa

TAI CHI

The last thing you heard from me was that I prepared your lunch box,
and that's four years ago. Questions for me, of course
They tell you I'm thinner,
I take free tai chi lessons
in the park.
that my food is a bottle of wine every day.
They tell you I like to cook.
For tai chi classes the City Council asks to wear white
that's why you don't see me in the snow.

From the Book "AL ESTE DE LA MARIPOSA", ANTOLOGÍA DE POESÍA RUMANA, IV International Poetry Award Gabriel Celaya, Diputación de Gipuskoa.

Krishna Prasai (Nepal)
President, Jara Foundation

Krishna Prasai made his debut in writing in 1975 with the publication of his poems in Jhapa-based periodical Suryodaya. Originally from Dhaijan, Jhapa and presently a resident of Anamnagar, Kathmandu. Mr. Prasai edited Nepali Samasamayik Kavitahroo, an anthology of contemporary Nepali poetry when he was just 24 years old and exhibited a rare literary talent he possessed. Till date, the works Mr. Prasai has published include Gham Nabhayeko Bela (poems), Ghamko Barsha (Zen poems in Nepali, English, and Korean, later translated into Sinhalese, Hindi, Burmese and Bengali), Prakshepan (stories), Anubhootika Chhalharoo (travel essays) and many other works published separately in periodicals. Mr. Prasai has also edited Chhariyeka Kehi Prishtha (essays) and three other works, besides translating one book.. He is the Chairman of Jara Foundation, and Treasurer of Devkota Lu-Xun Academy, a literary organization. He is also associated with Rotary International. Also, a stakeholder with several other literary organizations, Mr. Prasai has got his works translated into several languages like English, Korean, Sinhala, Hindi, Assamese, Maithili, German, Burmese, Bengali, Marathi, Guajarati, Arabic, Tamil, Romanian, Philippine, Spanish, Italian, Serbian, Uzbekistan, Vietnamese, Chinese, Japanese, Russian.

MY VILLAGE: A PLANET BEYOND THE BOUNDARIES

The sorcerer has still been figuring destiny
Counting kernels of rice,
Checking if something has gone wrong,
When the sun was on the rise, or fall.
Or, if some items lacked in the Gothdhup , last year!

Cocks had been offered to Sagune and Sime-Bhume ,
Cash offers made too, to appease evil air,
And promises to deities fulfilled.
Budhibaju is our family deity, after all.
What a spell could it be, at such an age?
Sikari presses hard, if ever it attacks
The Banjhankri has always been sweeping
Dakini and Sakini away, with rice kernels
The ghouls of the dead still haunt the village.

Such whispers are still rampant here.
I won't simply believe your claims, Sainla Dai!
That, development has reached the village –
a place, where time is still computed
With the sun's position above,
And where times are either propitious and evil,
a place, where some mantras have to be chanted
To effuse grains for good stars;
still, a cock has to crow
for my village to wake up!

FORLORN SAGARMATHA

"The ship denied me a ride
Not because I was heavy
But he says
I look beautiful in Korea
Even without an make-up. "

I wrote her back—
"I am ardently missing you!
I am the same old Saraksan of yours.
I would love to see you
My dear Sagarmatha
Albeit only for once!"

Katarina Saric (Montenegro)

Katarina Saric (10.03.1976.) prof. of slavic literature and philosophy, master student of political science, is montenegrian civil rights activist and writer of socially engaged literature, designed for performance and theatre. She has published 12 books, most of which were translated and awarded and represented in numerous literature portals and platforms.

WOMEN'S COURCES

CRUISE

I stand riven
between an ex gaffer:
"Don't babble!"
and a future shaver:
"LOL"

I count the present
on the fingers on the prison rails
on the knitting needles and my aunts' gobleins

It will be over it will be over it will be over…
tweets the cuckoo from my father's wall clock
while a worn-out vinyl revolves

I will stab her eyes with this needle
Me. The spinster.
(I will, I swear on my mother)

SENSELESS NOISE

And you will allow the sticky looks of contempt and envy borne of the blemish blindness
and despair piled up in backbone and wrinkled arms
You will allow the misfortunes and torments
yours and those of the others
You will shoulder both what you have to and what the others load in your saddlebags
equally here as everywhere else
in this wide world
one and the same life for everybody, through and through
You will be seizing the life of the others and the others will be taking it from you
ground in the same mill
till we meet our maker
till the very end
and whoever receives the ticket to hell and whoever to heaven
You will allow everything down the water
when everything and everyone flow away and leave
every Tom, Dick, and Harry
But you'll remember only those silent days
when all of this is over
in which you were lucky to find your own teddy
to cuddle under the covers
and everything suddenly pauses and stops
becoming a senseless noise

FLASH-BACK

I cannot stand rainy afternoons
jazz and always the same flashbacks
Looking back at our car drives at sunsets while with my folded knees curled on the seat
I'm finishing up cigarette in flight
nailed to your profile your beard, two or three days old and that cavity above your upper lip,
one funny hair from the mole on your nose,

I cannot stand tasteless chewing gum
strawberries and the bursting of balloons that sweet teasing
without inhibition
Petting my thighs at the traffic lights
in a standstill
Lolling out
in stunts
when I throw my head out of the window
and the wind ruffles my hair

They remained cramp tied I cannot stand
tears or hangouts by the road chips for jukeboxes
and cappuccino from the machine poetry evenings
And always the same lesions that break my shins at every new step
Or long-distance love

I cannot stand this accursed weakness that burns every bridge
but in vain its attitude
it strands me on the very bar spats me on that very shaft
with a spray of mud through an eternally open wound
Which again only pours me out
instead of killing me

I cannot stand rain
neither the sound of jazz
These flashbacks intermittently always along those unchangeable rails
The burst in the temples
and the smell of burnt by the road
always from those unchangeable ashes

Kari Krenn (Argentina)

Argentine writer, author of the novel "INMARCESIBLE".

Poet, specialized in contemporary oral and written poetry. She is the author of the book "Poémame, entre Angustias y Esperanzas" published in 2019. Kari Krenn, in addition to being a writer and teacher, is a tango dancer and has cultivated artistic expression in all facets. She worked as a specialized cultural promoter, in vulnerable social contexts.

A tireless traveler, in her photographic memories she unites landscapes and the ways of the people. He carries his word of peace and good will, seeking brotherhood between peoples. From his contact with the daily lives of people who live in remote and exotic parts of the world, his poetry is born, which seeks to promote love and respect among all human beings. She is published in more magazines and international anthologys in more Foreign Languages.

*BIOGRAPHY

"Before being thought,
I vibrated,
next to the first beat
from the earth.
I pierced the catacombs
of the times,
cohabiting between dreams
of my ancestors.
From the four cardinal points,
in the suburbs of their souls,
I was weaving
and the cycle of all the moons
they randomly silenced,
and made way for me.

I know.
It was written.
Eternity took shelter
in my atoms
and a past nostalgia,
it escaped me in a breath".

On time

It is not late.
I'm still standing,
retracing labyrinths of pain;
rebuilding myself
without miscalculation.
I've seen myself succumb in your lap;
sinking silent
in the maelstrom of time;
as if every sin in the world
had been faded
inside me,
making up distances ...
causing absences...
I persist one more time
giving up,
letting the storm get stronger.
I choose the sky
and the swallows in my soul,
they take flight.
They pass the height of the word.
That is still beating between my lips
and with a lovely wink to life
I exhale verses.

Kazimierz Burnat (Poland)

Kazimierz Burnat – born in Szczepanowice on the Dunajec River. A graduate of the University of Wrocław and the University of Economics in Wrocław. Polish Poet, translator, essayist, publisher, journalist, organizer of cultural activities... Author of 21 books of poetry. He translated 7 books from Czech and Ukrainian. He wrote the prologue for 80 books. Co-author of 300 anthologies and monographs published in Poland and abroad. Translated into 43 foreign languages. Instructor of literary workshops. Juror of literary contests. Organizer of the International Poetry Festival „Poets Without Borders" in Polanica Zdrój. The laureate of a dozen or so literary awards. Honored with many medals.

Member of the Bureau of the Polish Writers' Association and Chairman of the Evaluation Committee, the chairman of the Society in Lower Silesia. Member of the Union of Journalists of Poland.

Fathoming

I am lacking a few moments
to own
distance in reverie
over the embers burnt out

I close my eyes

and sense the fleeting whisper of tomorrow
the moon gives in
to soft light of the Morning

with warm pulse
I am inscribing myself within its freshness
to add new meaning to intimacy

I nestle into the trunk
my own piece of sky

Internal tear

Their love
plunges growt
of unreal expectations
intensyfying thirst

with the stream of consciousness
short-lived as a rainbow
they moisten realm of insufficiency

his arythmic heart
writes the last poem
full of inexpressible
self-dubts
will he make you happy
or walk away in failure?

careworn organism
mind animated
(mayby will bring the heart rythm back)
mayby God's surprise
from sky's palate
will bring death into agony
give chance to reach The Beggining

lasting in suffering
parting as apparent relief

Kamrul Islam (Bangladesh)

Kamrul Islam, Professor of English literature, was born in Bangladesh. He is a published bilingual poet, essayist, translator and short story writer. Twelve books of poems (including selected poems), four of essays and one of short stories have got published till date. He has been honored by Gujarat Sahitya Academy and Motivational Strips on India's 74th Independence Day. Honored on the 60th Independence Day of Nigeria for his contributions to world literature. Haven for the world writers has also honored him for his dedication to world literature. His poems have been translated into Spanish, French, Italian, Romanian, German, Hindi, Portuguese, Odia, Nepali, Philipino, Arabic, Gujarati, Assamese and some other languages and published in different magazines at home and abroad. The President of World Union of Poets for Peace and Freedom (based in Italy) has appointed him Honorary Cultural Ambassador of Bangladesh for the year 2021. Union Mundial de Escritores UHE has honored him bestowing international Cesar Vallejo award-2020 and appointed him World Cultural Manager of UHE. He has won many certificates of excellence and awards from many global poetry platforms.

Wings Of Cloudy Dreams

...a flock of doves,
and the coos,
the clouds and rains in the valley-
a craft of embracing death,
The shadow of a evergreen ghost
burns the race of tomorrow.

Your good days go by
the distant moonlight,
the spurs flying far off the shore,

I only see half-dead palm trees
in lightning,
I see blood-dust, secret ashram
in the shadow of cosmetic evening.

Wings of cloudy dreams
launch the dawn,
The serenades humanize
the black winds
in tune with the feathers of doves.
Gradual purgation shapes
the crazy veins,
when rattling bones leaning towards
the green silence…

The Woods' Gospel

A butterfly runs over the soft branches
of my thoughts leaning towards
your angelic face,
I have seen rains on the wings
of day-dreams of some old fairies
believing in the honesty of fallen leaves
on the desolate graveyards,
though you are still in my breath
like a binary soul of a dove that
obliquely looks at the erroneous sounds
of this mundane chaos .
In traditional gesture, if the
anatomy of love becomes a wild wave
I must welcome the woods' gospel
brushing aside the fears of death…

Lucia Daramus
(Romania -UK)

Lucia Daramus is a British-Jewish -Gypsy- Romanian writer and poet who is living in England, a classicist, a linguist, a freelance journalist, and an artist. She has Asperger's Syndrome. Her work has been published in various magazines in Romania, France, Germany, England, Canada, USA, etc. Recently she completed her course in Creative Writing (Memoir, Biography, Autobiography) at Oxford University. Her MA is in Linguistics, and BA in Ancient Greek and Latin, Babes-Bolyai University, Cluj-Napoca. She has published poetry, essay, short story, play, novels. Her recent novel is The Cortege of The Lambs, a book about Holocaust, and recent poetry book is Flying With Memories.
http://romanianwriters.com/author.php?id=121
https://www.amazon.co.uk/Flying-Memories-Lucia Daramus/dp/1528934148
She won prizes for poetry, including Romanian prizes and international prizes like the Canadian Prize for Poetry (Gasparik). She has also won an International Prize for Poetry, 2018, at The International Book Festival Dublin. She has published ten books in the Romanian language and three books of poetry in the English language.

Hope

Stars, stars, stars
and lanterns of fishermen
under the dark sky
flickering all night
on the gloss of the ocean
drops, drops, drops of light
romp in water and under water
fragile, fragile and shy gleam
quivers under the row of boats

as a silver castle.

The infinite is silent
in the ocean, dark ocean
only a thrill of life is moving
in the womb of vessels –
there are fishes, ocean fishes
which carrying the dream of Jonah

all beings are sinking in sleep
the fish net is full with stars
stars, stars, stars
and lanterns of the fishermen
beyond the night lights
a hope, a hope in the tunnel of life

Music of All Languages

I am from the East and South and North
when the wind dances so, so slowly
and is singing the story of its people
the fields, like in England, are green and shaggy
the clouds are whirling on the sky
and the sky is so, so fragile and blue
like my soul which is keeping the entire planet
But you, you don't understand this
because of your inner deconstruction's revolution
mister, mister Boris Johnson
I am just a woman
staying in front of a strong man
what can I do, what can I do, what can I do?
my powers are only my words! Words, words
what can I do, what can I do?
On the streets there are many conflicts
a special culture fights against another one
everywhere is a fight , yes a fight!
Mister Boris Johnson
I am not a terrorist, I am a European
domnule Boris Johnson, nu sunt o terorista sunt o europeana

Señor Boris Johnson, no soy un terrorista soy un europeo
Signore, io non sono un terrorista io sono un europeo
Κύριε, δεν είμαι τρομοκρατής είμαι Ευρωπαίος
I am from The East, and South and North
when lambs are jumping with happiness
and peasants knead ancestral clay
with their hands, worked hands.
The door of their soul is open
for each human ! – because
my country is Romania
when Brancusi crushed the stones
to make his Golden Bird flying over the world
my country is Poland
when Chopin touched with his
fragile fingers the sounds of our nature
my country is Germany, and Britain, and Italy, and Spain
Spain, Spain, Spain when Picasso
and Salvador Dali painted
my country is Denmark, and Greece
and, and, and....
because I am a Muslim
Buddhist
Jew
Muslim
Christian
yes, mister Boris Johnson
I am a European, I am a European
and in my veins are flowing
the musics of all languages!

Lidia Chiarelli (Italy)

Lidia Chiarelli is one of the Charter Members of Immagine & Poesia, the art literary Movement founded in Torino (Italy) in 2007 with Aeronwy Thomas, Dylan Thomas' daughter. Installation artist and collagist. Coordinator of #DylanDay in Italy (Turin). She has become an award-winning poet since 2011 and she was awarded a Certificate of Appreciation from The First International Poetry Festival of Swansea (U.K.) for her broadside poetry and art contribution.
Six Pushcart Prize (USA) nominations.
Her writing has been translated into different languages and published in Poetry magazines, and on web-sites in many countries.

https://lidiachiarelli.jimdofree.com/
https://lidiachiarelliart.jimdofree.com/
https://immaginepoesia.jimdofree.com/

September Dawn in Turin

*"Not knowing when the dawn will come
I open every door"*
Emily Dickinson

Silky and dark clouds
flake away
in the distance
where
the mountain profile
is a frame for the city
still asleep.

Only the Mole Antonelliana*
challenges the sky
of September
and rises high
above noble palaces
witnesses
to ancient history.

In this motionless hour
a blade of light
tears the sky
shivering in the unreal silence

Turin opens to a new day

*The Mole Antonelliana is a major landmark building in Turin, Italy, named after its architect, Alessandro Antonelli. Construction began in 1863, soon after Italian unification, and was completed in 1889.

The Enchanted Garden

(remembering Flor 61 Garden in Torino)

"Peacocks walked
under the night trees
in the lost moon light"
—Lawrence Ferlinghetti

And then there were the lights
that lit
slowly
in the garden of a thousand colours.

They lit
warm, vibrant
on the stones of paths
on the petals of tulips

on the water of fountains
caressed by a gentle breeze.

The lights
switched on for me
as I walked
on the flowered avenues
and subtle fragrances
wrapped me up
in the silence of the night
then the flags
moved by the wind
became
the variegated forms
of an incomplete painting.

Cluster of old memories
that today are recomposing
while I hold tight in my fingers
the last, dried
rose of May

Previously published in: Lidia Chiarelli – Immagine & Poesia – Cross-Cultural Communications, New York 2013

Liang Shenling (China)

Liang-style Poetry, a famous poet in contemporary China, real name Liang Shenling, native of Nanning, Guangxi, China, now a free-lance writer. He has been invited to attend the "Academic Meeting on Literary Language", which was hosted by Zhejiang Normal University. Some of his poems have been translated into English, Italian, Spanish, Dutch, and French, etc. He has published several poetry collections such as A Nail Is Advancing, etc. Inheriting the Chinese poetic tradition of combining musicality and image into one and absorbing the theory and composing method of "new free verse" proposed by Liu Yilin, gradually he is forming a unique form of Chinese poetry by fusing "external rhythm" and "internal melody" — "Liang-style poetry".

Pain

In preexistence there is no sunshine, the moon invisible
Your form untraceable, your countenance out of touch
This is the bitter root left by me in remote antiquity
Like the cells of revenge, fission and heredity
A drop of blood is hurt, another drop is like a fish bone stuck in the throat

Without your despair and your existence is beyond reach
The demerit of preexistence is peeling off like nails
This life I have my life, but I cannot live it for you
Like thanksgiving, for hunger and cold to feel satiety and warmth
Like pray, through the hell and the heart goes through paradise

Leaving this life, the earth of dead cave is buried inch by inch
The yin and yang which refuses to be cut off, without your breath

Without darkness but no light is seen
Awn on the back, poison into the heart, being put to death by dismembering the body to reveal the bone
Not to miss it in the next life, I shall not be able to die for you

On Qinghai-Tibet Plateau

Only the eagle warns the distance between me and the sky
Those stories and legends make me firmly believe
The soul of plateau people draws people closer to the sky
In high air, the wafting sutra streamers and scriptures
Is the height above me in my life

But my heart is still hovering over the plateau
Carelessly handle the silverware and fondle the agate
Sanctity clears away the dust over body and heart
Beg for a heavenly bead, put on a Khatag
The low human life seems to be rising secretly

Upward looking, I find the sky kissing me passionately
This is an eternal memory of soaring
When I chase fantasy to be named on the plateau
I walk in the posture of a crawling train
Pious like tender grass sucking lamb milk

Translated Zhang Zhizhong

Ledia Dushi (Albania)

Ledia Dushi was born in 1978 in the northern Albanian town of Shkodra. She studied Albanian language and literature and she continued and finished her master's and doctoral studies in ethnology-folklore. She is a researcher at the Institute of Cultural Anthropology and Art Studies in Tirana, Albania. She is also a translator. Her well-received verse is written primarily in the dialect of Shkodra, gegë. It has been published in the volumes: Ave Maria bahet lot (Ave Maria Turns to Tears), Tirana 1997; Seancë dimnash (Winter's Session), Shkodra 1999; Me mujt me fjet me kthimin e shpendve (If I could sleep with the bird's return...), Tirana 2009 and a volume of her verse has also appeared in Italian, Tempo di pioggia (Rainy Weather), Prishtina 2000, Rain in the dark, Transcendent Zero Press, USA 2019, N`nji fije t`thellë gjaku (In a deep thread of blood), Onufri Publishings, Tirana, Albania 2019, Femna s`asht njeri (Woman is not human), BardBooks, Prishtina, Kosovo 2020. In the 1998 she was awarded with "The Silver Pen for First Book" from the Ministry of Culture. Her poems are published in Lichtungen – Zeitschrift für Literatur, Kunst und Zeitkritik, Nr.103, XXVI. Jahrgang, Graz 2005, and Orte. Schweizerische Literaturzeitschrift n°186: Lyrik aus Albanien, 2016. She also participated with readings in Leipzig Book Fair 2011 and Frankfurt Book Fair in 2006. She was invited in Literariches Colloquium in Berlin, Germany (2004) and in Internationales Haus der Autorinnen und Autoren, Graz, Austria 2005. Her poems are translated into German, Polish, French, Macedonian, Greek, Serbian, Italian, Chinese etc.

***

who knows what's of the water
smitten house 'neath the stones
a musky dusk
drowned the eyes

cold dead watery things
the anguishing coast
the wailing seagulls
an unbroken moon
yet to shuck itself, solely in blood
sprinkles of liquefied words
within the mouth
the smell of grape, when trampled on
a body smashed in heat
every drop of it drains into women
a vein snatching breath
falls down to the womb
and it wastes into giggles of women
into bird crumbs water colliding
into the cliffs past the waves
there a breath chirm or a noise chirm
the pond is clumsy don't chirm a word
for islands, the pain we unleash
surrounds it by land

***

…it's the foggy sound of the lake in dawn
echoing on the things headed to the sun
floating floating floating entangled entangled colliding
it's the ions bonding into one against the fog
getting in every hollow every skull
all the mornings in the world happening without me
the whole world's now a foggy lonesome lake
of branches and nests and birds on it's harness
taking your eyes and mind and heart and gloomily sounding a morning
to the world

***

canto…
been dreaming of me holding onto two falcon feathers nearly falling
nearly in ramble nearly in the white of a nightly moon covering my head
i sing a few songs sing a few songs that sprout of a place deeper than
the inside

dreamily i hold on to names women names and to sung women
women ill with a dark illness wet illness falling off the tree
and the moistened invite her to languish circling in flare
been dreaming of myself hanging onto two floating feathers in the air
eye to eye with a falcon

***

the language is dead and useless
to what the Soul since the beginning of time
keeps locked, since immense eternity
the sky's no secret, he's undisclosed
everyone's a temple of themselves
standing under You who spring from above
their ears ought to hear you, their Souls ought to shine drawn
in delirium and essences
enlightened by each and every cosmic blast
and you hang on you hang on you hang on
nearly falling you hang on to a thread of blood
in the air in the air staring at the sky of talking stars
aloft you stand in the air on a deep thread of blood

Translated into English by Genta Hodo

Luca Ariano (Italy)

Luca Ariano (Mortara – PV 1979) live in Parma. He published: Bagliori crepuscolari nel buio (Cardano 1999), Bitume d'intorno (Edizioni del Bradipo 2005), Contratto a termine (Farepoesia, 2010, Qudu, 2018 prefaced by Luca Mozzachiodi), in 2012 for the Edizioni d'If the poem I Resistenti, written with Carmine De Falco, that it was the winner of Premio Russo Mazzacurati. In 2014 for Prospero Editore published l'e-book La Renault di Aldo Moro with a preface of Guido Mattia Gallerani. In 2015 for Dot.com.Press-Le Voci della Luna published Ero altrove, with a preface of Salvatore Ritrovato, finalisist at the Premio Gozzano 2015. In 2016 for Versante Ripido / LaRecherche.it published l'e-book of Bitume d'intorno with the introduction of Enea Roversi.

Translated by Max Mazzoli

Which season are you lagging behind in?

A late snowfall from the dormer window
with a warm forehead ...
the terror of mermaids for you too.
You find yourself almost in the summer:
sudden storms and animals
coming down to the plains between squares and weeds.
The city, a row of avenues
with signs "To Let", "For Sale"
and you can't find those bars and shops anymore.
Queuing up at "We Buy Gold", in the pockets
ancient jewels symbol of other seasons,
sacraments to celebrate.
Where did those Sundays go?
Vanished like the prayers of a saint

to stop lava flows,
but already a new one to invoke
for miracles under catacombs.
Those Egon's drawings burned like fever
in your chest ... forgotten models,
to be sketched in a portrait
drunk in some cafe before the war,
at the end of another secular empire.

***

You were no longer used
to walking...
like when, as a child
after a debilitating spell of flu,
you yearned to run out in the street
after a football.
It will never be like being in your avenues,
your neighbourhood, those Deco villas
too solemn:
they are certainly not semi-detached...
your myopic eighties world.
Your mother won't be there to call you back
for dinner, your father tired from work,
another day between life and death
but always smiling for your benefit.
You're looking for his steps in closed cafes,
silent arcades that did witness
farewell kisses at sunset.
Who knows when you will again see
his figure arising from behind millennial marbles,
now that even a mild temperature
frightens you like distant sirens.

Linda. S. Goldberg (USA)

Writer, producer, educator L. S. Goldberg highlights footnotes to history and resurrects overlooked figures and events that left an indelible impact on our world. Produced, co-wrote, co-directed History of Fraunces Tavern & Early New York, with Lynn Sherr, correspondent, Philip Bosco, Tony winner, narrating film shown at Fraunces Tavern Museum for more than a decade. Finalist, semi-finalist in renowned competitions: Nicholl Fellowships, Austin Heart of Film Festival Screenplay Competition, Chesterfield Film Company, New Century Writer Awards, Scriptapalooza, New Works of Merit Playwriting Competition. The production of her play Yesterday Iran/Today Iraq at Midtown International Theatre Festival received rave reviews The John Harms Center for the Performing Arts selected That Lady from St. Louis for a staged reading and excerpts were published in Xavier Review. Recipient of state humanities' grants and academic assistantships and honors; arts management consultant to Circle in the Square, Ensemble Studio Theatre, Second Stage; member of Dramatists Guild and New York Women in Film and Television. Taught drama, film, writing and literature at universities in Boston, New York, and New Jersey; this multi-hyphenate currently relishes exploring new venues for creating theater works in a social distanced Zoom reimagined world and participating in poetry readings.

3 Americas

"I can't breathe."
"I can't breathe."
"I can't breathe!"
Pandemic. Economy. Election.
Election. Economy. Pandemic.
Economy. Pandemic. Election.
Shakespeare's line "sorrows . . . come in battalions"
Meets the moment.
Confederate statues
Pulling down,

Falling down,
Coming down.
Fallen monuments leave a scar that festers
And a wound that never heals.
Dismantled mon-u-men-ts do not change
A man's heart and soul.
A gulf so wide—no bridge, no tunnel,
no hand outstretched can overcome–
Tearing at the seams of a nation.
Will it hold?
Will it survive?
Will it exist?
Will it be a mere blip
In the history of the world?
A brief shining light
Like a meteor that burns itself out?
Freedom Exhales.

"Treading Water"

I loved winter when weather created an indoor igloo!
I loved staying in and letting the world drift by.
I loved the coziness of watching flakes dance by my window.
I loved the patterns they made against the glass.
I loved the hush of silence.
I loved curling up on a cushiony couch under a warm afghan by the fireplace.
I loved reading until my heart's content.
I loved drinking a hot toddy or a glass of wine as the fire crackled.
I loved the solitude with my own thoughts.
I could stay forever in my igloo
Until the day a pandemic arrived.

Leda García Pérez (Costa Rica)

Leda García Pérez is Costa Rican and Spanish. She is writer, lawyer, communicator and actress, with a career in the cultural world since 1970. She was a member of the Estudiantina of the University of Costa Rica. As an actress, she participated in important theatrical works such as "Las nosgonas de Paso Ancho" and the high comedy "A perfect crime." She is director and founder of the Literary Portal and the International Poetry Festival HOJAS SIN TIEMPO. She is creator of the PATH OF THE POETS on Tortuga Island, coordinator of the FIA LITERARIO in 2017 and 2018, co-founder of the Poiesis Literary Group, co-founder of ADECA (Central American Writers Association). She has published the poetry books With me in the nude, Voices of oblivion, Ineî Poems, Infidel Poems, Songs of stone and petal, Praise of custom, Sleepwalking Poems, Crazy Poems that are loose. Unpublished books: Naughty Poems, The night of the bodies. She has been participated in different anthologies in Europe, Latin America, Mexico and the United States. Her poems have been translated into Arabic, English, French, Bengali, Italian and Swedish. She is member of the Costa Rican Association of Writers (ACE). She is president of the House of the Peruvian Poet, Costa Rica section. She is the manager in Costa Rica of Prometeo de Poesía, (Spain).

HAVING A LOVER WITHOUT HAVING ONE

Having a lover without having one
quenching the thirst
until the end of existence
stealing auroras from the landscape
allowing intimidation by his swords
and his honeys
crossing the dimension of everything
levitating

because a poet is born dead
and is resurrected
when the poem requires his presence.

FORCING ME TO DIE

Forcing me to die
to turn more moon
more earth
more woman
May the storm be my ego
merciless, flowerless
and I the miniature.

UNFINISHED CROSSWORD

Unfinished crossword
sign of doubt in wanderings
where we are the foot
the stone
the temporal dust of the roads
nothingness amidst the end.
Life is transiting the wind rose
with the sea on your skin
and running loose in the undertow
while the eye awaits your return.
I lived all that I lack
the day after.

Translations by Marie Pfaff

Laura Garavaglia (Italy)
https://www.lauragaravaglia.it/

Laura Garavaglia was born in Milan and lives in Como. She is a poet, a journalist, and the founder and president of La Casa della Poesia di Como. She organises the International Poetry Festival "Europa in versi". Her publications include the collections of poems: Frammenti di vita (Fragments of Life – Il Filo, 2009), Farfalle e pietre (Butterflies and Stones Lietocolle 2010, prize winner in Alda Merini's competition in 2011), La simmetria del gheriglio (The Symmetry of the Kernel Stampa, 2009, finalist in Luzi's competition in 2013), Correnti ascensionali Updrafts (CFR, 2016), Numeri e stelle (Numbers and Stars Ulivo, 2015, prize winner in A. Farina's competition in 2017), Sayi ve Yildiz, a collection of poems translated into Turkish (Şiirden Yayıncılık, 2018), two books of poetry translated into Japanese: Duet of Stars (Hoshi no nijuso: za sutazu dyuetto (Nihon Kokusai Shijin Kyokai), Duet of Formula Shiki no Nijuso: Nihon Kokusai Shijin Kyokai, three books of poetry in the Romenian language, Ridul adînc al vieții (CronEdit 2019), Numere si semne (Europa, 2019), Muzica sferelor (Editura pentru literatură şi artă 2019), in Albanian Amplitude e Probabiliteteve, Bogdani, 2019, in Hungarian Csendkvantumok, (AB ART Kiado, 2020), in Spanish La simetria de la nuez (La Garua, 2020) and two books translated in Ukrainian an Serbian. She's director of a poetry serie of foreign poets "Altri incontri" for I Quaderni del Bardo Publishing House. The books published to date are: the trilingual anthology of Vietnamese poets (Italian, Vietnamese and English) "The mountain and the river on our shoulders", 2020 translated by A. Tavani, (IQdB, 2019, the book of poems "Blue" by the Hungarian poet Attila Balasz (IQdB, 2020) and edited the book of poems "The mythical age" by the Kosovar poet Jeton Kelmendi, "The unknown" by the Vietnamese poet Kieu Bich Hau, the novel "Moon Boy" by Alexandre Korokto.

She is a member of the International Prize for Poetry and Narrative Europa in versi, of the literature award Antonio Fogazzaro and literary award Kanaga.

Poetry

Sometimes words are eyes
gazing at the world aslant.
Deep down they dig
different perspectives.
Sometimes, however, words
hover in mid air
and fail to reach
into the corners of life.
And verse is dust
in a beam of light.

Yusuf

Yusuf is sitting next to his mother, his body lying faceup in the field.
Sunshine's carving his childlike gaze.
In the morning lightening in the sky, a blast:
perhaps a thunderstorm, but no rain
melting the soil into endless dark rivulets.
War deletes the borders of sense.
Perhaps it was a game, his mother had been sleeping
for hours, her arms folded on her belly
and wouldn't wake up.
And the black chasm had swallowed
the poor things of home.
Yusuf still doesn't know, his father
and his brother killed far away
beyond the dunes of blood
from sunrise to sunset.
His mother had been telling
tales of love, tales of peace.
Yusuf is now waiting for her voice.

Leoreta Xhaferi (Albania)

Leoreta Xhaferi was born in Pogradec, Albania. After she finished her studies for early childhood education at the university "Fan S. Noli" in Korça, she completed a master for language-literature and two years of Political Science at "Political Academy of Tirana" earning the title "Political elite". Short stories and poetry are the most popular genre for this author. Through the diversity of life and the mentality in her creations she manages to be a fierce social voice, almost rebellious, defending woman's rights and promoting woman's social emancipation. The most evident stream of her poetry is the free structure and laconicism of a coherent spirit. It shows the perpetual reality, reminiscent occurrences, as well as her artistic spirit. All of these, raise her poetry and place it at the center of postmodern universality. She is the author of the poetry book; One day is coming and Inorganic matter. Her active life as an author, comes to the reader through essays, opinions, psychosocial analyses and literature. " I am the humble one in front of values and virtues but without a doubt I am the rebel in front of vanity" – the author.

In my mother's place

You didn't sleep this night too
I am the guard of your night, looking through the darkness
To find who've killed your sleep for so long
Did I tell you that I've discovered the first killer? It was me...
I fully condemned myself with all kinds of punishments, except death...
"All humans vanish when the time comes,
overcome the wickedness, my dear and survive"
I was just a child when you told me this.
for many reasons I learned early how to fake my happiness in front of you.
What is going on my dear mother, why aren't you sleeping?

then I try to put my feet into your shoes, and start thinking about my children
There were no more questions left.
I figured out why you weren't sleeping.

I am leaving...

I am leaving,
dragging my feet
there is nothing left for me here, no reason to stay
Abandoned,
I'm going as far away as possible
from everything that is mercilessly, exasperatingly, torturing me.
Sorrow, like a noose around my neck is choking me.
I run way, on piles of rubble, submerged in the well of sorrow,
Forgotten, like a lonely passenger, saddled on the getaway...
I am hearing notes of music,
the tune of songs we used to sing together, simultaneously with one voice
whereas now we have become two separate, distant voices.
My sacrifices have been drained and I am leaving in pain
like an elongated shadow on the empty streets
Far, so far away, but not to the grave
With regrets, do not search for me
I will never come back to you
I am leaving, innocent
The wounds are painful and heavy
Together with my sacrifice drained of substance,
That you never tried to recognise
I am leaving, in my train
Although I may already be late.

Translated into English by Merita Paparisto

Lyubka Slavova (Bulgaria)

Lyubka Slavova is born in 1972 in Plovdiv, Bulgaria. She wrote from a high school student – at first only prose, then – mostly poetry. She periodically joins literary sites and shares some of what she has written. It was only in 2013 that she sent several poems for various competitions, some of which brought her honors. She continues to participate in international and national competitions and she has won a number of awards. Her poems are published in various anthologies, almanacs and in periodicals. Her first book – the collection of poems "The Dream of Cloud Birds" was published in May 2014 as a prize in the competition "Love at the end of the cable" (2013). Her second book with poems – "The direction in which I love you", was published in November 2017 by the Foundation "The Letters", Sofia, Bulgaria. She is the Secretary of the Writers' Association – Plovdiv, Bulgaria.

Confession

I wrote you a letter –
Sunny, even blinding…
So that you couldn't read between the lines
About the storms in my soul.
I smiled radiantly at you
With my eyelids half-closed…
So you couldn't see
The night's insomnia in my eyes.
I touched you carelessly
With the gust of wind…
So you couldn't feel
The trembling of my fingers.
I walked with you,
My head was downed…

So you couldn't talk to me.

You don't have to forgive me.

Drawing

Draw me a wind of colorful hopes,
draw me a song of sea waves,
draw my dreams in blue – boundless,
draw me fondness, even if it hurts.

Draw a prayer with the blood from the heart,
draw a holy blessing with the veins.
You have to draw, don't stop, don't ask for a break –
for today you promised me to draw love.

And when your colors are finally over,
ask me for sunrise and sunset, and sky.
Draw with them a starry end of the night,
seal a child's dream in a drawing.

You paint this colorful life for me.
I give you the colors of sun and rain.
You paint laughter, tear-drops and thunder.
I share the dreams of blooming rye.

In this strange drawing, you and I are together.
In this strange life, I walk next to you.
Let everything in the earth be strange.
I am love for you. You are the world for me.

Lali Tsipi Michaeli (Israel)

Lali Tsipi Michaeli is an Israeli poet. She immigrated from Georgia to Israel at the age of 7. She has published six poetry books so far. Attended international poetry festivals. She was part of a residecy program for talented writers in New York at 2018. Her books have been translated into foreign languages in New York, India, France, Italy, Georgia, Ukraina, Russa, Romania, Turkish, China, among other countries. Michaeli was defined by Prof. Gabriel Moked as "Urban-Erotic Poet" in his book "In real time" and considered innovative by critics. The poet and critic Jonathan Berg diagnosed a new poetic language in Michaeli's poetry and writes in Walla!: "Michaeli is very busy with the new: in the search for new ways to express and reflect reality, this is true both in the formal side and in the content related to the content of her poetry. Michaeli's poems are not "disciplined", the basic order that leads them is movement of consciousness and search in language of expression to that Free movement". In the Rabindranath Tagore International Poetry Competition she won the Poiesis International Award for Excellence In Poetry (2021). Lali taught Hebrew language at Bar Ilan University, at Tel Aviv University and at Ben-Gurion University. She has one son and lives in Tel Aviv by the sea.

Oda on the mask

Luck stops the mobile targets
anosmics the smell of cities
And the windows close on
The possibility
That
once and for all
I will spread my wings and make a leap
        For my freedom
I will free myself from the memories
And I will carry a blessing

I do not believe what you left me
Keeps me alive
If I do not create something new I have no
Right of existence
The soul dies before the body
You're chasing me
That I succeeded
cut up
Chains
From my feet
I left your path and started
To go alone
In an unpaved road where you do not know
To spell war
I am a tribal soul
In a white robe

In your dress shrouds

Everything looks transparent and sealed
And only you
Flying
Naked from there, light bodyless
Leaving a ghostly
Frantic cursory glance
On the soundtrack of the bluebird
Nobody has caressed you in frills you've ordered from Chanel
Designed, cut, finished – all custom-made
The curve of your belly & line of your waist the sketch of the fabric stands on end
And I am not calmed
With you everything is new and unblemished
So much so
If it weren't for the clogs

Translated by Alexa Christopher-Daniels

Lily Swarn (India)

Internationally acclaimed, multilingual poet, author, columnist, peace ambassador, radio show host, has four books in different genres to her credit. Gold medallist from Chandigarh, with two University Colours for Dramatics and "A Trellis of Ecstasy" is applauded by Chief Minister, Punjab Journal of Common wealth Literature, London called it a "Veritable Delight". Lily's poems translated into 16 languages, feature in international anthologies.

Lilies of the Valley, (essays), "The Gypsy Trail", (novel) launched by Governor Punjab "History on My Plate", are widely acclaimed. "A Versatile Genius", "Our Poetry Archive", Atunispoetry.com, Mind Creative (Australia), Poem Kubili, The Garden of Poetry and Prose (USA), Incredible Women of India, Learning and Creativity, Different Truths feature her work. Member, administrator for organizations in Ghana, United World Movement for Children. Radio Show host in USA, interviewed by Red River Radio, USA, Sher e Punjab radio, Vancouver. Invited to recite by Sahitya Akademi, Lily's Urdu ghazals are now sung by prominent voices. Celebrated internationally in "25 Wonderful Women of Excellence," "Women of Essence" books, Lily is now working on her 5th book.

Her inspiration is her son who died young.

Just a Woman ?

So you want to talk about her anatomy ?
That statuesque lady who looks like She stepped out of a temple sculpture ?

Go on, slur your words and smirk
Lecherous glances and suggestive innuendos will help
Or better still

Rake up her "hoary "past
An ex boy friend or her intimate relationships
Tear her to shreds with your wagging tongues
Make mince meat out of her reputation

For she is not human at all
Just a woman after all !

Who cares why her sari is creased today ?
As terribly as her broad forehead is ?
Or why her mother simply won't come out of
that horrendous coma ?

And that her husband won't let her children
Be born because they were girls ?
Investigated in their embryonic state and rejected ?

That she first goes to cook for her vacantly gazing dad
And then waits yawningly for her alcoholic man to stop belching
So that he can stagger to the table to gobble down a few morsels

That she truly doesn't value the fact
That you choose to call her a firecracker a "pataakha"
within earshot
Instead of getting up to wish her politely
For that's what gentlemen should do

Well, definitely not men who commoditise women
Inebriated on their own hollow masculinity

How would they know that tears simply
Help to strengthen a woman's resolve
To irrigate her enormous reserves of patience
Not to drown her in a morass of self pity ?

Lilla Latus (Poland)

She is poetess, translator, author of reviews, song lyrics, articles about travelling. Many times awarded both for her poetry and engagement in cultural activity for local community. Published nine books of poems. Her poetry has been published in many magazines, online literary pages and anthologies (USA, Australia, India, The Czech Republic, Italy, etc).

On the edge

I broke a bottle

its sharp edges
look like peaks
of unknown land

I can put them
onto my wrists
and check
the depth of
life

Until tomorrow

today the air is so bad

all letters sent to the hearty address
are coming back to me

even time
is running away

and as far back as

yesterday

life made sense with
my hands

tomorrow…

tomorrow
is the most beautiful
day of the week

A girl with raindrops in her voice

She used to tell me about Plato and Aristotle.
Her Slavic accent sounded like gravel in the
Rain. Ing,ing, ing…
Feeling a fading shadow around my neck
I see a bright cave paved with desire and
Fear. In her language love and hatred are feminine
Nothing was neuter. Golden mean in motion.
I was Alexander but not great enough to conquer
The furthest reaches of her soul.
Leaving was a move excluding one of
The possible versions of future.
All places of my happiness are taken and create
Gloomy theory of forms.
Sitting in a brown study with blind shutters,
I can hear raindrops searching for a dry land.
Falling, tapping, dying, ing, ing, ing…

© *Emine Tokmakkaya (Turkey) "Existence or energy, of the Universe in the love on escape colors of cosmos nature"*

She lives in Istanbul and Turkey for education. She is graduated from the Faculty of Education and Art of Ankara Gazi University. She is an Art Educator and She create creative and curating international art projects. She worked as a painting and art history teacher in professional high schools. She retired and worked as an art and graphic design teacher for 24 years. Now she paint full time, prepare international art and culture projects and participate in international artistic and cultural events.

**Prof. Dr. Academic:
Milutin Đuričković (Serbia)**

Milutin Đuričković (1967, Dečani). A Serbian poet, short story writer, novelist, essayist, journalist. He graduated at the Department for Serbian Philology in Priština, where his master's degree. He earned his doctorate at the Faculty of Philosophy in East Sarajevo. He works as a professor at the College of Professional Studies for Educators in Aleksinac.His books were translated into 50 languages. He edited magazines "Lighthouse" and "Our creation". Member of the Serbian Rojal Academy of scientists and artists, Association of Writers of Serbia and the Association of Journalists of Serbia. He published 60 books for children and adults (poems, novel, story, critic, monography, anthology...). Lives in Belgrade.

PEACE

"Peace is always beautiful."
(Walt Whitman)

There is the Hellenic sea listening to us:
seagulls, shores,
ships, chronicle.

My hometown is
just a story
in the silence of centuries.

An old olive tree
told me.

REMEMBRANCE

Vet snow
is falling on the bed.
Water is gurgling.

Day like
any other.
Fiery rapsod.

Unfathomable silence.
Mild northern wind blows.

While
expecting her,
someone crosses
my threshold.

FREEDOM

You, always
watching the sky
full of birds.
You, not feeling
the flow of time,
yet knowing
all the old roads.
You must be
a tramp.
The olive branch
that I bring to you,
is a symbol of peace
and freedom…

**Maram al-Masri
(Syria – France)**

Maram al-Masri (born 1962) is a Syrian writer, living in Paris, She is considered "one of the most renowned and captivating feminine voices of her generation" in Arabic. Born in the coastal city of Latakia to a well-known Sunni Muslim family, Maram al-Masri studied English Literature in Damascus, although she interrupted her studies when she fell in love with a man of Christian faith. The relationship failed because of the opposition of the man's family (interfaith marriage was forbidden in Syrian law) and in 1982, Maram al-Masri emigrated to France, where she married a Syrian, whom she divorced later. In her book Le rapt she picks up the issue of having been unable to see her son for 13 years, because he was taken to Syria by his father after she remarried. She has another two children with her French husband, from whom she separated, too.

She wrote poetry from a young age "to distinguish herself from the other girls and to attract attention",publishing in literary magazines in Damascus. Her first collection was published there in 1984 under the title I alerted you with a white dove, but her public breakthrough came in 1997 with the book A red cherry on a white-tiled floor, published by the Tunisian Ministry of Culture, as it was considered "too erotic" by Syrian publishers. In 2002, the book was published in a Spanish translation which obtained an immediate positive echo with several reprints, and shortly afterwards, the French and English translations appeared. Maram al-Masri started to publish regularly in the French market and took up writing poetry in French, too. Although her writings "do not address the Arab reader because their language and their thoughts are different to mine", most of her work is still written in Standard Arabic. Her poetry has been described as "direct, unadorned writing, with its emphasis on the quotidian", where the "utilization of simple, almost child-like metaphors, contrasts sharply with the conventions of traditional Arabic love poetry". "That a woman write so unreservedly about sex" also "lends a fresh, unexpected quality" to her poetry. The Guardian described her as "a love poet whose verse spares no truth of love's joys and mercilessness" Besides publishing regularly in Spanish book market, some of her works have been translated also into Italian, Catalan and Corsican, with some samples in German, and she is a frequent guest at poetry gatherings in several European countries, from Ireland to Italy. She has received several prizes, like the "Adonis Prize" of the Lebanese Cultural Forum, the "Premio Citta di Calopezzati" and the "Prix d'Automne 2007" of the Societe des gens de letters.

Maram al-Masri has taken a firm stand against the Assad regime in Syria [9] and considers that "every decent person is with the Revolution". Her poetry book Elle va nue la liberté [Freedom, she comes naked] (2014) is based on social media images of the civil war.[9] Although she defines herself as an Atheist, she justifies the use of religious slogans in the Syrian uprising as a "last opium" which cannot be taken away from people brutally oppressed by a dictatorship.

Selected works

I alerted you with a white dove (Andhartuka bi hamāmaï beidā') (1984)
A red cherry on a white-tiled floor [Karzaï ḥamrā' ʿalá balāṭ abyad] (2003)
I look at you [Anẓuru ilayk] (2007)
Wallada's return [ʿAudaï Wallada] (2010)
Freedom, she comes naked (Elle va nue la liberté (2014)
The abduction [Le rapt] (2015)

The Bread of Letters

1

Who will tell the trees they are guilty
for having let fall their leaves,
who will accuse the sea of abandoning its shells on the sand?

I, mother-woman, woman-mother,
with two breasts for pleasure
two breasts for maternity
who gives the milk of music
tells stories
explains games
clarifies feelings
and the grammar of thoughts.
I, who am woman voluptuous tender,
virtuous and sinner,
with my mouth
I give to eat the bread of letters,
consonants and vowels,
phrases, synonyms and comparisons.

Who will accuse me,
I who make a gift of my body
to love?

2

The act of writing,
is it not a scandalous act in itself?

To write,
it is learning to know oneself in the most intimate thoughts

Yes I am scandalous
because I point to my truth and my nakedness as a woman,

yes I am scandalous
because I cry my sorrow and my hope
my desire, my hunger and my thirst.

to write
is to describe the multiple faces of man
the beautiful and the ugly
the tender and the cruel.

to write is to die in front of a person
upon whom you look, unmoved,

it is to drown in sight of a boat that passes close
without seeing you.

To write
is to be the boat that will save
the drowning.

To write
is to live on a cliff's edge
clinging to a blade
of grass.

We sow

she sprouts
she grows
she explodes
she gives birth
to an infant in a poem.

Between her thighs
it flows
like a waterfall,
a small body
naked,
hot.
He cries

Mark Meekers (Belgium)

Studied Philosophy and Letters (Modern History, KU Leuven). 80 Publications (27 collections of poetry, 1 novel, 3 art monographs, collections of essays, anthologies and collections). He wrote short stories, reviews, chanson and song texts, was on numerous editorial boards and was chairman of the jury for ten poetry competitions. His poems have been translated, set to music and included in many magazines, newspapers and anthologies. He was founder and chairman of the poet collective Mengmettaal (1991-2006), chairman of the Dutch-Flemish Association Concept, first village poet of Doel (2007-09), poetry ambassador of Flemish Brabant (2009). Guest of Honor at the "Woordfees" (Windhoek 2013). He has been awarded many times for poetry, essay and short story: "Hugo Claus and Mark Meekers are the most awarded Flemish poets" (Het goud van de Vlaamse Letteren / De Standaard). His visual poetry forms the bridge between literature and visual art. He is also active as a visual artist under his real name Marcel Rademakers. He was co-founder of the international group "Lumen Numen" (Antwerp, 1957) and founder of the international group Fusion, artistes peintres du Sud-Ouest (Dordogne, France 1982). He has exhibited at home and abroad (25 solo exhibitions, 145 group exhibitions).

TROUGH A MANGLE

first he shook a big bang out of his divine
sleeve. my 206 bones were shaking, but
did not give up the ghost. in astronomy
compassion is an unknown concept.

he sees it great, likes contrasts. than he plays
cunningly, in a tiny way, goes viral: does he
want to infect us? nose to nose with god,

inhaled and coughed up. his corona doesn't

fit around my head. god no longer appears in
my table of contents. I'm left behind more lonely
than myself. hope does not give a fixed
handle to put a ladder up against. fear
has broken steps. nothing climbs higher
than a bird. should i sew wings onto myself?

nothing i leave behind, no bubble, no hole,
but no bad word about this delicious
absurd existence. no tear that is worth silver.
nevertheless i don't want to miss you,
not for an angel nor celestial body
in the universe.

BACK AND FORTH

the pond too square to wink, where
deer and wild boar come to drink their
mirror image, women once washed
their gray bodies out of the sheets.

the stone as a benchmark, around which
the fields and the winds turn. the heifers
shiver on their young legs. who planted
that curiosity in their eyes?

the new is already falling down
dries, ochres. the processionary
caterpillars set the dog's eyes on fire.
insects sniff glue on a flycatcher ribbon.

hail storm marks every leaf with wounds.
war between the layers of air. chestnuts
lose their tongues. the oaks leave
their boast behind, go bald. the silence of
the forest shabby as a coat without a lining.

3D PRINTING

in vain they had tried it with an angel:
a sticky tuft of feathers. god cannot be
put into words, but cán be put in a 3D printer.
they really wanted to see him,

touch a light image, burn their fingers.
they typed in his parameters:

righteous, ubiquitous, full of love.
immortality in plastic, metal, concrete?

preferably in human cells. all priests
superfluous, no censers, crosses or
blessings, just a red painted nail
pressing the button. the buzz resembled

a long outspun prayer: no three-dimensional
image, but sensational emptiness.

too small a device, too low resolution?
perhaps he exists in a fourth dimension?

Translation: Eline Rademakers

Moaen Shalabia (Palestine)

Moaen Shalabia, Born on 14 October 1958 in Maghar town – In the Galilee region. Palestinian poet, one of the Arab Palestinian national minority who lives in Israel. Finished his studies in Haifa University – (Business Administration and management). **He published:** *Poetry:* The wave is return – 1989. (Al-Aswar Palestinian Culture Quarterly_ Acre); Between two butterflies – 1999. (The Arab Modern Foundation Jerusalem Alquds); The memory of senses – 2001. (The Arab Modern Foundation Jerusalem Alquds); Rituals of Solitude – 2004. (Al-Aswar Palestinian Culture Quarterly_ Acre); The immigration of the naked longings – 2008 (Al-Aswar Palestinian Culture Quarterly Acre): Stuck poems – 2014 ("Culture" for publishing and distribution – Tunisia); By Azure Water – 2020 (Siirden Yayincilik – Turkey)
Prose: Meditations – 1992 (Renaissance Publishing and Distribution – Nazareth); Narrow evening – 1995 (Abu Rahmoun, printing and publishing – Acre); Spirituality – 1998 (Albatof – printing, publishing and distribution).

My Foggy Window

Behind my foggy window,
The desire of revelation urges me
To uncover a planet that went deep into the clouds;
Remnants of a smell that scratch my body to go through,
Like a dreamer who goes through the mirrors of absence!

Behind my foggy window
A space for the moon splits in front of me in the darkness,
Steals a glance at her rising specter from below the rain.

Behind my foggy window,
She moves in front of me like the glimpse of the 'ah!' in my chest;
The sea pants in me like a trans-lust horse,
While the eternal blue erases the shadows of the sand,
And I depart to wherever the words carry me into the elegies
of memories.

Behind my foggy window
I collected the wood inside me and set fire to it;
I arranged my Persian carpet, some of my writings, my tobacco,
my senses,
A handful of music and the fragrance of her clothes,
And ran my hand even over the walls.

Behind my foggy window,
A broken intuition that is stricken by distress, anxiety, fear,
and longing befalls me
For someone who infiltrates towards the visible vague and
rises till grief;
It looks over my Self but I soon imagine that I am No one, No one!

Behind my foggy window,
Snowflakes fall on the coats of my heart and loss pours down
The taste of rain intensifies; sorrows sail into my soul –
And I cry:
My lady, My lady! O woman who takes off everything,
except her femininity;
The wind will fill my clothes and on the bed of love,
the whoop of creativity will spring!

Behind my foggy window,
She comes to me from nothingness, carrying her fiery wound
To awaken "Tammuz", who has never been absent, in me,
"Tammuz", who will certainly return!

**Maria do Sameiro Barroso
(Portugal)**

Maria do Sameiro Barroso is a medical doctor and a multilingual poet, translator, essayist and researcher in Portuguese and German Literature, translations studies and History of Medicine.
She has authored over 40 books of poetry, published in Portugal, Brazil, Spain, France, Serbia, Belgium, Albany, USA, and translations and books of essays.
Her poems are translated into over twenty languages.
She was awarded national and international prestigeous prizes.

BLUE STRING

I was born to a bright world
behind the closed curtain
out of the darkest bushes of the night,
surviving the hoovering whirls,
the marsh fields.
Then, I grabbed a soft blue string
and came up slowly,
breathing deeply,
inhaling the sacred scent
of yellow healing amber,
keeping green emeralds,
blue good luck sapphires
and malachite protecting eyes,
Once, I lived under the ocean.
I couldn't breathe.
Life was exhausting, painful.
No silver lines showed up.

Just a dead bird.
And the silent beating of the night
concealing a sheltering wing.

BYGONE DAYS

I write from a golden age
as old as childhood,
veiled and mysterious
like a garden of Hesperides.
But I never forget about the sick
animals of the night,
nor about harpoons of stars
waking me up.
I always retain a memory
of sea pebbles,
round glasses of aroma,
velvet orchids, amber rows
and fish swimming
under the boat hulls.
My islands are memories
of camellias, transparent doors,
sparkles of light,
and demiurge birds flying over
forgotten nightmares
and dreams of bygone days.

Mahmoud Said Kawash (Palestine)

Born in Mirun - Safad, in the Upper Galilee of occupied Palestine. His previous place of residence was Beirut - Lebanon, and the current place is Denmark. He holds two degrees in management and English literature. He worked in the fields of higher education, translation, and written and audio media, along with journalistic writing and preparing political, cultural and social studies and research. He was previous director of the Arabic-speaking radio for the Arab community in Denmark, and news and talk shows presenter in it. He has many studies and researches on Arab national thought and Arab affairs, especially Palestinian. He has two books, one in politics and the other in literature.

MY NOSTALGIA FOR YOU!!

When your absence complies with me in the presence of longing
The letters of my poem wear your perfume
The strings of pens head on lines towards you
To form a letter that leans on my soft spring shadow
Which searches for you behind the desert silence
To let me live in an oasis of leaves
I water with a blossom that bears the flavor of my blood

My nostalgia for you is a letter which pours out the river of my flowers
Draws the first smile that sees the sunrise of life
As if you are the first word to inhabit the dictionary of love
The moment in which my eyes fall asleep
The vision which reflects itself on the edge of my pen
The ink pot that utters the meanings carrying your flavour
Most probably the spirit was indwelling you until it touched you
to give birth

Yes, I will break silence as long as you are with me
To practice the ritual of splashing ink with you
To stimulate poetically the pulse of moments inside you
And no matter how the footsteps of that pen go, I will travel with you
To share my covenant with you
To keep pouring my soul with you
To draw you letters in the colour of the sky

Oh man, whom I failed to place in my chest, so my poetry recited him
My message to you is sinking between a dream and a sea of papers!!

ODE TO FREEDOM

In our country, the pride dies in the souls of the politicians
They eat the "haram" mixed with the complaints of the people
Pray in the sanctuaries, where the prophets died
Spend the nights on the praise and tons of supplication
Fall asleep at dawn within the arms of hypocrisy
While our country reaps death with tears and blood
The roar of the victorious heroes has reached the sky
Our country boils "a revolution in the hearts of revolutionists"
Who raise their voices above the throats saying:
Our ears got bored of the bells and the sound of candlesticks
Our delegations came back filled with piles of losses
We are revolutionists singing our own revolution
Refusing to sing the tone of solace seventy years more
We love our country and never give up our love for freedom

Michela Zanarella (Italy)

Michela Zanarella was born in Cittadella (PD) in 1980.
Since 2007 she lives and works in Rome.
She published the following collections of poetry: Credo (2006), Risvegli (2008), Vita, infinito, paradisi (2009), Sensualità (2011), Meditazioni al femminile (2012), L'estetica dell'oltre (2013), Le identità del cielo (2013), Tragicamente rosso (2015), Le parole accanto (2017), L'esigenza del silenzio (2018), L'istinto altrove (2019).
In Romania the collection Imensele coincidențe (2015) was published in a bilingual edition. In the United States, the collection translated in english by Leanne Hoppe "Meditations in the Feminine", was published by Bordighera Press (2018).
Author of fiction books and texts for the theater, she is a journalist of Periodico italiano Magazine and Laici.it.
She is one of the eight coauthors of Federico Moccia's novel "La ragazza di Roma Nord" published by SEM.
Her poems have been translated into English, French, Arabic, Spanish, Romanian, Serbian, Greek, Portuguese, Hindi and Japanese.
She won the Creativity Prize at the Naji Naaman's 2016 International Award. She is an ambassador for culture and represents Italy in Lebanon for the Naji Naaman Foundation.
She is speaker of Radio Double Zero.
Corresponding member of the Cosentina Academy, founded in 1511 by Aulo Giano Parrasio.
She works with EMUI_ EuroMed University, a European inter-university platform, and deals with international relations.
She was President of the Italian Network for the Euro-Mediterranean Dialogue (RIDE-APS), Italian leader of the Anna Lindh Foundation (ALF).
Honorary President of the WikiPoesia Poetic Encyclopedia.

Then, Silence

We know of a destiny
that seems a season that persists,
a repeating, divine and ancient,
a shadow tracking down
in the face of life.
The expected color
is on the muscles of a dream.
Inside the moon
other worlds, a sound of sculpted waters.
Then, the silence.

The Canals are Bare
(to Alda Merini)

The canals are bare,
they don't have any more pupils
thirsty of love
from protecting.
The dust preserves the aroma
of silences woven together by the sky.
On the back of a road, imprints of rhymes
they go back to drinking
sips of will,
breaths of syllables,
they go back to kissing dimensions
with the benevolent look
of a woman,
who teaches her soul
to remain dawn
devoted to the earth.

Mordechai Geldman (Israel)

Mordechai Geldman was born in Munich to Polish parents who had survived the Holocaust. His family immigrated to Israel in 1949 and settled in Tel Aviv, where he has lived ever since. Geldman studied World Literature and Clinical Psychology and works as a psychotherapist using psychoanalytical methods His poetry tends to be meditative and includes many haiku. He was influenced by Zen Buddhist esthetics and philosophy. His poetry sings with many voices – lyrical, philosophical, sensual, erotic, religious, ironic and others. He has published 18 poetry books, a book of short stories and 6 non-fiction books. A two volume collection of poems from his books was published in 2011. His last poetry book is the third volume of the collection of his poetry written till 2019. His poems were translated into many languages: Chinese and Japanese included. His book "Becoming One" was translated to Portuguese ("Teoria Do Um") and published in Portugal on 2017. A large collection of his poems in English "Years I Walked at Your Side" was published on 2018 in Suny Press, State University of N.Y. His non-fiction books deal with subjects as the self in psychoanalytic theories and in Yoga and Buddhism, psychoanalytic interpretation of literature, doubles and symmetries in Shakespeare's plays, his favorite Israeli poets and artists, etc. As a visual artist Geldman is engaged in painting, ceramics and photography. Geldman was an art critic for the Israeli daily Haaretz, and curated exhibitions for many Israeli artists. Awards: the Prime Minister Prize; the Brenner Prize for literature; the Amichai Prize; the Bialik Prize for Literature.

THE CAFÉ

I walked to the sea again –
I left home where I was locked down
fearing the plague
whose creator is unseen as a demonic god
but I was not infected

I was as pure as a Tibetan hermit

the sea was full and empty
and I was full and empty
the plague enabled us to merge
without other nomads present
or couples clinging to their hug
no one was seen till the limits of sight
a deep loneliness aroused dark waves
and we were starry as a galaxy
there both of us were swept away
by the magnets of gravitation
and we stayed in the dark hole of truth
and didn't worry at all

a tune of a Ney flute
that the wind carried from a distance
from the lips of an hallucinated flutist
aroused great longings
for the smell of coffee
in the cafe where I wrote many poems

A SMALL JACKAL

On the river's bench
a small jackal stopped to look at me
wanted that I'll look at him
to know his hardship
he was very hungry
probably infected with rabid
and I unconsciously
innocently like green grass
wanted him to look at me
and see that my life too
is not easy at all
thou I was still not infected
with the pandemic plague
that is destroying our world
and killing and killing

We looked at each other
but he didn't howl
and I restrained my sobbing
the universe was too big for both of us
but for a short moment
we promised each other something
that we will never fulfill
and everything was enormously clear
like the azure sky that was our roof

POEMS

a small pebble
a peephole to galactic infinity
a heart waiting for transplantation
a Jasmine bush in a spring night
a skull full with emptiness
the howling of abandoned dogs
a raku cup for a tea ceremony
a note in a green bottle
an eye without eyelids
sparrows chirping under the table
a parable resisting interpretation
the look of Orpheus backwards
the darkness covering the sea
a love letter to your soul
a written confirmation of my being
an epitaph
and on and on

Prof. Masudul Hoq (Bangladesh)

Masudul Hoq (1968) has a PhD in Aesthetics under Professor Hayat Mamud at Jahangirnagar University, Dhaka, Bangladesh. He is a contemporary Bengali poet,short story writer, translator and researcher. His previous published work includes short stories Tamakbari (1999), The poems Dhonimoy Palok(2000), Dhadhashil Chaya which translated version is Shadow of Illusion (2005) and Jonmandher Swapna which translated version is Blind Man's Dream (2010), translated by Kelly J. Copeland. Masudul Hoq also translated T.S. Eliot's poem, Four Quartets (2012), Allen Ginsburg's poem, Howl(2018), from English to Bengali. In the late 1990's for 3 years he worked under a research fellowship at The Bangla Academy. Bangla Academy has published his two research books. His poems have been published in Chinese, Romanian, Mandarin, Azarbaijanese, Turkish, Nepali and Spanish languages. At present he is a Professor of Philosophy in a government college, Bangladesh.

Jesus

Seeing the dusty footprints of the man
I'm here; In this desert rock country

In his glittering white cloak
The garden of heaven is hidden
Lots of flowers there!

Running after the man's dream
Polar and desert
Ice and sand
All has become the sea of our hearts!

Happiness

Our village is further east across the Himalayas
Wandering in the Zhou and Devdaru forests
The fog comes to the village by touching the ice

We find the shadow of good fortune in it
When winter comes, we look north
Kanchenjunga surrounded by clouds is hanging in the sky

This time in December
In the garland of light awakened in the fog
I will decorate the forest with zhao and fir trees

If any happy bird before the Christmas
comes flying towards our village
we will decorate the forest with zhao and fir trees.

December twenty-five

Shepherd and I are two brothers in human birth
He and I were born in December
He is before; I am after

While protecting the wood industry from damage
He became the Jesus of the cross long before me!

After much later I cry loudly for the pain
Of losing my brother while reading holy scripts.

I think this time in our northern hemisphere
When the twenty-fifth of December will come by lighting the festival brightness
I will make the small day bigger!

Merita Paparisto
(Albania – Canada)

Merita Paparisto was born and grew up in Elbasan City. She has a Bachelor degree in Finance from the University of Tirana. Writing is her hobby and her passion. She has published three books: "Cristal in the fog"(2005) "Beyond… "(2018), "Solstice" (2020) as well a book with short stories written by her "The foolishness of broken years" (2020).
Merita has also translated and published a book with short stories, from well-known authors such as Joyce, Capote, Chopin, Virginia Wolf, O' Henry, Poe, etc. titled "Selected short stories"(2005). Other poetry translations have been published in different online magazines or portals.
She has a blog,(*http://www.kamomila-kamomila.blogspot.com*) where she posts her creative works as well as her translated works.

A ballade for my grandma

I combed your hair and braided your grey dreams
on petite braids that become thinner and thinner every day
I touched your sight, that curious one…. under your eyes…
I polished your nails that were getting as old,
as the arthritis joints of your hands.
And yet, your silent, frozen sight over this world
that whirled much faster than can be perceived by you…

your sorrow was sealed in your chest's box
the box that you entombed under the rose tree.
The last memory of touching your perfectly weakened bones
and your white delicate skin
is crackling on my fingertips
like the whisper that you had borrowed
from the running wind.

But I remember you having those warm blue circles of energy
that poured over and surrounded me forever.
Those warm waves that I miss so much
in this cold and wild world
I was crumbled in in hundreds white dots of hope
over the black sorrow of your dress
I was clinging to you with my baby hands
to shelter myself in your generous grey caves.

The white and black buds that you planted in me
are missing your blue light so much grandma.

Would you be able…

Would you be able, letting me
be planted into your brain?

Me, the tiny wild earthy seed…
chestnut with the thorny skin

Your brain is white coral
cliffs and caves, cliffs and caves

The famished roots of seed
debilitated in the darkness of the abyss

The sloppy, murky thoughts speaking
With the little voice: whispering in my ears
"You're seeking to be planted
in the wrong place…
the brain is not the heart"

Hence:
"swallow the darkness and survive,
swallow the darkness and survive"

**Małgorzata Borzeszkowska
(Poland)**

Małgorzata Borzeszkowska, a History and English teacher and poet from the north of Poland (Gdańsk) , has been writing poem for over 20 years. She published 3 books of poetry – "At the gate", "Inscribed in a landscape" and "On the border of silence and light". Two of them were awarded. Poems were published in many anthologies and magazines. She was awarded in numerous poetry contests. Her poems are also published on the Internet in Helikopter, Pisarze.pl, Fabrica Librorum and Litteratuer. Incidentally, she is also a member of jury in poetry contests. She belongs to Gdańsk Poets' Club.

Unstoppable

life unstoppable
in a pot of an old rotten willow trunk –
self-seeding twigs of rowan and elderberry –
a duopoly of germination, growth and blossoming

life irresistibly grows up, breaks out, overflows
with a stream of green leaves, it scratches
low clouds,
seeps the light entices

it's banal, obvious and predictable,
that we are all like those willow trunks, from our decay
something will be born one day,
a rowan basket?
or maybe dead
nettles

Confession

I own a square of sand
three drops of salt water shaken from the coastal dog's hair,
shells in a mini version, but matching the color
of my eyes and nails,
dry-wet tree trunk engraved by a storm
and its ghostly shadows in which the gulls make their nests

I have that and more:
a red polka dot swimming costume and a bottle of sweetened tea,
two hard-boiled eggs and bread with cheese and sand in my teeth,

jellyfish like translucent anemones
thrown from the green garden by the seventh wave,
your footprints in the sand framed in ice crystals

I have them all and I don't know if
I will be able to move my shore
to the other side,
when the strong winds have finally died down
above us

and time will be utterly smooth

Metin Cengiz (Turkey)

Metin Cengiz, short bio: Poet and writer (b. 3 May 1953, Göle-Kars). He wrote particularly on the problems of poetry. His poems are translated into nearly 40 languages and his book has been published in 14 languagaes. He wrote 18 poetry book and 16 theorical and essay books. He has received numerous prestigious awards in his country and other countries. Metin Cengiz: Poet and writer (b. 3 May 1953, Göle). He wrote particularly on the problems of poetry. He attended numerous International festivals and symposiums. Her poems have been translated into more than thirty languages.

POETRY: Collected poems 1, 2008, Collected poems 2, 2010; Images are my home, 2011; States of the world, 2013; Sorrowful Poems, 2015; Poems for Mercan, 2018; Life is dream, 2018.

ESSAY-CRITICISM-STUDY: He wrote theoretical and study books on over twenty poems.
Some: Modernism and Our Modern Poery, 2002; Poetry, Language, Language of Poetry and Poetic Meaning, 2006, Globalisation, Postmodernism and Literature, 2007; What is image? 2009; Culture and poetry, 2010, Philosophy and poetry, 2010; Thought of poetry in Plato and Aristotle 2012; Poetry and criticism 2018, Read the poem through the effect 2019, The writings of the street (Poetic correspondance), with Celal Soycân (2019)

He is published in more foreign countrys.

LOVE

Wherever, whenever it was I forgot
Grasses scorched by the sun

Trees and their shadows melting
Wind breathed into its raki, drank it up
No scent of wild rose
No song of the grasshopper
Just her voice ringing in my ears.
Just her eyes over the never-ending steppe.
The horizon grew red with her, the sun
Danced her light over our heads.
Summer since I last saw her.
Summer since I learned I had a heart.
But she was composing another song
One that life had already written for her.

THE SAME FATE

I am asleep
Sharing the same fate as the tree in the garden
On its branches the light sleep of birds
On my branches thoughts the night has bestowed

I wake up
In my dream the hungover cool of rain
Yesterday the sun held its breath
And slept in the shade of my thoughts

Mariela Cordero (Venezuela)

Mariela Cordero Valencia, Venezuela (1985) is a lawyer, poet, writer, translator and visual artist. Her poetry has been published in several international anthologies and she has received some distinctions among them: Third Prize of Poetry Alejandra Pizarnik Argentina (2014). First Prize in the II Iberoamerican Poetry Contest Euler Granda, Ecuador (2015) Second Prize for Poetry, Concorso Letterario Internazionale Bilingüe Tracceperlameta Edizioni, Italy (2015). First Place in International Poetry Contest #AniversarioPoetasHispanos mentioning literary quality,Spain (2016)She is the author of the book of poems El cuerpo de la duda Ediciones Publicarte Caracas, Venezuela (2013) and Transfigurar es un país que amas, Editorial Dos Islas Miami, Estados Unidos (2020) Her poems have been translated into Hindi, Czech, Serbian, Shona, Uzbek, Romanian, Macedonian, Bengali, English, Arabic, Chinese,Hebrew Russian and Polish. She currently coordinates the sections #PoesíaVenezolana and #PoetasdelMundo in the Revista Abierta de Poesía Poémame (Spain).

Love the shadow

Invasions of light are usually corrosive
to what lives in the shadows.
It is easy to love the dark,
the coldness with the smell of torrid vegetation.

Peace and danger amalgamated
in the mouth of the inviolable black horizon.
Swim forever in an ocean woven of gloom,
protected only by the irregular flapping

of birds dressed like the night.

Without hurtful illuminations the meaning can be spilled,
you can embrace languid hopes
and caress the symptoms of a rainy and exquisite love.

In the shadow we are all dark stars.

You once followed the course of the packs

You once followed the course of the packs
Guided
By that smell of furrows
Possessed
By the dizziness
That was spilling
Above the crowd
You learned to bite
And to dismember as the others.
The Dawn
Tore the veil
Diminishing
Of the night
To offer you a horror
Newborn.
You killed your own in the dark.
You were part
Of the weakness that you devoured
You were
The prey.

Prof. Migena Arllati (Albania)

Migena Arllati is a poet, publicist, albanologist. She works in education as a professor of Albanian language and literature.

She was born in Elbasan / Albania on 06.09.1974, in a family with civic and educational traditions. She has been living in the city of Gjakova in Kosovo for 25 years with her husband Behar and four children (Bora, Rina, Triumf, Argen).

She studied at the Faculty of Philology, branch of language – literature at the public university "Alexander Xhuvani" in Elbasan. Graduated for diplomacy at the Albanian Diplomatic Academy in Tirana. Has completed her postgraduate studies Master of Linguistics at the State Center for Albanological Studies in Tirana. Actually, she is Phd cand. – Doctor of Linguistics. Until now, she is the editor and reviewer of about 80 volumes of poetry and prose by Albanian and three foreign authors. The author has so far published ten books:

Volume of poetry: "Thoughts in the Frame" (Publishing House "Bridge", Prishtina 2012); Monography: "Born to Become a Doctor" ("John N. Kazazi", Gjakova 2013); Language Study: "An Overview of Phraseological Expressions in the Gjakova Verb" (Association of Intellectuals "Jakova", Gjakova 2014); Study publication: "Patronymics, family surnames in Gjakova" in co-authorship with prof. M. Rogova (Association of Intellectuals "Jakova", Gjakova 2015); Literary criticism and reviews: "Etern'Ars", vol. I, (Association of Intellectuals "Jakova", Gjakova 2016); Encyclopedic dictionary: "Authors of Albanian literature for children and young people, 1886 – 2017", co-authored with prof. dr. A. Bishqemi (Association of Intellectuals "Jakova", Gjakova 2017); Volume of poetry: "They do not love gods" (Adonis Publishing House, Elbasan 2018); Literary Criticism and Reviews: "Etern'Ars" – vol. II, (Jakova Intellectuals Association, Gjakova 2019); Albanian-Italian Poetry: "The Possession of Whistle" – "Brezza di mormorii" ("John N. Kazazi", Gjakova 2019); Albanian-English Poetry: "Honeycomb love" (Pristina, 2020); Albanian-Franch Poetry: "Crystal red" – "Le verre rouge" (Pristina, 2020).

MY LIFE, A POETRY

My life
like a cigarette, you scorch in these hands,
the light ash, lightens and distinguishes
smoking the illusions, unexpectedly, unpredictably

Yesterday, it was me
part of the same story
when crossing the paths
one by one

Today it is me,
you are the history
my life that aches
to the light of eyes remain

Who remains tomorrow
apart from these verses filling the paper?
Approaching me as laurel leafs
hair crown, amongst the crowded angels

The poetry as acquired from Mehmeti,
the verses as borrowed from Podrimja,
crests of magic as lustrated by Shkreli,
engraved poets in my wildest dreams

My life, poetry
what else can I expect of you?
Death I spot far as I laze,
I scrabble and search for a new chorus

My life, but a branch of olive tree
thick of dreams and desires
crashing years under the same name
pushed to abysses, languishing through swards

A heap of worries in my back I should through
invite the first vagrant to join me

the coin of luck to toss away
the gamble of this world we shall throw

A tweet afar, doesn't let me go through
attention of the skylark it gets to stop the song
you gorgeous, o holy poetry
unwritten words don't diminish in oblivion!

MEMORIES!

Rain's falling
bringing back my memorie,
The rain falling from sky,
falling from long time past
fallin over me!

The shadowy autumn of Vivaldi
emerging suddenly.
An abstract tune,
strays away blended with the cloud,
and the steam of my meditation

Rain falling down,
and I entirely get melted

The ran falling and
I feel the emptiness.
On the solitude
Only me
And rain of my old memories!

Maria Del Castillo Sucerquia (Colombia)

Maria Del Castillo Sucerquia (Barranquilla, Colombia in 1997) is a bilingual poet (Spanish and English), short story writer, proofreader, mentor, oriental medic (Neijing, Spain), ancient Chinese language student and translator (from English, Italian, Portuguese, French, German, Greek, Arabic). She is translator of many writer around the world and she is consider as the brigde between writers and spanish-speaking world. Her poems have been published in national and international anthologies, journals, websites and magazines, and have been translated into Kannada, Bangla, Arabic, Greek, Italian and English. She has participated in national and international festivals, recitals and webinars (Filogicus, Libresta, María Mulata, Bharatha Vision, Azahar, Atunis Poetry, El Heraldo, Muelle Caribe, Crisol, Uttor Kota, Sol y Luna, Sabdakhunja, The Poet, and other) She collaborates with translating and literary criticism in several literary magazines such as Altazor (Chile), Cardenal (Mexico), Cronopio (Missouri), Golem (Mexico), Vive Afro (Colombia), Mood Magazine (Mexico), Palabrerías (Mexico), Raíz Invertida (Colombia) and other.

Holy Grail

while I was sleeping
the bird of fire delighted
between its wings
dream blazed—burning
terrors and elegies

I blossomed into flaming
violet while my
name, in silent flight
within my soul,

>   drank and sang
> until dawn

I Beg

my poor love, sitting there
crowned by the rain
in your head blooms a gale
sadness springs from every nail
sunlight striking
the glass with splendor
a mead tunnel screaming to infinity

Drown me in your sea!
                    …salt, glow…

The Weaver

Light travels from
your lip to my lip
in a thread of drool

from your body to mine
weaving an Elohim
the size of
Two.

Alchemy

a rainbow
in my bed
naked gold

Translation: Douglas Cole and María Del Castillo Sucerquia

Mbizo Chirasha (Zimbabwe)

Editor. African Contributor Poet /Essayist at Monk Arts and Soul Magazine (UK). SACRED SPACES (edited by Sophie Lévy Burton at Monk Arts and Soul, UK). Ditch Poetry (Albert University, Creative Writing, Canada). Full of Crow (Canada), Scarlet Leaf (Canada). Poetry Potion (Canada). Poetry Soup (USA). Poetry Hunter (USA). Trip Wire. Journal (Latina America). International Poet of the Week (THE POET MAGAZINE, UK). HOBO LITERARY REVIEW (USA). Cultural Weekly (USA). Poetry Bulawayo (Zimbabwe). Wrath Bearing Tree (USA). Iminspired (UK). Poetry Question (USA) Atunis Galatica (edited Agron Shele, Belgium). Black Well Pamphlet (Oxford School of Poetry, UK). Litnet (South Africa). Ofi Press (Mexico City). Fem Asia Magazine (UK). Ink Sweatand Tears (UK). Squackback (USA). The Poet a Day Zine (founded by the late Maestro G Jamie Dedes, Brooklyn, and USA). Demer Press International Poetry Series (curated and edited by Hannie Rouweler, Netherlands). World Poetry Almanac Series (urated and Edited by Hadaa Sendoo, Mongolia). Poesi. Is Journal (edited by Peter Semolic, Slovenia). Stellenbosch Literary Project, SLIPNet (South Africa), Tambira (Zimbabwe). *https://en.wikipedia.org/wiki/Mbizo_Chirasha*

RONDAVELS OF POVERTY : dedicated to my rural villagers

I)
See, Ideological tutors discarding their dignity in crank jugs
Comrades dying between rude stitches of hypocrisy and conspiracy
Father's phalluses chopped by cyber- punk slang,
Mother's cotton tuft -hair wisdom castrated by hard pliers of poverty
Liberation euphoria fading with the whirlwinds of corruption
-seized cartels
Poverty THRASHED mothers, scratching lives out of the barren
red clay earth
Daughters groaning under the grind of forced intercourse,
Their sorrow soaked lives trembling against nights of death
Owls singing satirical verses of doom,

Hyenas reading page- poetry of gloom
Spoken word verses throbbing alongside the frail beat of bald –shaved
Red hills, burning under the depressing charcoal of hot summers
Red glow of fire shimmered over the roasting earth like an expiring day
Shame -creased faces told rending story of hunger
Rivers are motionless skeletons of dry sand,
Droughts folded their legs onto the doorsteps of our land
Silence, graveyard silence, silence of decaying mass, a dying mass
Rondavels drenched by rituals of grief
My land is a sorry tale of sufferance,
Its manhood deposited into hot pants of PENNURY
Heartbeat of this land throb like the crack of a broken drumbeat,
Crushed between hunger and disease
Mothers enduring under the weather like determined cassava roots.

II)
A country once a revolutionary granite,
Now, exfoliated by political scars and moral sores
Super -human autocrats spitting out rotten gospels of freedom,
Their combat clad, steely booted green horns, toyi-toying
Their high-kicking liberation dance, jabbing the ideologically
spoilt wind
Napoleonic kings of the land, sloshed by hypocritical revolutionary
Hymns indoctrinated by the pseudo-socialist political lingos,
Nights of death pounced like stray baboons over village-rondavels,
My mind suffers from nostalgia, a disease, an ailment
A disease of memory
Memories of yesteryear
Memories of red dagga and pole huts farting beautiful smoke,
Aroma of fresh cow dung, dampness of fog under our cracked feet
Jiving and chattering of mother monkeys and cackling of wild hens
Domesticated dogs howling to shadows dancing
under guise of moonlight
Owls singing their baritone announcing the black veil
of the sleeping earth
Doves hooting their morning poetry slam, celebrating the rays of a renewed day.
Rhythm of black villages
Memories ....

Marija Najthefer Popov (Serbia)

Marija Najthefer Popov was born in Serbia on March 11, 1958. So far, she has been published in more than two hundred joint, domestic and international poetry collections; published in an extremely large number of domestic and foreign magazines and literary sites. In 2018, she published her first book "I WRITE TO A WOMAN". This poetic book explains the world of women, creativity, existence and love, elegance and meaning that directs and gives all the colors of life. The author, within her poetic mission, sees art as a spirit of freedom and lyrics, nature as a trace of that splendor that enables the merging of its elements with the spiritual world. The author has received numerous international evaluations and recognitions; it has been translated into many foreign languages. She is currently preparing for future publications and dealing with other synergies, in various journals on culture and international anthologies. She is the author of the capital ANTHOLOGY 2021 / SERBIA with the participation of over 300 eminent poets from Serbia and around the world (In preparation) She is a member of many literary and poetic associations, an honorary member, president, ambassador of peace in the world ... She is a great advocate of love and friendship, respect and esteem of all people without distinction, on the planet, and he believes that poetry is a language that unites the whole world and does not make a difference. Being a poet is God's choice and gift. Blessing! She lives and works in Zrenjanin, Serbia.

Silence And Me

They took me yester night,
They loved silence,
They were passionate,
I had no hope,
They deceived me for a long time,

By delusion,
It was only heard,
Fast departing train,
Woman with reservation,
In the hand, as a hope
Stunned were my senses.
They took me yester night
They vowed silence,
It was clear,
They were not longing either,
They glowed for a long time,
Blood flowed,
It was only heard,
Church bells, yes the bells,
That same woman
With faith as a source of life
Shut up, nothing more,
No idea,
That was it, the last train.
They took me yester night,
They left words,
Clear
Not a whisper for long,
They didn't speak,
It was only heard.
All hope was broken,
A woman resolutely,
In complete silence,
Slammed the heavy door,
Behind her,
They stopped waiting,
With their strength,
Silence
And I with him sensed the answer.

Passion

Your song is written with a murmur,
Drops of sweat from your skin,
In my opinion when they drip,
So it multiplies.
Air currents and kinks
Sighs in the rhythm of chorus,
Drums in the senses,
And roaring like waterfalls,
Moves up whirlpools, rapid to the gorges
Through the fast rivers' buffs,
Through the wild beasts,
It cuts and tends to get into my foot sheets,
The middle of the thighs,
He gritted his teeth,
Then permanent scars,
From my throat, a scream,
The scream of the wilderness dies down,
It stretches out, like a raging sun,
In the middle of the spring,
And dries everything
Shoals and ponds, in the depths
And drives speedboats
On the open sea,
The waves are rise, the riders drown,
They hit the shores, narrow straits
And they swallow floods,
Sharp rocks foam,
Here is the end in the rhythm
Of the wild call, the universe stretches,
And slides down the manuscript from sweat
It is thrown onto her knees,
Amid foam spilled on the rocks.

Marianella Sáenz Mora
(Costa Rica)

Degree in tourism from the Castro Carazo Metropolitan University and the Latin American University of Science and Technology.

Judge for the Costa Rica Ministry of Education Student Art Festival and the Moravian Art and Cultural Festival in 2016.

Selected for anthologies and translated into other languages, including Braille. A plastic art collage piece grew out of her future poetry collection, Transgredir (se) (Violating [Yourself]). She also writes microstories, haikus, and children's stories and does photography.

Publications: Migración a la esperanza (Migration toward Hope, 2015) and Perspectiva de la ausencia (Perspective of Absence, 2017).

Translations by Kailyn Stuckey & Marianella Sáenz Mora

I Confess

I pursue your memory
that flutters damaged around the house
cracking the mirrors
while I wander for this eternity
of wounded hunger
in a body not ignoring your absence
and its prints scattered in the breeze.

I live the hope fully
of the refugee and his longings for a homeland
exiled from a love that isn't really mine,
indolent and infinite in the parallel experience
of shifted latitudes.

Here in the confessional of my silences
unconquerable and false, like my fear.

Recognize

Accept that I am hurt
just a little
and that it doesn't depend on me
except to take the budding start
that cautiously protects itself from doubt.

Take refuge in introspection,
in the revolutionary act
that allows me to see the light,
when it's May again
and earth and skin awaken
their hopes of water.

Recognize yourself as another one
attached to the anonymous, dogmatic
hope of statistics.

Miljana Živanovič
(Croatia – Switzerland)

Miljana Živanovič was born in Trpinja, Vukovar, Croatia. She lives and works in Switzerland, at the urging he publishes his poetry for the first time in 2017, although she has been writing since school days.
"A Walk in the Saffron Valley" is her first solo release.
Her poetry from that time is being prepared, and the books "Journey through the poetry of the world" and "Travelogue Plus" too on the international level are biographies of important people seen and written from her point of view who leave a trace in her life and work. She is a member of: Literary Club Scene Crnjanski – Belgrade, Literary Club Art Horizont – Kragujevac, Golden Pen Knjazevac – Knjazevac, Association of Free Artists of Australia – Australia, Association of Writers of Serbia – Serbia and Association of Serbian Writers in the Homeland and Diaspora – Belgrade.
She is published in more magazines and International Anthologys and her poetry are published in more international Languages.

The stage and me

I'm flipping through the pages
who have been browsed so many times,
folded at the ends,
significant moments marked ...
I already know the text by heart.
Scene and me.
The lodges are empty ...
Dim light to hide shivering,
water on the lashes,
worn out old clothes,
And ... me without shoes ...
And the voice is harsh, cheeky, defiant.

It's almost like I'm shouting.
I started the sentence at the end of the chapter ...
The mask of indifference suits me well.
And I stopped ...
I told all of you too much.
I remembered that this was just mine ...
Because ...
I direc and act in this play
theatrical performances.

From thë book "A Walk in the Valley of Saffron"

Self-portrait

White canvas laughs ... ready brush and palette.
A sigh and a hand move ...

I need to paint myself ...
With a friendly, sweet smile,
Special.
Because of the order
I'm not upset anymore.

Mixed colors merge together.
Almost dazzling as a spark
Beautiful line, graceful ...
My eyes adjusted to every movement,
Passion...passion movement,
Rhythm on canvas ...
The "painter" diligently paints.
The portrait is finished
I'm glad the "painter" says, "Just look!"
The model looks expected.

But then my smile quickly disappears ...
The portrait says with a lot of sadness:
"My eyes must be chestnut
And my bust must be steel

My hair is gray
Don't deny it! "

I'm correcting the portrait,
To satisfy my model.
And I paint with a brush what is required of me ...

I'm so sorry ...
If only I could drop the brush !?
Stuck with its beautiful patterns
Angry about this imposed noose ...

I'm painting the throne ...
Your look becomes royal,
Dignified, not carefree,
The mouth expresses a calm gratitude.

Your descent from the canvas ...
Wrapped in royal blue.
I notice our resemblance in similarities...
Your boundless loyalty ...

Filled with gratitude,
And the announcement of your recognition ...
With a bow,
You pay tribute to the "painter's" presence.
"Good afthernoon Your Majesty, thank you!"

Mario Meléndez (Chile)

Mario Meléndez (Linares, Chile, 1971). He studied Journalism and Social Communication. His books include: Notes for a legend, Underground flight, The paper circus, Death has its days numbered, Waiting for Perec and The magician of loneliness. Part of his work was translated into various languages. For several years he lived in Mexico City, where he directed the series Poetas Latinoamericanos in the press Laberinto Ediciones and made anthologies of Chilean and Latin American poetry. At the beginning of 2012 he fixed his residence in Italy. In 2013 he received the medal of the President of the Italian Republic, awarded by the Don Luigi di Liegro International Foundation. During the period 2014-2016, he directed two collections of Latin American poetry for Raffaelli Editore, from Rimini. A selection of his work appeared in the prestigious magazine Poesia de Nicola Crocetti. At the beginning of 2015, he was included in the anthology El canon abierto. Last poetry in Spanish (Visor, Spain). In 2017 some of his poems were translated into English and published in the legendary Poetry Magazine, from Chicago. In 2018 he returned to Chile to become general editor of the Vicente Huidobro Foundation.

from Waiting for Perec

I
Trailer of past lives

The unconscious is a madhouse
with an ocean view
Each fish that leaps from the water
carries a straitjacket

1

I saw a blank page
wandering through fields
of unreality
It looked like a ballerina
ready to give birth

2

I saw Pizarnik emerge
from a shallow pane of water
Huidobro carried her in his arms
It was night
Death slept naked
on God's corpse

3

I saw Death parachute
over a field of ashes
It was mid afternoon
The crows yawned inward
and Vincent painted his ear
with the blood of Christ

4

I saw God dig a grave in the void
His hands were shaking
It was February
Death wrote its epitaph
on a four-leaf clover

5
I saw the Pope waking
from a horrible nightmare
God had told him

he read Rimbaud
It was a new year
The Pope slept hugging
his plush Christ

6

I saw Death dragging
Vallejo's coffin
The coffin was vacant
but weighed an eternity
It was November
The worms gargled
God's ashes

7

I saw God kissing Death
in a cafe in Paris
He wore a beard of centuries
and carried an umbrella
to keep loneliness at bay
It was summer
His shadow fanned itself
with van Gogh's ear

Trans. by Eloisa Amezcua and John Allen Taylor

Marion de Vos-Hoekstra
(Netherlands)

Marion de Vos-Hoekstra was born in the Netherlands and is married to a career diplomat. They both served in North Yemen, Tanzania, United Kingdom, Mali, Spain, South Africa and The United States and now in the Netherlands. She trained as a teacher of French and as translator French, English and Dutch.

She is also fluent in Spanish and German, plays the piano and the guitar, is amateur ornithologist and makes drawings, aquarelles and oil paintings. Nature, human nature and her nomad life are her main inspiration.

She attended several poetry workshops in English among which a Masterclass in New York at Poetshouse and a course at the prestigious 92Y Institute. She is the author of five poetry collections (in English and Dutch), 4 with Demer Press, and is published in several anthologies and magazines (25) all over the world. (South Africa, Australia, UK and US)

She gave presentations at:

"Woordfees" of the University of Stellenbosch, South Africa, Bloemfontein Literary Museum, South Africa, Literary Cafe, Cornelia street, Manhattan, New York US, Dutch club, New York US. Vlaanderen Huis, "De orde van de Prins" New York US, Dutch section Columbia University New York, US, De Haagse Kunstkring, The Hague, and at the libraries of Wassenaar and Nijmegen.

Zanzibar

I trace my steps back to long before the tourists came.
Balmy Trade winds brush my face.
On the horizon, Dhows fade in a hazy mirage.

The virgin whiteness of the sand blinds my eyes.
The shell cemetery is littered with pieces of Chinese pottery,
and Dutch VOC coins from ages of East Indian Trade.

In the forest, the air is saturated
with the smell of vanilla, nutmeg and cinnamon.
Red Colobus Monkeys observe my sleeping son.

His white curls fall on the shoulder
of an elegant black man with Omani features,
a Frangipani flower in his cropped hair.

His pace, almost dancing cradles the innocent.
In the slave market, a number, a price,
silent vestiges of an islands' gruesome past.

Maria Dayana Fraile (Venezuela)

Maria Dayana Fraile (Puerto La Cruz, Venezuela, 1985) received her undergraduate degree in Literature from the Universidad Central de Venezuela. She received also an Master degree from University of Pittsburgh. Her poems and short stories have been awarded various prizes, including the Festival Literario Ucevista, the Premio de Cuento Policlínica Metropolitana and the Semana de la Nueva Narrativa Urbana. Her first book, Granizo y otros relatos, was the winner of the I Bienal de Literatura Julián Padrón. She has published Ahorcados de tinta (2019) and La máquina de viajar por la luz in CAAW (Miami).

Forbidden Fruit

I wanted to eat from the night
         and I kept the palms of my hands always extended
while I slept
lifted skyward
        they waited awkwardly
                for the luminous flights of a cricket

              and the defendants evaded themselves
irreperably
      at dawn certainty
             only opened itself to the horizontal figures
and these
      when they awoke
remembered nothing
they barely managed to glimpe
sweetening the coffee

                    with meager plastic teaspoons that grew like tangles
in the signs indicating

the bus stop

Office 3 P.M.

Feel like crying
Feel like hiding these ink birds
                            in my hair
they play with matches
                              stab pencils into light sockets
Feel like rinsing this afternoon's mouth
                          with sugar water
(so that only I can hear her)

Feel like biting into the Times New Roman font
hard
to find its skin
                    to lick it

Majlinda Zeqiri-Shaqiri (Kosova)

Majlinda Zeqiri-Shaqiri, born in Leskovac, Republic of Serbia.
She has completed primary school in Medvegja, in the Serbian language, and afterwards she has finished her high school studies in the General High School "Hivzi Sulejmani" in Kosovo. She has completed her undergraduate and postgraduate studies at the University of Prishtina "Hasan Prishtina, in the Faculty of Philology with the academic degree "Master of Philological Sciences" at the aforementioned university. She currently works in the Ministry of Local Government, in the Kosovo Government, holding the position of Senior Officer in the Department for Municipal Performance and Transparency, Prishtina / Kosovo. Her poems and writings have been published in various magazines, newspapers and websites, ammong them: Gazeta Rilindja, Prishtina, Revista Mirdita published by the Academy of Arts, Science and Letters "Mirdita", Tirana, Dituria magazine, Boras-Sweden, Historical Traces magazine, published by the League of Albanian Historians based in Switzerland, Alternativa magazine, Gazeta Letrare, the website and magazine Medvegja, Pirusti News website, Tirana / Albania, Floripress Agency, Kosovo, etc. Her poems are part of Atunis publications, the database that makes her part of the wider community of contemporary local and foreign authors, Belgium. She has been awarded with several literary prizes, including the award of the Academy of Arts, Science and Letters "Mirdita" Tirana, from the nationwide poetry competition "Year of Fishta 2020" and she has also recently published her first poetry collection "Në Sytë e Diellit / In the Eyes Of The Sun".

A Mythological Tale

An autumn melody
Melancholy of a broken verse
A wanderer's rustle beyond the mountain

A tale engraved in the dusk and its shadows
First Chapter

Groaning torrents, a smiling face
Ornaments of a withering flower
Form ancient mythologies
Second Chapter

Becoming the voice of your silences
Under the yoke of the iron empire
The stubborn Ares from Greek mythology
Quenching the thirst of thunders
Third Chapter

Escape

Undressing the night, taking off her silk garments
Black
Like the fumes of a smoker in rags
I left her naked on a small stone
Black
Like the turmoil of thunderclaps
Above the clouds
Becoming ashes
And next to the naked shadows
The night undresses
A rendezvous with its lustful self
She…
Has finally escaped…!

Translated into English by Elvi Sidheri

Mónika Tóth (Romania)

Mónika Tóth was born in Covasna on 14th April,1980. She is graduated high-school in Humanities at Körösi Csoma Sándor in Covasna and then she studied accountancy in her hometown. She is interested in culture and fond of reading, painting, philosophy and photography. She likes Romanian, Turkish, Russian, South-American and Norwegian literature. She is passionate the poetry. Her new book of poetry "Soványít hiányod" is published with Hungarian language. Her new book of poetry "Tu eşti roua dimineţii" is published with Romanian language

"When I write, the world closes in around me, and there remains nothing".

Come back to me

Come back to me
I will learn to live without you
But not now...
I can't
I am not ready
Just please come back
I will do anything
I beg you
Come back...

Winter

winter's sun
blessed
tiny rays

I sit

As I sit with an empty soul,
not sad,
not glad but pissed,
thinking back on happier times
when those who are gone hugged

I love you

I love you
I love you when you're wrong
as much as when you're right.
I love you when you're up,
I love you when you're down.
I love you when you smile.
I love you no matter
what you say or do.

I lost

heartbreaking silence
I lost my inspiration
I am worthless
I am empty…
the disappointment will never end

our hearts

gilded night
I love you again
our hearts have found each other

Ngoc Le Ninh (Vietnam)

Le Ngoc Ninh is PhD of mining science, his pen name is Ngoc Le Ninh, given birth October 24th 1969. He was born in Hai Nhan village, Nghi Son city, Thanh Hoa province, Vietnam. He lives in Ha Noi Capital and working at General Department of Environment, VIETNAM MONRE. He is a member of Ha Noi writers association and also a member of IWA – BOGDANI. His poems were published in Vietnam, USA, Belgium, Spain, India. He received a poetry prize 2019 from IWA-BOGDANI for his poems and other prizes.

THE FUNCTION LOVE

I want to tell you
Our story about two functions
On the unfinished graph
In time of our early love.

The days we got to know each other
The increasing function along with remembrances
At night, we breathed in the wind's soul
Loving each other! Hearts in praying!

The function love at the intersection
Our emotions in happiness
My blood boiling with excitement
Your fire burning up in blue.

The days we got angry with each other
The decreasing function along with sufferings
Evening falling sadness on the grass
Red eyes coloring over the trees.

The season we broke up
The function love separated forever
Shattered in young grass time
Storming across the domain without us.

THE SOUL OF NATURAL CREATION

I went through the dying forests
Absent birds and without sounds of beasts calling their flock
Hearing the moans from the sprites of thirsty beasts
Listening to the resentment and hatred boiling up in the heart of trees

Who dried up the rivers and streams?
Pebbles and stones lying on the barren became isolated
Who burned the green forests creating misty smokes?
Trees came to the ruined age making the beasts' eyes in tears

I collapsed by the side of the murky stream
Smelling fishy blood tinting red the eyes of sunset
Hearing the whine of every kind of birds tired
Listening to the sound of beasts invoking the spirits

In the past, I left love affairs to starve out in exhaustion
The blue time faded breaking up my heart!
Now it is impossible to let mountains and forests groaning anyhow
Those beasts' souls are looking forward to the revitalization.

Nevin Koçoğlu (Turkey)

Nevin Koçoğlu is a Turkish poet, jounalist, environmentalist and human rights activist. Born in Gaziantep, she lived in Istanbul during her childhood years and moved,when she was an adult,to the Turkish capital Ankara where she currently lives. She completed a B.Sc. degree in Public Administration at Anadolu University in Turkey and is studying at the same university for a second degree in Sociology. Koçoğlu's poems are translated into Arabic, English, French, German, Italian, Kurdish , Persian, Serbian and Spanish. She is the winner of Vahittin Bozgeyik Poetry Award, 2012.
She participated in poetry festivals in Turkey and number of other counries where she read her poems. She has many contributions to various international anthologies. Her poems are published in a large number of prestigious literari journals and magazines.
Kocoglu is actively campaigning to build village libraries in all the regions of Turkey.
Her books: Tanrının Vişne Bahçesi (1st Ed.2013),(2nd Ed.2014), (3rd Ed. 2018); Kurdish translation published (2014) Persian translaton published (2020); Tuz ve Gece (2015) (Printed with Persian translation); Kuğu Kardinalinin Ölümü (2020).

And I testify

I
Whither away all the trees once they 'hibernate in water'
and your heart whithers away,
the heartbeat pendent on the highest offshoot...

II
When the eyes of the skys fall into the water
I came to know that green is more akin to the pain than the black
and that unforgiveness was what was oozing out of that crock
I counted how many times the scorpion whirled towards tha ashes
inside the circle of scarlet flame

III
The golden daffodil under the naked tree
the purple hyacinth falling out of my hair,
the lace on the weaving loom,
would it know how hard it is to be cleansed from the scarlet?
while carrying the fire inside your palm...

IV
Here I am,
in the shadow of your countenance
in the silence of flowing nothingness

And I testify..
that the cracks of my walls
can only be plastered with solitude

V
And now-
one must die like a dead tree leaning on a river bank,
close to heavens, far away from you

One must die

Translation: Hale Koray

Nina Lys Affane (Algeria)

Nina Lys Affane, French teacher, writer-poet and correspondent in the written press, has published several books and a very large number of press articles in newspapers, (in socio-economic, scientific and cultural). **Works:** "In talks with love" 2011: 140 pages, art edition (the rent) the money from all the books sold paid and donated by Nina lys to the cancer patient; "at the edge of time" ANEP edition (Algeria); 135 pages, (dedicated sale at the Paris Book Fair in 2016 and 2017); 137 pages "confession", published in 2017 by Dar moulaf Beyrouth (Lebanon), book sale, in Beirut, Paris, Algiers book sale and book rent paid for the association of hereditary anemia patients (2019); "crash of the senses" 2018, words color edition, Montreal (Canada) 100 pages; "Havre des sens 2018" book edited in collaboration with writers from around the world (in Montreal) Canada; Chosen from among 50 poets for an anthology of female creation published in Bulgaria for the capital of European culture) Plovdiv 2019; participation with several texts in a book by North African Mediterranean writers, under the theme "migration" book published and distributed in Canada,; Also, Nina lys AFFANE, participated with poems, in several anthologies of poet writers (sometimes in solidarity with the sick) published: Morocco, Tunisia, Lebanon, Egypt, Turkey, Romania, France, Portugal, Canada…

My solidarity

I think of the sick, the vulnerable, the poor in this word
I feel like I'm in a war!
Against something we hardly know!
I am sad for the whole of humanity!
I'm here to help you
if you need it … I'm ready to give you a hand,

Where you are in any nation
any corner ...
I will help in any way!
I know !
when life becomes less beautiful
And a life so wicked so cruel!
so find in us the strength of kindness which is like a sun
Know that the most effective remedy
Lies in us, and in the heart of the other
and his
The love of those close to the human being in us
and their support
is the sweetest of the affections for the tomorrows
When illness knocks on the door, you have to know how to find happiness
illness, hard test that brings us back to basics
Being sick is a sign that reminds us that nothing is forever
Invite in oneself hope and hope so that the pain so intense ceases
Illness teaches us that living in good health is a wonder
Know how to appreciate the present time and love yours at all times
Only solidarity and Faith in God
Faith in Love can save us and heal ...
Illness certainly carries a lesson
A lesson in life that will transform us into great
Courage and persistence are the best of doctors and medicines
that do good
heal and regain the good health of humanity
This pandemic, a test, an intense fight to fight and we will win by arming ourselves with solidarity!
We must love to live and live to love
Courage, I think of you sick every moment, every moment!
Certainly, soon we will celebrate together the happiness and the flowers of a new Spring ...
my solidarity with all of humanity.

Nahid Ensafpour
(Iran – Germany)

Nahid Ensafpour was born in Teheran and has been living in Germany since 1985. On arriving in Germany, Nahid was struck by the close connection between Goethe and Persian poetry, in particular, with the work of the poet Hafez, that is especially evident as the inspiration for Goethe's West-Eastern Divan, a lyrical collection of some 235 poems. Motivated by a desire to tell others about her own experiences and history, Nahid herself began writing poetry. At the age of 18, she enjoyed an education in classical Persian singing. In 1991, she graduated from the University of Munich, having obtained the official German language certificate from the German Education Authorities and the Foreign Office. In April 2015 she completed her correspondence course studies at the Cornelia Goethe Academy, Frankfurt/Main with a degree in Creative Writing. In tandem with pursuing her career, she is currently studying New German Literature and Philosophy at the distance-learning University of Hagen. Nahid is a member of the "Licio Poetico de Benidorm" World Writers' Association and of the Leipzig Schiller Association and the Goethe Society in Cologne. She writes poems, prose and translates poetry. Her poetry have been published in numerous German and international anthologies. Many of her poems have been translated into several languages.

The Bridge

"for A"
From the bank
across the river
came a loud cry
confused, unknowing
how I could help her
no-one else

came to her rescue
louder and louder
still she cried
till a raging strength
took hold of me
and I grew and grew
far beyond myself
and arched
across the river
to become a bridge
but just as she was
about to cross
I broke.

My turbulent soul

Oh, brutal storm of my turbulent soul,
your rage reaches down
to the depths of my heart,
and breaks all that is still whole in me,
I can only watch you impotently
shuddering at your power,
how can I tame you
and tear off these chains?
you shackle me,
your heart is full of greed,
ruling my life, shattered,
I tremble you tyrant,
and finally, I bow down
you sweep me up
and I am yours.

Translated from German into English by Marion Godfrey

Nurie Emrullai
(North Macedonia)

Nurie Emrullai was born in 1992 in Kicevo, North Macedonia, and recived her BA of Albanian Language and Literature and is in the end of the MA of Albanian Language. Mostly she writes poems, most of them are published in different magazines, one of them is The Literature Magazine of Tirana Illz, and the other the magazine Akademia, Kosovo.

She was the representative of literature in the CEEC Literature Forum in Ningbo, China. Also she was represent with her poems that speaks about women, in the exhibition "Vajza, jo nuse", that was on 8 March '18, in Zurich, Switzerland. She was part with her feminist poems in "FemArt 2019" in Kosovo.

Her poems are translated in Macedonian language, in English and in Italian. Currently she pursue some important courses that have to do with poetry and literature. She published her first book of poetry For the other half of the moon, in 2019.

Alive

Oh earth!
Layer upon layer
Layer upon layer
and I reached my skin.

Pilgrim

Take me,
Were the Gods are in peace with themselves.

Were the evening is not so painful,
Just to sleep.

Take me there,
Where bread is eaten by desire,
Not of the lack of everything else.

Let me go there
Where love is still alive,
And just for the sake of it fruits bloom,
And not from the fear of the branches withering alone.

Take me there
Where people brighten the light and
they feel the soul alive inside them.

Take me,
Were the Gods are in pace with themselves.

So I can recount them the number of our years...

The last man

Where is the moon at this dawn,
Or it doesn't want eternity?

Where is the promise of eternity
For the last man who stays awake?

Nigar Arif (Azerbaijan)

Nigar Arif was born in 1993 on the 20th of January in Azerbaijan. She studied at Azerbaijan State Pedagogical University in the English faculty in 2010- 2014. Nigar Arif is a member of the "World Youth Turkish Writers' Union" and graduated from "III Youth Writers' School" in "Azerbaijan Writers' Union". She is also a member of the "International Forum for Creativity and Humanity" in Morocco. Her poems have been partially translated into English, Turkish, Russian, Persian, Montenegro, and Spanish and have been published in different countries. She was a participant of "IV LIFT-Eurasian Literary Festival of Festivals" which was held in Baku in 2019 and "30 Festival Internacional De Poesia De Medillin" in 2020 which was held in Colombia, "Panaroma International Literary Festival 2020" in India at an online platform. She participated at the "Word trip Europe" project, "100 poets around the World for love" and "Fourth Global Poet Virtual Meeting 2020" as well.

Close Your Eyes

Close your eyes, baby...
Let your looks pour into your soul
to see those at your age.
Don't look at great pictures,
at the shades
showing an ant as an elephant,
like a giant you called.
Don't be afraid...
There can't be shadows of shades, my child,
Close your eyes,
Close your eyes...

The Wind

Hey wind, knocking door to door,
is that one door you're looking for,
is that enough for you?
Where are they now,
those open doors
from the hot, sunny days of summer?
Where are those that loved you,
to dine with and to rest;
who once were pleased to welcome you
and treat you as their guest?
Hey wind, knocking door to door,
where are your lovers now?
Now the weather's turned to winter,
have they turned cold as well?
Don't knock, my dear, don't knock,
no one's opening their door,
no one will look out for you, nor call on you,
no more.
Who, I ask, now the weathers changed,
would call on you at all?
Go dear, go.
Just wander round these dull grey streets
and break dry trees in anger;
just wait as winter turns to summer and your friends,
dear wind, with the sun, will grow again once more.

Olga Lalić – Krowicka (Serbia-Poland)

Olga Lalić-Krowicka – born April 2nd, 1980 in Šibenik, Croatia. Graduated from Slavic Philology at the Jagiellonian University in Kraków. A honorary citizen of the Imperial City of Sirmium (Sremska Mitovica, Serbia), double stipendist of the Minister of Culture and National Heritage. Author of over ten poetry volumes, a drama collection, fairytales, etc. She has translated poetry and prose of Polish and Balkan authors.
Her poems were translated to Bulgarian, English, Macedonian, Slovene, German, Ruthenian, Slovak, Spanish, Lithuanian, Belarussian and Russian. She draws, paints, photographs, designs book covers, etc.
She also exhibited her art works twice in Valjevo, Serbia. She lives in Dukla in Podkarpacie.

A letter from heaven

Hmmm, the dragon, oh no, it will burn the wool of the white
Leo, not either, because it'll bite the day fluffiness
Maybe the little elephant that the big cat catches
Ah, it is dangerous,
The cat can catch it before it comes to you
and then what?
Well, a Slavic water nymph, look, she lets her hair down ,
She plays the flute so wonderfully
No, she will play loudly and you get ears ache.
So what am I going to send you?
Aaaaaaa, a cloud of smile.

The two sick

one is lying in the street
in a pool of blood
with a broken leg
everyone helps
they call an ambulance

next to him
there is another sick
he laughs up to the clouds
and the clouds laugh at him
but they won't help
they will kill his brain
with a human hammer

Quite

Don't believe the honorable lies
which are dripping in pathos.
This anxiety is not the sea ships
that don't like the space.
Don't believe in
the cheers of honor
the sun which ruins the rain
it must always rain
to put out the hot sadness.

Translated by Alicja Maria Kuberska

Panagiota Christopoulou- ZALONI
(Greece)

Member of Society of Greek Writers
Laureate Women of Letters (From U.P.L.I.-USA)
Award "ALI ASLLANI" of University "Ismail Qemali" – Vlora-Albania

Panagiota Christopoulou – ZALONI was born during 1942 in Saint George Istiaias Evia Island. Greece. She studied economics at the University of Piraeus. She is active with literature and culture for several years.

Has published her work in 79 books and participates with her poems in 61 Anthologies

Translated and published in Serbia her poetic collection « chrysalis » within the framework of the 38th Festival of Poetry of Smederevo Serbia, where she participated as a Greek representation.

Also translated and published in Serbia by Dragan Dragojlovič her book «At the length of Love».

Five books have been translated and published to Albanian language, where were shown and won the reading public of Albania

Her work translated in many languages is published in various literary publications abroad, for example in Serbia, Italy, China, India, Albania, Romania, etc.

Her work was honorably presented by great entities in many Greek cities and to the Balkans.

As president of the literary club XASTERON and also as director of the literary magazine «KELAINO» operates in the area of Culture and Letters (events, presentations, lectures, festivals, national and international congresses).

The poet also is painter of Byzantine icons and fights for a better world where love will reign.

Warm days

Warm days
I am having friendship with them
Till them
They betray me.
Like a fresh baked bread
Are smelling
And make me drunk.
Angels are holding
The hand tenderly
Sweet words are singing to me
To be dancing together.
Warms days…
The souls are in love.

Wilderness

My horizons are going away
My dreams are distinguishing.
My thoughts are wearing grey hat
And my voices the sculptured are muted.
They are not calling the kiss of love.
The flowers in my hair withered
How? How to go to my temples?
My saints are weeping…
My seagulls?
Where my seagulls have been?
They always have accompanied me…

Codes of wilderness I am interpreting.

From the beginning

It was about contradictions
Though they merged harmonically

Oh! The hearts
When hearts are beating
All becomes alike
And identical (completely)
Like that at least, are been seen.
Augmented (their) life
Though, in contrary
Should have been diminished
Addition instead of subtraction
How nice!

Escape sobs

Green leaf
Travels in the foam of the sea.
It will be lost…
Escape sobs
He swims in the open sea to catch it.
But the wind blows.
And pushes it far away
In sunless places and times
It will be lost…
Escape sobs
He swims, he tries
Will he catch it?

Translated into english by Antonios Zalonis

Petraq Risto (Albania – USA)

Petraq Risto was born in Durrës, Albania, on 1952. He graduated from the University of Political-Juridical Sciences for Journalism, and from the Academy of Beautiful Arts for Theater Criticism. Worked as a journalist, Playwright for children and publisher. Now lives in USA. The poet and novelist Petraq Risto is one of the most important and prolific voices in Albania. Petraq has authored thirty books of poetry, novels and short stories, and has been the recipient of many prestigious awards in poetry. Risto's poetry has been praised by literary critics nationally and internationally for their individuality, sincerity, spontaneity, and universal themes. The literary world in France, Mexico, Romania and USA has recently recognized Risto's poetic genius. Many of Risto's poems have appeared in prestigious literary journals in the United States. Risto is recognized for the unique treatment of his subjects and the rich and metaphorical language in the likeness of the magic realism school, which suits the agitated Peninsula of the Balkans.

The Tear

When God created man's eyes, from God's eyes a teardrop fell.
At that moment a thought crystalized – for God to be crumbled
into teardrops.
He thought, should tears of joy be pink or sky-blue,
tears of sadness gray or black?
Perhaps, said God,
joy and sadness can stay united,
how can I create new tears?

He thought to make the tears of Love warm,
the tears of Hate cold.
But, since these conditions often get jumbled,
God the inventor retreated.

He judged that some tears should be large to flow from great people,
History could speak of these tears.
Again, He retreated from fear that Kings would
imprison these great-teary-eyed-men
who carried the surname freedom.

He decided tears should be created equal,
transparent as dew, evaporating as rain,
trickling down cheeks, tears would create maps
to keep souls from wasting away.

Written on the Wall

When you find the old book written on the wall,
do not forget to look from the other side,
to read the same book from a different viewpoint,
and to understand why the wall does not collapse.
Then, you can lean on the wall
to naturally transmit to it your heartbeats
and the heavy words written in stone,
to engrave them in the shape of the window
This way, others can also read the wall.

You are a Small Peace

You are a small peace folded up inside the map of war
and I'm the wounded next in line.
Let me drink from your breast the stellar serum
to awaken the star and replace the wound.
You're a small peace folded in the map of war
and I am the surrender: the white flag.

Translated by Sidorela Risto

Padmaja Iyengar-Paddy (India)

Padmaja Iyengar-Paddy, a senior ex-banker and a former urban governance consultant, is currently an Advisory Panel Member, ISISAR, Kolkata, India and the Editorial Counselor-India, International Writers' Journal, USA.

Her maiden poetry collection 'P-En-Chants' has been recognized as a Unique Record of Excellence by the India Book of Records, for never-before-attempted movie reviews and management topics in rhyming poetry.

A recipient of several awards, Paddy has compiled and edited 6 international multilingual poetry anthologies of which 'Amaravati Poetic Prism' 2016 to 2019 have been recognized by the Limca Book of Records (published by Coca Cola India) as "Poetry Anthology in Most Languages".

Her poems, short stories, some of them prize winners, and articles have been published in various international anthologies, print journals and e-zines.

CALLING ...

The deeper I delve into the mysteries of the sea,
The more it opens up its hidden treasures to me.
The deeper I delve into the depths of my heart,
The further it makes me an inner journey chart.
The deeper I delve into the recesses of my mind,
The greater am I led to discoveries of a new kind.

Waves after waves keep emerging from the sea,
That keep hitting the shore with a nonstop glee.
My heart is a melting pot of feelings sizzling intensely.
My mind is a beehive of thoughts buzzing constantly.
Hitting waves, sizzling feelings and buzzing thoughts,
Are incessant and also keep tying themselves in knots.

I sit on the seashore watching the waves rising and falling.
I sense my heart and mind yearning for an unusual calling.

CONSUMING DESIRE

Consuming desire
Raging like a fire
Engulfing everything
Charts its own course

Consuming desire
All pervading
Over powering
Treads its own path.

Consuming desire
Charging ahead
Raw and unabated
Evades a closure

Consuming desire
Self-destructive
Burning and scalding
Refuses to diffuse

Consuming desire
Flashy and blinding
Painful and grinding
Follows its own destiny

Pankhuri Sinha (India)

Bilingual young poet and story writer from India. Two books of poems published in English, two collections of stories published in Hindi, and five collections of poetries published in Hindi, and many more are lined up.

Her writing is dominated by themes of exile, immigration, gender equality and environmental concerns. After doing her BA from Delhi University, and PG diploma in Journalism, from Symbiosis Pune, Pankhuri did her Master's in history from SUNY Buffalo, and has an unfinished Phd from the University of Calgary, Canada. She has worked in various positions as a journalist, lecturer and a content editor.

An oil drenched sea bird

An oil drenched sea bird
Is what she felt like
Is what the morning felt like
Made up of the froth and filth of an oil spill
Of unbearable anger
Erupting in flames
On the tarmac of the road
And in the sea
Inside the pages of the book
She was reading
And in the room
She was reading
Of an office fight
Enlarged
Enhanced
Engulfing others
Needlessly dragging others
Framing the innocent
The naïve
Killing people
Leaving birds unable to fly

Maiming them
Maiming my voice
My wings
Chopping all skies around me.

Talking with everything at stake

Talking with everything at stake
Like the last chance of making a baby
Completely visible
In matrimonial negotiations
Is a very strange position
Specially
If you have been trapped into it
Like the last year was so full of telling people
You cannot talk
Just cannot bear
The ringing of the phone
Alarms go off in your head
Strange buzzers
Implant like things
Tracking devices
Such was the zeal with which the phone rang
Such was the precision
With which the phone rang
Telling you of a strange surveillance system
That even with that last year of baby making
Going by
You simply could not talk
Although there were other platforms
Where talking meant
Talking with all at stake
And much being held
Many, many strings holding your voice
Outside the room
Or was it just released
Prior to the walk in?

Rudina Çupi (Albania)

Rudina Çupi is an Albanian writer. She has studied Albanian Language and Literature at the University of Tirana.

Her artistic activity includes four poetry books: "© All rights reserved" (2015); "®"(2010); Shkopsitje / "Unbuttoning" (2006); and "Don't remember me the death" (1993).

Rudina is the author and translator of several children's books too and didactic book. For several media she writes critical writing, journalistic articles, interviews etc. and she love to organize reading activities with children.

She worked in some main Publishing Houses.

Art and women are major culprits...
A football commentator opines like a poet.

1.
Art made usable!!!
After all, it's what adults do best with
precious things: possessing.
Why should we judge them?
Perhaps a Nobel prize is more valuable
when sung in the shower... Go ahead and sing!

But whom to blame for the fadeing of hope,
except the ones who are able to create?

From "Madonna and The Child Jesus"
to "The Lady With The Dog"
there are only a few children in the arts
and, consequently in the yards,

(having kids is so classic!)
not that they aren't interesting,
but when women saw how sons were used to fight wars,
and daughters to place guilt upon,
women began to economize creation
to teach everyone that life is given to be blissful.
People created non-adopting couples
and the world is relieved, really...
Nevertheles, art and women are major culprits...

2.
The family is a belly.
It and the churches emptied daily
reduced to uninhabited wombs.
The womb, a word soon to be forgotten.
"Test tube" is much more modern
and the blame cannot be placed all on science
that there would be only animals embarking Noah's Ark,
or for the fabricated pacifiers,
audio lullabies and fairy tales,
the invented mothers for pay...
Of the weaks, only children are left.

The happy ending and women are major culprits ...

My Aquatic Child

My aquatic baby, all white,
freedom you are now spreading
surfacing across wide-shored beaches.
Lying on his back, playing with midair toys and sailing ships,
troubled, thrilled, abyssal.

When the shores take you,
closing and closing upon you, threatening
to crush and dilute you like a river,
my fluid baby, do not lament or thunder,
tears will decipher you,

you will feel sweet water like all rivers
running along a path
and ironically, the nostalgia for the ships of the past,
you'll confess to the logs on your back.

Learn not to lament, my aquatic son,
when you melt like snow and dissolve into steam on the glass
or passing between two slabs of soil so narrow
as if between two hands kissing in prayer
then remember you are destino: to leave ...
So leave, leave constantly.
Travel to discover new oppressed forms of yourself
until you realize the advancing force you have within yourself
to carve underground rocks
to find your way with your nails carving away
until you have invented a rift and found light.
Then explode, marvolous, tall, colorfull, a waterfall;
reigning with a fog crown
a swan with a helo.

Translated into English by Shpresa Ymeraj

Rahman Shaari (Malaysia)

Rahman Shaari was born on 5th Sept 1949, in Perlis. Received primary education in Perlis, then at Alam Shah School, in Cheras, KL. He entered Sultan Idris Teacher Training College in 1970 and continued his education at the National University of Malaysia (UKM) in 1973 and gained his Bachelor's degree in Literature 1976. After working at the Ministry of Education for 6 years, he continued his stuies at UKM, and obtained his Master's degree. He was appointed as a lecturer at the Faculty of Education ini 1988. In 1991, he attended a course on international writing at the University of Iowa, USA. In 2003, he was appointed as a Professor at Media Studies Department. Rahman Shaari received the S.E.A Write Award in 2007. He is currently the President of Malaysian Poetry Association (Penyair).

Translated into english by Dr Ramilah Jantan

Deep Effect in My Heart

Quiet around me
No one passed by
Effect of covid attack

I see tree one by one
All freezing
Breeze becoming lazy ?

Or it is my heart that froze
Burdened by duress environment
Conscience touched
World speaking sadly

In the lock up
Self talking to myself

Repeated questions in silent language
The answers are boredom
Surrounded by meaning after meaning

Weak and slow
Is my movement
Seized by restlessness and doubt

I observed once more
From this window pane
Hundred of cars stalled
Quiet for many days
Colour all the quietness

For a long time I am not hearing
Challenging idea
Meaning cover by meaning

For a long time not seeing
Friend's face
Happy and full of fun

All left in memory

I waited for weeks
For worry and anxious voices
Random by sad news

If canary whistle
At this very moment
Surely will leave deep feelings in the heart
But worry still exist
If covid pandemic didn't end.

Rozalia Aleksandrova (Bulgaria)

Rozalia Aleksandrova lives in Plovdiv, Bulgaria. She was born in the magical Rhodope Mountains, the cradle of Orpheus. Author of 11 poetry books: "The House of My Soul" (2000), "Shining Body" (2003), "The Mystery of the Road" (2005), "The Eyes of the Wind" (2007) , "Parable of the key" (2008), "The Conversation between Pigeons" (2010), "Sacral" (2013), "The Real Life of Feelings" (2015), "Pomegranate from Narrow" (2016), "Brushy"(2017), "Everything I did not say"(2019). Editor and compiler of over ten literary almanacs, collections and anthologies. She is a member of the Union of Bulgarian Writers. In March 2006 she created a poetic-intellectual association "Quantum and Friends" for the promotion of quantum poetry in civil society, Plovdiv and Bulgarian phenomenon. Initiator and organizer of the International Festival of Poetry SPIRITUALITY WITHOUT BORDERS from 2015. Every year the Festival publishes an almanac, which unites thematically the bright verses of the poets from Bulgaria and the world.

**THE STATUS QUO
OF MY SILENCE**

Originally.
Like a storm.
No shelter.
Like a flash.
And help.
And the swing of dreams.
Among the trees.
As a reptile,
crossed my shelter.

Like a missing.
of you.
In a babie's cry.
Speechless pillow.
I want you again.
Unabandoned.
I want you here.
Among the fears.
Seconds are buzzing.
Seasons have become entangled.
Blue sky.
Like autumn.
Cloud Warriors.
And land.
The Inconsistency
Of wind.
Deceiving and groaning.
Drops grow.
The Covenant of the Rain.
Wet Silence.
No trace.

On the peaks
glowing.
Spending hopes.
Voile feather.
Purifying
distances.

I am in the world.
And it is in me.

Ricardo Plata (Mexico)

Ricardo Plata (Mexico City, 1994). He studied Hispanic Literature at the Universidad Autónoma Metropolitana. He is author of the poetry collection Para habitar mi nombre under the Literalia publishing label. He was a fellow of the Festival Interfaz: The signs in rotation. He is founder and CEO of Cardenal Literary Magazine and of the National Meeting of Young Writers- UAM-I. He has published in the magazines Círculo de poesía, Punto de Partida, Buenos Aires Poetry and Mood Magazine.

A prayer for abandonment

I never released myself
from my loved ones,
I think about abandonment
as an excuse to come back,
so that time can make of the chest
a moor of open hopes.
I think about abandonment
as a night with three suspension points
which opens the windows of grief.
People who loved me
looked at me as if I was a tall house,
three-story high
which they could dessert,
they departed leaving the doors open
because they knew I don't have
the strength to close them.
I was always the prelude
so they could find love,

I was the place where they concurred crying,
the place where they swaddled their heart,
and when they left,
I, also, wanted to uninhabit my self.

***

The Television's statics
settle in the room,
right on the corner where our words join.

I honor the wisdom of your body,
the experience you have gained from your other lovers
to untangle your hair and disentangle your daily clothes.

An angel paralyzes every time you undress,
there's a thirty degrees sun
raising from your feet
and a moon climbing up your stomach
completing each one of your phases.
You remind me of the woman I dreamt of in my childhood
and you describe your waist which maddens every time someone loves it,
show in my stomach the madness of your pelvis
so the caress will taste like a January's evening.

Translated from Spanish to English by Daniela Sánchez

Rajashree Mohapatra (India)

Rajashree Mohapatra loves to devote her time in painting .For her, painting is a mode of creative expression and can communicate souls . She believes that artists play an important role in making of the society .Most of her paintings can be found on the cover page of prestigious Anthologies, published in different parts of the world .

BE MY LOVE !

O Night!
When light is smoothly withdrawn,
the darkness spreads from your wings

When the bright moon ascends
in a cluster of light
You cling to the sky as love to life

A silence wraps me
A blessing all around me

O Night!
Out of your silence comes
my beauty , my grace
Comes the depth of my eyes
Aura of my being

I close my eyes
and sleep into your lap
Into its fathomless depth ,
I rejuvenate every moment

O Night!
Be my love
Cast me in your core
Meet me in my dreams
Let the endless sky bow down before us ...

Now ...

Now ...
Everything around appears motionless
I stand as a statue in impenetrable darkness
Who knows how long
I would burn myself

Standing on the altar of agony
I stare into empty sky
With a broken heart.

I dream of you ...
With eagerness in your eyes
you are coming back ...

I stand waiting on this quiet shore now
My heart desperately search for you
And soul desire your sweet embrace
My anxiety for your passionate touch
Of course knows no bounds ...

©Irina Hysi. MA (Albania) "Dancing in the Autumn" (70x50)

Member of Board of the International Poetical Galaxy ATUNIS
Albanian poet and painter. Graduated in master's art management, the Mediterranean University of Albania. The veil between deep inspiration, poetic intuition, and appearance and image realization as a painting often accompanies the category of all the artists who possess these types of techniques, but resizing and expressive forms with the language codes and the spirit of the music make this art to touch the highest constellations creatures of the creative spirit.

Susana Roberts (Argentina)

Susana Roberts- Argentinian poet-writer-translator-peacemaker Resides in Trelew-Chubut-Patagonian, Argentina, dedicated to the Culture of Peace. Dr. Litt Honoris Causa-WAAC-2009. Member of Life of WAAC.Ca.EEUU. Ambassador of Peace by Mil Milennia.org- Pea.org-(Senate of Argentine Nation (Unesco-Unicef). Vice. Dir. IFLAC-Argentina and Latin America/ Honorary Member Global Harmony Association-Russia/ Member SELAE: European Society of Writers and Artists/. Honorary Member of Global Harmony Association (G.H.A).-Russia. Universal Ambassador of Peace n 537 -Circle of Ambassadors-Geneva-Switzerland. Member of Noosphera Ethical Ecological World Assembly-Russia.(NEEWA) Member Presidium WFSC (World Forum of Spiritual Culture) -Kazakhstan. Member SELAE. Society of Latin American and European Writers-Italy. International Cultural Ambassador – SIPEA. Ambassador "The Love Foundation" -Tampa-Florida-USA. Bilingual publications in many countries. Participation in many World, National and International Congresses. Honored award with the 1st prize to the translation by IPCRT -China. Winner of national, international Prizes, S.A.D.E(Argentinian Society of Writers) awards including 1st Prize in English- WAAC, WCP in Trujillo-Peru 2014. Activity and trajectory awarded by the Government of the Prov. Del Chubut-Argentina during 2013-2016. Prize Grand Master Award for World Ladies Grand Masters in the Senate of Argentina Nation- CABA. 2018. Honored by India Intercultural Association of Writers and Kafla Editorial with the International "Sahitya Shree Award". International Honor Lady of Roses Award-Buenos Aires-Argentina MS Production. "Heroe of Peace" by Global Harmony Association. Visitor of Honor of many countries, Mexico, Perú, Spain, Kazahastán. Staff Member of Atunis Galktika Poetry. International Newspapers and Magazines: In Spain-Greece, Kazakhstan, Uzbekistan, Belgium, Albany, India...Etc. Co-author of many books and anthologies. Book prologue's writer. Bilingual Books: Rostros / Faces. El vuelo del Ave / the flight's bird. Arte y virtud en la evolución humana/Art and Virtue in human evolution – in French. Epub-France-Alter Editions).

Intention

For those who try to spread Peace
In the world
I will be always there
inside the empty and powerless knots
in the ink of the bookseller
crying out for justice
always the same oblivion
there is a trap of loneliness
and then, the world will make us a portrait
... slowly
we are like alms passengers
with wishes and complaints
Witnesses of a fragile light, hardly appears

Since I was a girl I knew that the pen
and bare feet will be speaking to the earth
I tattooed my skin to conquer the painful soul
in the crowd I felt my eyelids dropping
on the same humidity of empty gatherings
And I suffered within the same horror
that many people suffered

since then I understood that
narrow minds multiplied
very far, and over miseries of the same place

is like a grass that sprouts in every report
from every point of the planet, ...pains

now harmonious dreams face the tough and
obedient plot of the paper
refracting beneficial light
that, however, many people find it difficult to understand
will be the spirit of kindness expanding
or the sad fate of humanity in agony.

Stanislav Penev (Bulgaria)

Stanislav Penev (1953,Varna,Bulgaria) is a poet, a translator,and an editor. He graduated from The University of Sofia "St.Kliment Ohridski" in "Bulgarian philology" and "Phylosophy". Having a long professional life dedicated to teaching Bulgarian language and literature in Varna, he is also a socially engaged person focused on the problems of Bulgarian literature,as a part of the modern cultural developement of the country.

He is the president of the society of the writers in Varna, the president of the editorial council of the "CAL" (КИЛ)- a journal for culture, art and literature.
Since 2009 he has been the president of the literary society of Varna (SLOV). He is also the editor-in-chief and the main organizer of the journal "Literature and Society"-a national edition for literature, art and social life, which is published in Varna. He is a member of the union of the Bulgarian writers.

His first volume of poetry "Intimate Cosmogony" (1992) was translated into Polish and published in Poland (1993). Six of his poetry books:"Coasts" (2008), "Wharf" (2009), "Bulgarian Sea" (2010), "Hopes on the waves" (2011), "The sky leaves slowly" (2011), and" The soul arises to sail away" (2011) were translated in England, Russia, Germany, USA, Armenia by the author and translator Vsevolod Kuznetsov, and were published in Russia.
During recent years, his works have been translated and published in many countries, such as Italy, England, Croatia, France, Poland, Ukraine, Belarus, Latvia, Italy, Hungary, Greece, Armenia, Serbia, USA, Canada, Australia, Russia. He has got a lot of prizes for literature; in 2020 alone they are three of them: the big prize of VI-th International poetic festival "Spirituality without limits" in Plovdiv, 2020, for achievement in spirituality and poetry.

***

In the sky
The parachutes of clouds
Gleam.
The sail-boats –
Sea-gulls
Heavy with waiting –
Follow them lazily.
In the hold
Of the summer
There is plenty of room
For memories…
But not a hope
For another
Obstacle,
Except
The intangibility
Of the horizon.

SUMMER

I see the eyes of good fortune
Painting high-tides.
Goodness and humanity
Have again spread their sails,
Full of sunrises.

As a fruit of a mirage and urgent illusion,
I bear the catharsis of life.

I love summer apples
Even when sour.

Sunita Paul (India)

Founder of Aabs Publishing House
www.aabspublishinghouse.com

Hailing from the educational, commercial and cultural centre of Eastern India, Kolkata, Sunita Paul is an author, editor, publisher and humanitarian of international repute. She has authored 6 books and has edited more than 35 anthologies. For her contributions towards literature, Sunita was awarded the prestigious Nazi Naman prize in the year 2017. She was also the recipient of the Literary Laureate Award for the year 2017 conferred by the World Nations Writer's Organization, Kazakhstan. Recently she received the IndianAwaz Award in Kolkata. In the field of humanity, Sunita Paul represents a number of organizations in India and abroad. She is also the National General Secretary of National Child & Woman Development Council (NCWDC) and National Human Rights & Anti-corruption Force (NHRACF) and the administrative persona in the World Institute Of Peace, Nigeria. Sunita is also famed as an organiser of International Conferences Pan India. She is Founder of Aabs Publishing House, Kolkata and member of Atunis Board.

My eyes remember

My eyes remember
My mother's kiss on my forehead so sweet and deep
Every night when I used to go to sleep
My eyes remember
My father's tensed face
When I used to compete in any race
My eyes remember
When my husband set his eyes on me
A silent promise to let me what I wannabe
My eyes remember
My kids' growing years
With hopes, anticipation and fears

My eyes remember
Each pains and fears
How I smiled with hidden tears
My eyes remember
The backstabbing of my hypocrite relatives and friends
Some twist and turns on every end
My eyes remember
Each time how I failed and again tried
How badly i survived when deep inside I died
My eyes still remember
The betrayal and the lies
How each time I was fooled with open eyes
My eyes remember
Each and everything
How life has taught me hard to live as a human being.

Darkness

Darkness taught me
The best lessons of life
Regardless of how dark is the night
However difficult maybe the grief or strife
Come what may, none can dim your inner light

Darkness taught me to stand strong
When life knocks us down
It showed me what's right and wrong
How to deal with the miseries without any frowns

I learnt from darkness that it's light which attracts the eye
But loyal shadows have more to say
Coz it's they who know how to distinguish between a truth and lie
In the light and shadow game, it's always darkness which shows us the way.

Prof. Sungrye Han (South Korea)
https://blog.naver.com/kudara21

Born in 1955 Rep of Korea. Poet, Translator (Japanese-Korean). Adjunct professor. She majored in Japanese language and Japanese literature at Sejong University and earned her master's degree in Japanese studies at Sejong University's Graduate School of Policy Science. Her works have earned her the Newcomer Award of Poem and Consciousness, Korea's the Heonanseolheon Literature Award and Japan's Sitosozo Award. Book of Poetry The Beauty in a Laboratory, Smiling flowers in Korean, The Sky in the Yellowish Red Korean Skirt, Drama of the Light in Japanese. Historical essay The Formation of the Ancient Nation in Japan and Japanese oldest anthology Manyo-shu and so on. Her poems express Korean tradition, life and death, sadness, pain and anguish in surrealism, modernism and avant-garde forms.

She translated many Japanese literary works into Korean and many Korean literary works into Japanese. This work includes more than 200 volumes, for example, poems, novels, essays, poem anthologies, books for children, humanity books, self enlightenment books and scientific books. In particular, she translated many poems and Book of Poetry between Korea and Japan.In particular, she translated many poems and Book of Poetry between Korea and Japan. Korean textbooks used in Korean high schools contain several translations of her for educational purposes. She has translated and introduced Korean and Japanese poems in literary magazines between the two countries since 1990. She is now an adjunct professional at Sejong Cyber University in Seoul, South Korea.

The Angle of a blind spot

The faded sunlight shines through the leaves
Underneath the tree, the leaves turn into a navy blue canvas
A hazy curtain hung
At the evening when red and black are blended

The hour of the devil, neither day nor night
Spiders are coming down low
A bird flies low
Lives falling down from the air

Under the influence of that power,
The heaven comes to the earth
The boundary between the earth and the sky is erased
Now is the time to forget what we said during the day
At the end of the earth's axis
Where the blood of day and night is blended
A dream that hasn't cooled down is being buried
The sunset drags its feet carefully
Not to spill over the blood in a basket
A person also flows holding up their lives in critical condition

I came to see a walking tree of mirage
Created by the yearning for the sunshine, but…
A tree that has its own feet
A tree that has its root on its body
To move along to get nutrients
Suddenly, a cluster of trees looks like a group of people
A death spot
Appearing on the skin immediately after death
I wonder if the spot has buried lives in it
A moment
When things look dimly
At the evening neither day nor night,
The angle of a blind spot
That cannot distinguish this world or afterlife

Satis Shroff (Germany)

Satis Shroff is a prolific writer and has taught Creative Writing at the University of Education and the University of Freiburg.
He is a lecturer, poet and writer and the published author. He is based in Freiburg (poems, fiction, non-fiction) and also writes on ecological, ethno-medical, culture-ethnological themes. He has studied Zoology and Botany in Nepal, Medicine and Social Sciences in Germany and Creative Writing in Freiburg and the United Kingdom.

The German media describes him as a mediator between western and eastern cultures.

Since literature is one of the most important means of cross-cultural learning, he is dedicated to promoting and creating awareness for Creative Writing and transcultural togetherness in his writings, and in preserving an attitude of Miteinander in this world. Writing experience: Satis Shroff has written two language books on the Nepali language in German for DSE (Deutsche Stiftung für Entwicklungsdienst) & Horlemannverlag. His anthology of poems 'Katmandu. Katmandu', German poems "Im Schatten des Himalaya" and travelogue "Through Nepalese Eyes" have been published on the website http://www.Lulu.com/spotlight/satisle. He is a contributing author on http://www.Boloji.com/writers/1338/satis. His feature articles have been published in the Munich-based Nelles Verlag's 'Nepal' on the Himalayan Kingdom's Gurkhas, sacred mountains and Nepalese symbols, and on Hinduism in 'Nepal: Myths & Realities (Book Faith India), and his poem 'Mental Molotovs' was published in epd-Entwicklungsdienst (Frankfurt).

You can find his writings under: *satis shroff literature.*

He has been featured in The Rising Nepal, The Christian Science Monitor, the Independent, the Fryburger, Swatantra Biswa (USIS publication), Himal Asia.

THE BRIDGE OF SIGHS

In Venice I stood on the Bridge of Sighs,
Thought about the Doge's palace
And the prison beyond the bridge,
I was imprisoned in my mind.
Thought about the Doge's palace,
In Venice I stood on the Bridge of Sighs,
I was imprisoned in my mind,
For a life was underway.
It was a far better choice I had made,
I was imprisoned in my mind.
The product of our genes,
For a life was underway.
I was imprisoned in my mind,
Swimming in a small amniotic sea;
For a life was underway,
I had to say adieu to a love.
Swimming in a small amniotic sea,
That was not to be.
I had to say adieu to a love;
Too many verbal battles.
That was not to be,
Malicious verbal daggers drawn,
Why, O why, couldn't we go asunder,
I had to say adieu to a love.
Malicious verbal daggers drawn,
In Frieden like civilised people,
I had to say adieu to a love,
At peace with each other.
In V
Venice I stood on the Bridge of Sighs.

Sophy Chen (China)

Sophy Chen (Lihua Chen), Chinese poet & translator, born in Shannxi in 1975, lives in Guangzhou and graduated from XISU. She editted and translated I Find Your Beauty In The Taste Of Your Eyes, Poetry Selection Of PENTASI B 2019 China World Poetry Festival & Sophy Chen World Poetry Awards and Sophy Poetry & Translation (C-E) World Poetry Paper Magazine and 10 poetry collections. She is the President of Sophy International Translation Publishing House and the founder of Sophy Chen World Poetry Awards. She will organize, sponsor and hold 2021 PENTASI B China World Poetry Festival & Sophy Chen World Poetry Awards in China.

Siberian Iris

Siberian Iris, your green leaves are the most grand green
in front of my house when winter is yellow withering, you become
the only green in front of me
Every time when I came back, it is almost winter, everything
is withered and silent
Only Siberian Iris give me a vast expanse of green as far as
the eyes can see
Whether it is in stern winter rain or heavy snow, it can not stop
your green
Suddenly I thought of your summer shadow, the shadow reflected
in the stream
Now I can hardly remember exactly what season you are flowering
But in my memory at the time, the most striking thing
about you was
The blue small flowers set each other off in the stream, there are
always water magpies
Sliding over in the flowers, water magpies and the flowers are
surely a good match

The beauty of that moment, only memory can make you
beautiful forever

It Turns Out That The Moon Is Hidden By The Cold Cliff

Last night , it was the 15th day of the first month of lunar year,
I translated poems overtime at night
In the mountain village the moon is bright and distant
The chill invaded my bone marrow at midnight, so I did not appreciate it
Tonight it is the 16th day of the first month of lunar year and the moon
should be round the most
But I suddenly found out that the moon didn't come out
Looking over the roof and the four sides of the canyon
There is no shadow of the moon, where is the moon
Is the moon of the 16th day of the first month of lunar year covered by
dark clouds
The moment when I turned around, I suddenly found in the east
of canyon
There was a shallow halo on the black cliff of it
The halo is getting stronger and stronger, till
On the cliff the shadow of the trees can be seen sparsely, slowly
The moon rose a dim light shadow from the shadows of the trees, the
light shadow
Is getting stronger and stronger, bigger and bigger, and clearer
and clearer
Until its whole body is appearing in the dancing tree shadows
If you look at it from another angle, the moon oh
It hangs beautifully on the treetop of hillside
To see its cold and cheerless looking, I suddenly felt deep cold between
the canyon ...
It turns out that the moon is hidden by the cold cliff

Silvana Kühtz (Italy)
http://www.poesiainazione.it

Silvana Kühtz was born in Bari. She has a multi-disciplinary background (theatre and poetry training, engineering degree and PhD, communicationMSc, journalism).
Graduated in Engineering at Politecnico di Bari (Italy), attended the Imperial College of Science (University of London), leading to a Ph.D. degree and Diploma of Imperial College. She completed a Master Course in Communication (Aleph school Assisi, Italy). Since 1995 she is lecturer at Università della Basilicata, Matera, Italy, senior lecturer of Language Future and Possibility (an innovative course she created to enhance the quality of learning, creativity and self expression of future generations of scientists). Winner of the 2014 Alfonso Gatto Poetry Prize in the category for unpublished works, with this very collection. In 2005 she created the project Poetry in action, where poetry and other arts fuse and mingle to produce concerts and workshops. In particular the sensory concerts are a focal point of her activity since the beginning. Since 2017 she conducts Sensory Concerts for the Harvard Summer school in Siena, Italy. She has published books and papers on International Journals and is invited to contribute to conferences on the research topics investigated.

30 days one Earth and one home

Thursday 23.

I do not know where you stand in this clear night
but I know that you are inside a movement
supported by lintels against the peril of subsidence.
Come hell or high water, I will be there
should the lake boil,
I will be there

at least for one hour of silence in the dark
I dream for that circle to widen
while being absorbed by the wind
and thinking that I may be happy to be there.
Accept my tea and my almonds.
Getting used to you
head high
but always attentive to the feet at each step
is my prayer.
I started a journey and
clouds of yellow and black butterflies
freshen their wings
in a windmill of pleasure.
Open your eyes wide
their noise is so bare
that if you pay no attention
you will be left with a frozen heart.

Wednesday 27.

That not named is lost
but nothing has value if your
soul is stolen.
I dream that I fall on the heavy earth
to give dreams of gold.

The risks of one word too many
or one word too few
must be chewed on every day.
We are love seekers.

Translation: Nathaniel DuPertuis

Stefania Miola (Italy)

Stefania Miola is an eccentric and multifaceted writer passionate about art in all its many expressions. She defines herself as a truth seeker. He lives with his family in a small town on the outskirts of Turin – Italy. She has always loved reading the soul of art and giving voice to the soul through the words of her narration. She is mainly interested in the relationship between art and spirit following a dynamic path that embraces multiple disciplines: psychology, philosophy, spirituality, well-being. Fascinated by direct confrontation, she prefers the form of observation and artist / work dialogue as an opportunity for inner enrichment.
2020 member of the World's Nation Writers Union.
She has published three books of poetry: "The only sky-the true one"; "Violets in the desert"; "The perfume of white rabbit".
She is published in many magazines and global Anthologies and she is winner of many international Awards.

Letters from eternity

It does not matter how much time will pass
before we can meet again.
Somewhere , for some reason, all of a sudden
or according to the laws imposed by fate.
Really it doesn't matter.
One account is to be together
another thing is "feeling together".
Here, now.
In two eyes that contemplate the sky
or that they rest with amazement on a small flower
that it simply blossomed on the edge of a precipice
without wondering if there's a tomorrow.
You know, I'm just looking at you from a different place.

Far or near I don't know.
Distance is something that does not exist.
It's all so weird and wonderful.
I'll touch your forehead with a silent kiss
and I'll touch you gently face
with soaked hands of all the Hidden Colors
between the folds of my soul.
Give me a smile.
Your smile will echo
of happiness on my face.

Letter from a grandfather

My little love,
I write these few lines before I put my accordion over the closet.
I can no longer play it.
My hands are tired . Do not despair.
My music will become poetry in your memories…
If you have a dream, fight to achieve it with body and soul.
The dreams in the drawers are colorful flowers
that without water wither and die.
Don't look forward, look up filled with the blue of the sky
and the warmth of the sun.
Look at what looks good to you.
There will be difficult moments.
If you have to think, think of the positive things.
Watch meeting, look inside and pray to get close to your God.
Look over the leaf that falls.
Live the spring .

Dr. Salma Naimi (Algeria)

*Writer and thinker Salma Naimi
*Jurist and certified lawyer
*Academic researcher
in international management
*I studied Arabic literature, majoring in criticism
*Translator
*She studied languages at the International Institute in Algiers
*Traditional and modern costume designer –
*Painter
*She obtained many prizes inside and outside the Arab world in writing and drawing
*Best Costume Designer in the Emirates award.
*Best Literary Work Award.

Her literature:
-Novel deaf permises has three parts in arabic
-Divan our meeting trance
-Six novels to be published
-Book on customs smuggling law
-disgrace of Thought book

Touch me!

Touch me like you do,
I' will try so hard to forget you I leave my life ...
we had behind ,
I feel the day has come stop love you,
I forget things that we used to do,
but ...
But I'm afraid there's always something and makes me see,
your's more than just a memory in the past,
life doesn't ask why,
and never explain don't you know my heart doesn't think twice!!
cause when you're in my arm's

I understand don't have a voice for ….
tell you :
I lived great time with you…

Gonna whispers day…

Gonna whispers day!
can never the careless whispers Entering
At the good time to the heart…
I gnorance is kind the mind…
no comfort in the truth …
I'm never gonna dance again…
I want you to need me,
I want to be the the mind you see when you close your heart…
I touch your herat evrey singer night,
I want to be your fantasy..
but..
but you never your reality me…
I want to be your deepest kiss…
How I love you?!
I love you when we are together,
Doing things that we love. ..
I feel like I'm in heaven every time you're near. …
I need every day,
I need to hold you tight!
I don't want to let go, life. ..
No ,no ..
I just wanna die in my life. .
Here tonight
When I'm feeling gloom,
For everything that's mine,around me die.

Smaragdi Mitropoulou (Greece)

Smaragdi Mitropoulou was born in Athens. She has studied history and archaeology at the University of Athens and had postgraduate history studies at the University of Cardiff, in Great Britain. She serves in secondary education. She is also a Creative Writing graduate (Diploma in Creative Writing) from the Writers' Bureau College (Manchester, UK), and has studied theater writing at the International Theater Institute and directing at the Foundation of Culture in Tinos island. She has received awards in Greece and abroad for her poetry and prose. Also, she is Programme Coordinator of Writers Capital International Foundation. Up to now, she has written four books, which have been published and launched in Greece. One of them, "One moment just an eternity", has been translated in English and was published in 2020 by Ontime Books in Great Britain; it has become best-seller in eight countries. Her poetry has been translated into English, Chinese, Taiwanese, Bengali and Spanish language.

ETERNITY

Dressed in a white tunic
sunbeams embroidered
and bare feet
along the river I walk.
Dressed in a golden tunic
above the stars I rose.
Dressed in a red tunic
I tasted passion over the centuries.
With you
in the circle of heaven
in the circle of sea
in the circle of earth.
With you

in the walls of war
in the whisper of peace
in the blonde cornfields.
With you
in the sounds of music
in the homelands we loved
yesterday, today, tomorrow,
forever.
With you
on the pages engraved inside us
in the light, in the dark
in the miracle of life.
History
now begins.

BIRLAND

Under the desert sky
and next to the river that silently crosses the palm trees
a land blessed by gods
waits for the wayfarers.
Soil and water, sun, bread and love…
Through the roar of the wind
and wild waves
I, the stranger, have been wandering around for centuries alone
without my mother's amulet.
The night when the moon became one with the sea
an invisible hand led me here…
My soul found
a homeland to rely on
a port as a shelter
and the devout birds to greet
with a ferry-line full of dreams coming and going.

Sylwia K. Malinowska (Poland)

A graduate of the faculty of Journalism and Education at the University of Warsaw.
A lover of Sylvia Plath and Emily Dickinson's poetry, passionate and tireless in familiarizing oneself with literature and striving at becoming an expert in it. Her poems were printed in journals such as "Poezja Dzisiaj", as well as in numerous anthologies in Polish, English and Bulgarian. The author of the literary broadcast "Black Drawer" in Dublin. She also collaborates with HelloIrlandia , which promotes Polish literature abroad. Her poems were printed in journals such as "Poezja Dzisiaj", as well as in numerous anthologies in Polish, English and Bulgarian. She also writes poetry for the photo album by Beata Cierzniewska "Cognition" presented at The Cooper House Gallery in Dublin. The author of the literary broadcast "Black Drawer" in Dublin.

Exist

When you awaken the force in you.
When you realize that there is a great force in you, that beauty is you.
The strength is you.
Sensitivity is you.
Truth.
Force.
It's you.
When you feel you're all you've been looking for, you're full, the source of everything.
When you touch the corners of your existence.
When you dive into yourself and don't look away.
When you swim somewhere on the verge of non-existence.
To places that aren't there, but are inside you.
When fear takes over your being,
that you stop being in it, stop existing, understanding what it is to be.
When you wander in infinity.

When you cross all boundaries.
When you understand that there is no turning back.
When you give up.
Simply fall.
Cease to exist.
When you feel a real touch of yourself that hurts because being who you are hurts you.
Then you will really feel, touch, experience your beauty.
That spark.
Force.
Strength.
This unimaginable miracle.
Beauty.
Yes, that beauty.
Your existence.

Beautiful

Beauty is a power flowing from the knowledge of our nature. The brightness of the heart, the light melting in the distance. Empathy and sensitivity in looking at other beings. It is a conscious value and intention that comes from the heart in action. This is following the voice of the heart when the whole world screams...no.
It is the forgiveness that gives solace and acceptance that brings peace.
Love, someone makes us great and the power that allows us to go on.
This certainty pushes you in one direction although the common sense pulls you by the neck.
And although we do not know the future, we do not know what will happen next and we do not know why we are here, we know that it is our identity, the individual color that defines us in everyday life, separating the light line from the million others.
This power of striving for harmony and not perfection is beautiful.

Sakineh Asadzadeh (Iran)

I am Sakineh Asadzadeh, born (25/Aug/1989) in Iran, Ph.d in Private Law.
I am working in Ministry of Justice - Governmental Sanction Institution as a law employer (also I am the law member in specialized commission of legal council about the trade affaires in this institution).
I am the author of the law and poetry books (Hayalı Damlacik, Şiirden Yayincilik, 2019) in Turkish, (Fiery Sunder, Arshadan Publication, 2020), (Garnet Gray, 2019- Muskwillow Jujub, 2019 – Imaginary Dropper, 2018- New Moon/poetry collection, 2020, Narvan Publication) in Iran and (Legal status of Contractual Groups, Majd Publication, 2019), the political assistant in ministry of foreign and research assistant and translator in international association of universities muslim professors.
Also I am teaching a law courses in university. Awards include The First International Scientific, Literature and Arts Festival of Saadi/2020, Second National Festival of Superior Writes of Human Sciences (Allameh Jafari/2020), The 4th Festival of the Best Dissertations of Iran (Special Award of Professor Hesabi/2020), (Superior Researcher/2018), (Best Law Employers/2017).
I am so corious, humour, thoughtful and my favourites are Muzik, exercise, reading the law, literature and culture books and articles about them and etc...

Distillate of Bittern

The spirit of humanity was spoiled for the mixed ignorance
It's not the story of eating apple or falling apple
That this one's reward was life in the world
And that one's reward was gravity's discovery
The difference is about opinions...in stablishment and firmness
The stories have been told and the hearsayes are endless
From Tous, Karkheh and Bactria ...

I wish being human not humanity … in the battle of the egoisms
I'll not be sorry for the smiles of hyaenas
Because the politesse of vultures is devour
Whether devouring the meat or the bone
My grief is about abrogation the commandments not about breach them
Because the abrogator distroyed and the scofflaw trampled
Put the verdicts on the propylaeum of justice
For my plaint is more than my complaints
I'm distillate of bittern…A legend with the other mean of love
There's my mobility and acstacy in souls
My attitude is still warm as the same as the coolness of my forehead
I'm me even with my antithesises
I'm the part of soil in the needy body
My soul has full contents and this is enough!
My atlas is so vast with the constantly bright candles and lively colorful
I'm heavy champaign full of melodies of furerunner
My address is the same oaken home
Nearby the autumn's seasons, with the abullient furnitures
I habits to sit on the near the warmish nature
On the pinealy chair before the kiblah of sea
And for playing in the nights… about the crapulence and the pain
Yes…! Pain …
The pain of inertia …
The pain of conscious …
Passive inertia and factitious conscious

Senem Gökel (Cyprus)

Senem Gökel was born in 1982, Nicosia, Cyprus. Her first poems were published in 2005. Her poems and/or translations have been published in various literary magazines of Cyprus, Turkey and Greece, such as Varlık, Kitap-lık, Şiirden, Cadences and Mandragoras. In 2012, she received the Fikret Demirag Poetry Award from the Cyprus Writers Union. As a result of this award, a bilingual poetry collection (in Turkish, Greek) was published under the general title of 'Ποίηση / Şiirler' (2012). She also published a poetry pamphlet titled as 'Unutmabeni / Forget-Me-Not / Μη με λησμόνει' (2018). She has participated in several poetry anthologies and literary events as well as organised poetry events, such as 'Cypriot Poets: Transcending Conflict' at the National Poetry Library, London.

On Sundays and the Stale Petals

I killed a glance
and wore it on Sundays
I resonated upon water
like the petal of a flower,
staling in vase for days
I kept turning around. Then hushed.
I've left a leaky faucet behind;
we should have things to count at nights.

I got used to the sounds:
bees in the sunrise
garden bats in the sundown
sheets waving in the wind, like a whip
and the crackly creak of an empty swing
shaking the pole
of my heart.

Wells on the Island

Let my delusions stay on the floor. I
want to gather my fears
and fill sacks with them.

Because you, wisely, explained
that you will take them.
That you leave them under the earth

and you shall return without them.
You said, I should wait for you with great patience.

Until, with a marble stone, you crash these visions
as if they were shells of almonds.

Then without looking back
I will pass the corridor

I will arrive at the kitchen for a glass of water
which I will drink in peace

without suspecting
that it comes from those wells

Those wells
Where the unclaimed bodies, along with their stories, were thrown.

Translated by Zeki Ali & Niki Marangou

Slavka Bozovic (Montenegro)

Slavka Bozovic was born in Niksic – Montenegro, where she lives, works and creates. She graduated from the School of Economics, and since childhood she has enjoyed beautiful creations as a member of various recitation and acting sections. Her works have been presented in over two hundred regional, European and world anthologies and have been translated into several world languages. Also, her poetry has a significant participation in electronic magazines, domestic and foreign sites, as well as on radio frequencies, where they gladly listen to it on all meridians. She has also won numerous high awards and recognitions from various international festivals. She was awarded a bronze medal for 2020 by the President of the World Union of Literature, Silvano Bortolazzi, for her contribution to poetry. At the international level, she won the "Special Award" four times. She has published "Suitcase souls" and "Spark in the eye" He is also an academician of the Brazilian Academy.

Out of range . . .

In me there is one place
Where I live I am absolutely alone
The heavenly throne is rocking me
When darkness reigns in the vault.

Then the butterflies whisper softly
Happiness waves in the body
Emotions flutter in flocks
Like swallows in the middle of spring.
I love this holy place
This is where the source of empathy flows

I cautiously protect the spiritual throne
From sudden rain and thunder.

I walk the fields of dreams elegantly
I lay the birds on my chest
Poetry comes from the heart
Sunny, in God's eyes.

That hidden place in me
It has impassable passages
And the taste of the blue sea when it foams
Only special souls can,
to visit him.

Do not ask ...

If unrest touches you tonight
and the heart trembles with pain
know that one star is dying
on the horizon as you kneel.
And don't ask her anything tonight
on the slopes of sorrow while silent
tears heal the souls of the hearth,
that no one knows or doubts it.
She used to be very happy
she shone in her beauty
tender knees were bleeding
abruptly when she fell.
And don't ask her why she fell
and why it no longer shines on anyone
with ashes her love united
from the hearth does not grow an shoot.
Do not ask . . .

Sirojiddin Sayyid (Uzbekistan)

Sirojiddin Sayyid was born on October 1958, 30 in the village of Kundajuvoz, Sariosiya district, Surkhandarya region. People's Poet of Uzbekistan (2006). Graduated from Tashkent State University, Faculty of Journalism (1979). Literary worker, head of department, deputy chairman of the Writers' Union of Uzbekistan in the newspapers "Tashkent evening" (1980-89), "Literature and art of Uzbekistan" (1989-90; 1991-96) and the magazine "Mushtum" (1990-91) (2001) —03), first deputy (since 2003). His first collection of poems was The Map of the Soul (1985). After that he wrote "In the palm of cool rocks" (1987), "The land of love" (1989), "Asragil", "Love remains, love remains" (1990), "I burned" (1994), "Studying the homeland" (1996), His collections "Vatan abadiy" (2001), "Ustimizdan oygan aylar" (2003), "Swallows give your awnings" (200) and others have been published. Along with the traditions of Uzbek classical poetry, Sirojiddin Sayyid's poetry is dominated by features of folklore – populism, simplicity, sweetness of language, lexical and musical nuances of Surkhandarya dialect. A. He translated Voznesensky's Eternal Food (1990) into Uzbek. He was awarded the Order of Friendship (1999). Lives in the city of Tashkent.

MY MUMMY

Mummy, with you I couldn't stay,
On your eyes the dust I couldn't wipe too,
What is peace and rest in this world?
I took your peace, but rest couldn't give you

Springs are watched by our entrance,
Changing the dry leaves to fragrance.
When leaves tell wisdom scratching walls

With you I couldn't stay to caress once.

Here winter designs white table-cloths,
What games will the fate show again?
The fire in the oven will warm you,
I couldn't be as this fire to you.

When spring comes, brides will charm,
Toiling they carry water without harm.
When cradles swing with full of babies,
Worried you were, but I couldn't balm.

Gone were the years, it stopped to rain
Don't floods finish, run out and end.
The rains of your face have never ceased,
I couldn't come up as a wind when needed.

The way to soul is labor from beginning to end,
In a straw lying on a road a magic I've seen a lot,
Falling in love with others I've been reproached,
Striking my head at stones break it I could not.

Life was said like a bird on a bush,
The love's essence was said in vain.
The world was said yesterday's dream,
This dream's meaning I couldn't explain.

Were you tired by sunset again, mummy,
Dry and weak like a fallen leave again?
Weren't these sorrows enough, I came up
To share all my grieves not being ashamed.

Translated by Begoyim Kholbekova

Sue Zhu (淑文) New Zealand

Sue Zhu, Chinese poet, painter, organizer of international cultural exchange. She used to be TV presenter in China, now lives in Auckland. She is a member of the Chinese Poetry Association,The NZ–China Culture Exchange Association, The NZ Chinese Poetry Art Association, honorary director of The US-China Culture and Art Center. Founder of "NZ All Souls Poetry" club. Editor for some Chinese poetry clubs which come from China, Canada and New Zealand. Her poems were published in Chinese main newspaper and magazines such as People's Daily, Poetry Selection, Chinese Poets, China Daily, international paper media such as the World Journal, International Daily News and in many counties including United States, Canada, New Zealand, Singapore, Indonesia, Japan, Taiwan, Hong Kong and Macao. She is a multi award winner in the Chinese national poetry competitions. Pushcart Prize Nomination (USA) in 2020. She has won the II Meleto di Guido Gozzano Literary Prize (International Section) — X (2020) in 2020.

To My Daughter

In one afternoon
I wrote a long letter and sent a gift to You, my daughter
who are far away from me and just turned 16 years old

The choice apples throughout the ages
with their origins marked out one by one

One is from the distant East Eden
And a golden apple burning in a wedding banquet
Still another one handed into the dwarf's window by an old lady
There is one that once appeared in Socrates' class

There is also an imaginary one set by Fromm's goal that he was to try to jump up to reach
There is still another one discarded away by the careless Charlie,
just waking up Newton who was meditating
Besides there is one that once went across the Sahara Desert
with a traveller
Another one is a token of love under the apple tree outside the fence in 1942
And there is still one more from the garden, which we have been cultivating together

Those apples have their own aromas
which can be made into a uniquely flavoured jam
Accompanying you for your whole life
Have a good journey

English Translator: Jimmy Wei (New Zealand)

Starlight

In the day
You are silent
as same as those lamps

But night time
You were lighted up by darkness
Like me, withered
Complete the bloom.

Sofia Doko Arapaj (Albania)

Sofia Doko Arapaj was born on a village named "the second Mekat" Vlorë on December 6, 1969. Her passion for literature was evident since childhood with her first creations published in the newspaper "Zeri i Vlorës" and at various radio shows for youth. In 1991 she started her studies at University "Eqerem Cabej" majoring in Literature. Later with her family, she immigrated to Greece where she continued to collaborate with local writers leading to the publication of her first book in the Greek language "Ifestio". The critical acclaim received for her first publication as well as the publicity in magazines and readings on cultural radio programs encouraged the author to fully peruse her passion for literature. The most critical component of her literature is a lyrical vain which links the ancient and contemporary traditions, with cohesion and worldliness that differentiates her as an authentic artist of the present and future.
Published books : "Brishtësi" , publisher "Emal" – 2010; "Vrullimi i flakës", publisher "LNSHA" – 2014; "Nëntë detet e Orfeut", publisher "Lena Grafik"- Pristina 2016; "Shegët pëlacasin nga vetmia", publisher "Klubi i Poezisë" – Tirana; "Terminal", publisher "Klubi i Poezisë" – Tirana 2020; "Terminal", second edition publisher "Prokult Press" – Pristina 2021.

Translated by Merita Paparisto

Earthquake on Minoa's kingdom

I passed the threshold of horns
Minoa, sweetly waits for me
there are no servants around
I don't ask what's happening
look how I grabbed your glass,
how I went in to your cellar
look how I drank the wine of your heart
I healed the places that were hurting

Oh…
I heard your deep cry,
your moan pierced the sky,
because there was no hope in life
from your wife, Pacifai
both of us, hugged and cried
our nails were plunged into flesh
like that, mistreated, and hurt
until the palace became a ruin ….!

Orpheus gaze

I cannot
die Orpheus
because
I have in my chest
the arrow
of you gaze…
After the ceturies
no one waits
for your beheaded
head
at the sea shore…
You must come
you must
Orpheus
I have to hear
your last song…
………………
Even
if you don't sing for me Orpheus
I will still love you
because I know, I know Orpheus
you cannot give away your soul
without me there.

Shikdar Mohammed Kibriah
(Bangladesh)

Shikdar Mohammed Kibriah. Poet, essayist and story writer. He was born in 1968 at vill: kachpurai, post: Goala Bazar, upozilla: Osmaninagar, Dist: Sylhet, Bangladesh. He has been writing for 3 decades and his published books are 15. Among them 6 of poems, 6 essays and 3 stories. He's M.A in philosophy and professionally a teacher.

He is settled in his village home

Hybrid Dreams-1

My native world has worn a chador
Woven by soft thread of dreams, and
Just explored a vast green steppe,
Brightened a late afternoon, where
A zigzag already gone into the dark
belly of foggy dusk.
Having compact with the phenomena
The sleepy swamp, its marsh-paddy
Complete their last holy ablution, and
After evening prayer they are likely to
Lying in the arm of nature.
Vanishing fog I'm running to be absorbed
In a dreamy warmth and break traditional
darkness with a self-intimacy absolutely.

Hybrid Dream-2

Waveless wintry river alike a sleepyhead wife,
Boatmen paddle unwillingly shivering in cold.
Leaving aside sobbing water, sleepy storks,

Marshy paddy and human habitation
I'm, a post-modern Adam, going to be
immigrant in hybrid dreams.
Making an unthinkable garland in the sky
How the migratory birds fly
like that I have come here in this winter evening
To peddling dreams into the human colonies of
The world.
Obviously I'm a dream-hawker.
Have a dreamy warmth.

Do you think what's the colour of my chador
And how its comfort. Look at my coffee cup.
What could you see?
Greening warmth flying in the air and swamp,
stork, marsh-paddy, boatman, human beings
All of the things are floating in my dreams.

Pure Father

Here life is nothing but a shameless woman
Standing in a blind narrow lane who colours
Her lips with painful bloody rose of bad luck.

Art of toiling life makes a shortcut bargain
Ravings of night vomits a darker dirty dawn
To be prepared for another upcoming night.

Modern city walks through a tiring darkness.
Still tries to find out a meaning of noise and
Suddenly boxes in the air to have offloaded.

When I will be eighty-over and cover my face
With ashen sky or grey water wets my chest
Right then you, ideal leader will be emerged!

Then that of the good days as if our children
Could find the minimum means of existence.

Shanita Vichare (India)

Prof. Shanita Vichare is a well known academician, International bi-lingual poet, reviewer and author from Pune has been honoured by Gujarat 'Sahitya Academi World's most active forum in the world. has conferred this title on her.

She has been writing in many international journals and has maintained a high bench mark. Aneeta pursues an eclectic style in her penmanship and is Swell appreciated as a poet in International arena. She has published her poems internationally and in India. On 15th Aug 2020, she has received "Gujarat Sahitya Academy Award-India".
She explores the women of India in her narrative form and her social status, in her themes. Nature remains one of her major motif in poems and writings. Her Poems have appeared in Egypt, Albania & Greece in Europe's highly esteemed journal, "AtniusPoetry.com".
Aneeta Chitale is her Pen name for Shanita Vichare

Rhapsody!

By the fenugreek twigs-
When the humming bird calls
The rice pods sways
Deep in the mud beds

Cascades tumble by the
Hillside dale
Gamut of stars
Afloat on the clouds!

As the sunsets
The mind rests
In sweet repose
In quietude....
As one traverses....

The leaves, gently caress
By the hand as
The steps hasten
Azimuth!

The chestnut bend
The solemn traveller
Passes by-
In rhapsody!

Devi

God in his wisdom was fascinated by her, he made her according to his vision and devotion God immersed his divine magical brushes and coloured her in fantastical hues, she emerged in ten avatars!

Sun God wanted to bring her down, to turn the cosmic time, her womb to fill the earth with love and care, so she was made in the image of a mother- soft and benevolent....

She emerged as Goddess Saraswati, the goddess of knowledge to read the secret scriptures. She emerged from the ocean, as Goddess Laxmi! In the image of wealth and bountiful She was threatened by the demons and ghosts, So She emerged as Durga!

To Kill the demonic powers who had lived since ions, she faught like a 'Chamundi' The Goddess who devoured the devils & inhuman forms to illuminate the truth!

She still rises from the 'Jatas' of lord Shiva who stays in heavenly abode of Himalayas!

Shoshana Vegh (Israel)

Shoshana Vegh was born in Israel in 1957. She wrote poetry and diaries from an early age. Still, destiny meant writing to her in the wake of bereavement, and she started writing when her brother Tuvia was killed in 1974 in an accident at his military service. She graduate B.A and M.A in Hebrew literature. Her poems were published in an anthology in 1980. In 2000, she published her first novel, about the infatuation of a married woman on the Internet. In 2002 her second novel was published, and later poetry and children's books were published over the years. In 2009, she founded a publishing house called "Pyutit" that specializes in publishing poetry books. She wrote 17 books herself and edited over 100 books, poetry, and prose. She was awarded a scholarship from the House of the President of the State of Israel for her first poetry book, "The Coming of Madness." For the book "Sad Ones" from the Israel Foundation's scholarship.

Like a rose

I am like a rose flower
You never get to see all my colors
Inside me many beautiful Stamens
That you want to taste
Is you mouth and heart are equal my love
When you call me honey at night
Do you think about me
When you say i can make you sleep
Is it me who you are waiting for
Or my shadow the reflect in many shades

I am like a rose flower
Don't take me out of my garden

And after throw me at your home
I want to bloom at my garden
And to show my beauty to all
When you make love to me
Just be with me
And don't think about my garden
I am the rose garden
My love

Fraud

When you came across me
I thought the light in you
I didn't feel that you prepare
To still all that I have
First you took my heart
I saw only you
I couldn't open my eyes to the trap
And step by step you preoare
Your bullets to kill me
In the rikushet
As I saw the reall
Meaning of desire
I understand you always saw
Throw me the potential
To have another life
But you never had the chance
To go inside the new world
Because I realised before
The sunrise
You are just a fraud

Shurouk Hammod (Syria)

Shurouk Hammod born in 1982, a Syrian poetess, editor and literary translator, BA of arts graduate and a master degree graduate of text translation, Damascus University.
She has three published poetry collections in Arabic language and two published poetry collection in English titled: The night papers and Blind time, which is translated and published in Serbian and Macedonian languages. Her poetry has been translated into 13 languages. And she has translated 14 books so far, in addition to poems by more than 35 poets from around the world.

The poem I did not want to write

I am damaged, my dear!

I was not kidding when I said to you:
My heart is a matchbox that was wetted by tears.
My eyes are an hourglass
Time runs out in
whenever shadows of love pass in front of them.
I am damaged in an unfamiliar way,
So don't try to be my Night's Knight
Who comes on the Moon Horse;
I am tired of looking at the sky
as a sunflower.
And I buried my compass
so that the directions would not stammer in my head like a time bomb
Then I recover from my ice
That keeps me alive
Like a corpse.

Fake life of a real person

I joined parties I knew nothing about
I attended the Communists Meetings
Just because my friends asked me to spend longer time with them,
I celebrated Nowruz with the Kurds
and danced around the fire
like an Indian
Also just because I liked them.
I attended discussion seminars about books I have not read
because I like to sneak out silently to smoke a cigarette.
Fate gifted me many nightmares that I used to tell to everyone
under the pretext of interpretation
And the truth is, I don't care about interpretation as I care for the pleasure I feel
When all people turn to be the closest to my empty heart.

I flirt my sorrows

I flirt my nightmares
Pat their shoulders
Invite them to all my poetry-reading sessions
and let them sit in the first row as the closest friends.
Of course they did not hear of ingratitude,
So they share the same eagerness
crown me as their first priority,
Telling me stories I thought I had forgotten,
Dancing with my past on the stairs of tomorrow,
And as they feel the pulse of frost in my body,
They sing to me
Their stubborn songs
In order not to sleep.

Shodiya Sultonova (Uzbekistan)

Shodiya Sultonova was born in Yangibozor district, Khorezm region of Uzbekistan in 1979. Her books "The Station of Soul", "Image of Boredom" "Destination of Happiness" and "My Dearest Parents" were published. She writes both in poetry and fiction. Her poems included in International Anthologies.

***

Are you sleeping?
Did the hair of extraneous,
pervade your eyes and face?..
Your love that you depreciated before,
Did you remember her?!
I realize…
You stand up,
Directly,
While hiding the whoop in the cage of soul,
You wander inside your room,
The bitter smoke of tobacco!
No, it's not a tobacco's smoke,
The fumes of the burnt love!

***

It's dawning.
The sun sets. Life is passing.
The crown of misery that I am wearing,
I live quietly behind the door,
The black guard called "solitude".
It follows me wherever I move,
And it impales its spear ceaselessly.
When I went back home closing my door,
The dagger returns to my heart again!..
It's dawning.
The sun sets. Life is passing.
Days, give me a hope, could I fly?
While surviving in the world of torments,
Could I embrace the world of happiness?!

EXPECTATION

I waited for a long, so long,
I lived awake in at nights.
While following my heavy hope,
Spring blooms in my hair.
The river of torments on my eyes,
There is a moan on my throat.
My soul gets hurt by its pain,
It's not a heart but the cactus!
What a pity! The unlucky destiny,
It doesn't let us to be together.
The last tear became an ice,
Eyelashes wore the robe of hoarfrost.

I waited for a long, so long...

Teresa Jolanta Podemska – Abt (Australia)

Teresa Jolanta Podemska – Abt is a philologist, poet-writer, translator and a researcher-member of Australian Institute of Aboriginal and Torres Strait Islander Studies (AIATSIS). She holds PhD, BEd, MEd (course/w) and MA degrees from Unis of South Australia, Adelaide and Wrocław. She creates in many genres, won a range of literary and academic prizes and has been internationally published in Poland, Australia, Canada and US (Text Matters, Odra, Nowe Media, Czas Kultury, Rozmowy o Komunikacji, Postscriptum Polonistyczne, Rita Baum, Tygiel Kultury, Poezja dzisiaj, Winter in Australia, Contemporary Poetry, On life's Path, Poetrix, Love postcards, Kosmos Literatów, Metafora Współczesności, Inter, and many more). Her short stories, poetic prose and interviews also appear in such publishing websites as Polska Canada, Wydawnictwo j, Culture Avenue, Kobieta 50 plus, Puls Polonii, Przegląd Australijski, Polish Currier.

She authored books of prose and selections of poetry (e.g. Spaces of literary Wor(l)ds and Reality. Interpretation and reception of Aboriginal Literature, Składam człowieka, Żywe sny, Pomieszały mi się światy, Świat tubylców australijskich, to name a few). Her newest poetic play is going to be staged by the Old Theatre in Adelaide in March 2021. She is a proud mother of a jazz musician and an academic Kamil Abt.

writing with a character of non-Australian heritage
deliberations; for my father

I was in a hurry to get to the country
where time was born
beyond the seas
where in the crowns of trees
from forevermore hides the divine azure of mundane paradise

and from time immemorial a rainbow serpent watches
tall Walamanggara
first noticed
how far I moved away from my home

surprised by my appearance
in silent abyss of their land
the Walamanggara trees sobbed over me
with their own memory
of persistence
and a frantic death dance
the Mindiri
relate that the only one saved
later did eat here the first rabbit

in autumn
the first great mothers-goannas of the forefathers
celebrate
near the great water
the last dancer is immersed by eternal Dreaming
where the big-headed ant returns human remains to the earth
on paths of reconciliation
sky-high trees Walamanggara
wake a primaeval dream

from the depths of earth's enormity
a being as old as the world straining its eyes peeps into my soul
full of new power
I fall into dreaming
of the rocking with stories Walamanggara
as if a first woman woven from cobweb fogs
a river below rivers
forever hungry for my first name
I hear the speech of germinating grains

Whatever will be whatever will happen there is still love
whispers of lost words from my home flow to me
the winter's aura of the old sand clock ticktocks as if
from my home where the dreams of my great-great-grandfathers

fell asleep
although at the end of any song there is clarity
my great grandmother didn't escape death during the war
the sister of my grandmother didn't save her life
and I instead of dreaming of heavenly bluebird in my soul
was once copying my father's letters sent home from Auschwitz
I have no more land than my foot's length tiptoeing I love you and life

the Walamanggara trees lowered their hands helplessly
in their shade no one has so far told
about graves
of white wanderers from there
behind my back the red horizon
lazily chatters with Cosmos
unmoved by earthly stories
and crosses
that separate

embedded in the vastness
of fleetingness
I an eternal vagrant with no guilt
have lost here my name haggling it for a bit of else
and yet I will never be able to say
that under the slender Walamanggara trees
sang for me
even for one and only one time
moja Matka

Tadeusz Zawadowski (Poland)

Tadeusz Zawadowski – a Polish poet, editor, critic; born on 9.12.1956 in Łódź, since 1981 has been living in Zduńska Wola, where he was a co-founder of Literary Club "Poplar" and Artistic Creation Work Club "Without Aureole". Member of Polish Writers' Union. Awarded about 250 prizes in both Polish and international writing competitions and got many literary rewards. He is an author of more than 1500 publications in Polish, emigration and foreign literary magazines. His poems, critic essays were published in about 250 anthologies. They were also translated into following languages: Russian, Latvian, Croatian, Bosnian, Serbian, Slovenian, Greek, Italian and English. The author of 17 poetry books.

THE ART OF COUNTING TREES

I am in the woods
counting trees
it is good to count trees
when you cannot count people

moles on a meadow
dig pits
people also dig pits
under people

trees grow
upwards
people increasingly
fall upon
themselves

CHILDISH PRAYER

my childhood barefoot
run out on a meadow
as happy as a blackbird's voice
wet with dew
how I miss you
crying to heaven

LOVE BORDERS
To Ewa

I love you most in all worlds. no matter
which I am about to be in a moment. in each beyond borders of
comprehension. it is impossible to close love
in the grid of meridians and parallels put on
telescope eyes of scholars. to limit with
atmosphere or lithosphere. one world is too little
to hold something

borderless

IT IS OVER

shelves with books
taken off the wall

some homeless guy
is wearing my sweater

it is over

Tatiana Koshkina (Russia)
Nickname - Tatiana Vk

She is a poet, prose writer, essayist. Member of the Writers' Union of Northern America.
She was born in Russia, Tyumen region. Lives in Russia and the USA. The author of poems "My happiness is all in you alone" ("Publishing solutions", Russia, 2015), "Heavens' Watercolors" (Lulu, USA, 2018), a collection of short stories and reports "My eyes" ("Steklograf", Moscow, 2020). Tatiana also writes short and fantastic stories, fairy tales for children and adults, sketches and reports about her traveling experience in America, Mexico, France, Russia, etc. Participant of poetry festivals in the Crimea, Moscow, Siberia, Azerbaijan, Belarus.

Two Angels with the Wings Divine

I don't want to hurt you, even slightly,
I want your touches and your gentle strokes.
I want us to be bound tightly
With unobtrusive yarn of final hopes.

I want your arms to hold me when I sleep,
I want to wake up with a tender laughter,
To merge with you and let my soul leap
With happiness this day and many after.

I want to listen to your heart and then to know
That I'm the dearest treasure in your vault
When winter covers our heads with snow
And our flight comes to a sudden halt.
I don't want to fear the day
When comes the herald

Showing you the way...

There will be two — two angels with the wings divine
Which will above us in the heaven shine.

Rowans and Lilac

The old prophecy, made by the raven,
Said I would have to go far away.
Now Russia is not my last haven,
And I grieve every night, every day.

Rowans, bushes of lilac, my granny
And her cat are the guests of my dreams.
It gets dark here early; each cranny
Is invaded with ocean's screams.

Every dream is a thorn; I can hear
Birches wisp'ring to me every night...
Stop it, birches! There are palm trees here,
I must now love them — am I right?

Tareq al Karmy (Palestine)

Tareq al Karmy, 1975, a Palestinian poet from the city of Tulkarm.
He published 11 poetry files so far. Plays a Nay flute.
His poems have been translated into various languages and he has participated in local and international poetry festivals. Al Karmy's poems attempt to write poems without ending, in a way that creates a deliberate interruption in the poem, leaving space for the reader to engage in writing the ending of the poem and leaving him space for imagination.
This is a unique and unusual act in the landscape of Palestinian poetry that makes al Karmy one of the most interesting young voices in contemporary Palestinian poetry.

The smoky morning night

Asleep while asleep the piano
It's breath stagnates in the corner
from the living room
I will put on the earth
In order to climb
Up to you
Panting breath from the piano
On the staff lines
The lines that look like
On the rails of the train that crosses you
On this smoky morning.

I want a dream to die in the sunset

Where Twilight is an absolute wine bar
I want to die in the Twilight Bar
And near my mare, which is a taoist running the earth
By my horse, which has the hair and braids
I have loved one day
Give me my delicious death.

The moment is a warm cold

Taking in your shower from weeping clouds
and from the milky rain
The pouring rain will bury us under the sheet
Up to the knees
I'll catch you virgin tonight
Where the iron softens, and the reed softens
It is life babbling at the door of my time
Come, for the stones of my house smelt
cold like the teeth of a horse
come.
You are my heater
And my bones are firewood.

* Evening / winter Tulkarem

Taghrid Fayad (Lebanon)

Taghrid Fayad is a Lebanese poetess, but she was born in Kuwait and stayed there for a while. She had published there, her first articles and short stories, in Kuwaiti newspapers at the age of 13. After that she had moved to Beirut, and studied there: 1- English Literature and translation- 2- Psychology (Clinical) -3- Media. She later moved to Egypt in 2005, and is still living there. She is a poetess, a writer, and a translator. She has published 3 poetry books, and a short stories book, in Cairo, and became a member of the Egypt Writers Union. Taghrid is planning to publish her first novel, a fourth poetry book, in addition to her first poetry book in English "Follow your Dreams". She had established a cultural forum in Cairo, since 2015, that is held on monthly basis. It discusses important cultural, artistic, literary, in addition to some educational issues, through the first part of the event, then continues with a poetic and musical evening, in the second half. A lot of poets, writers, artists, journalists, diplomats, academic experts in various fields, and educated people from different Arab and African countries have participated in its sessions.

As Simple as That

The day usually ends,
As simple as that!
The sun usually rises,
As simple as that!
The sky is blue, as the sea is too!
Simple facts,
In our system they are!
Which nobody can change,
As simple as that!

She the dreaming soul,
Dreamt once to change!
To replace colors!
To grow trees in the clouds!
To braid the sun's rays,
As a crown!
To engulf people with love!
To do all that was to her,
As simple as that!
She did not notice,
That waking up, can vanish dreams,
As simple as that!
And can hurt even more,
As simple as that!!

Definition

Being in love...is the second turn to hell..!!
Being in love is the softest...weakest case of all...
To be in love, is to open a hole for all...!!!
All pain...all joy...all suffering...all happiness!!
And the most of all...all hope...!!!
Being in love is the next turn to hell...
Since living is the first wide gate...
Being in love is the second worst thing in life...
Since marriage is the first worst thing...!!!
To be in love, means having no choices
Of to be or not to be...!!!
Love is the tempest...that does it all...!!!

Tuğçe Tekhanlı (Cyprus)

Tuğçe Tekhanlı was born in 1990 in Nicosia, Cyprus. She has done her bachelor's degree at the department of English-French Translation and Interpreting at Hacettepe University. She got her postgraduate certificate from the University of East Anglia in the UK.

Her poems and translations were published in many literary magazines. Her poems were translated into various languages; Spanish, English, Italian, Greek, Romanian, and German.

In 2016, she has been awarded the bi-communal poetry prize with the poetry portfolio titled 'Derindim İnandırıldım Aksine'. The bilingual book (Turkish-Greek) including her portfolio and Andreas Timotheou's portfolio was published in the same year with the name 'Şiirler' by the Cyprus
Writers Union.

In 2017, 'Şiirden First Book Award' organized by Şiirden Publishing in Turkey, was granted to her same portfolio 'Derindim İnandırıldım Aksine' and the portfolio was republished by Şiirden in 2018, in Istanbul, Turkey.

She participated in many international poetry festivals and art projects.

Her poems appeared in an anthology called "Women Poetry" which was published by KAFEKÜLTÜR Publishing House in Turkey and later in 2018, in another anthology called "Anthology of Young Cypriot Poets" by the Publishing House Vakxikon in Athens, Greece.

In 2020, with her poems and translations she contributed to the anthology which was published in Spain and Cyprus with the name of POESIA SIN FRONTERAS V (SINIRSIZ ŞİİRLER V).

In July 2020, in Italy, her poetry has been considered remarkable for the International Poetry Prize Europa in Versi.

She is also interested in dance and seeking ways to combine dance and poetry as a form of collaborative art.

NE ME QUITTE PAS*

summer is still away from me
so the songs
the bow and the notes

I am stringing the jasmines
and the roses
the goodmornings
the things that I can not hide
like your fingers

your hands are playing a cello, flowing
they are on my belly
in my childhood photograph in which I didn't smile at all

accepting someone as they are
is sometimes away from me

je t'inventerai
des mots insensés
que tu comprendras

CONSIDER ME A BIRD

do not kiss me here
carry me to the forest
consider me a bird
foraging your beard

© Giorgio Fileni (Italy) Magma 70×90 Aplikacion stof e akrelik në telajo   https://www.premioceleste.it/giorgio.fileni

Giorgio Fileni was born in Chiaravalle (An) in 1957. He has always shown a predisposition for color and painting. He took part in collective and personal exhibitions in various Italian and European cities. Among the many awards he has received there are: "Special Mention for Excellence" at the 2013 Biennale of Chianciano, "La Palma d'Oro for" Art "of Monte Carlo , "International Art Award Virgil - Artist in History". Fileni is an artist always committed to experimenting, with his latest works he focuses on a technic made with feathers. The artist in search of lightness puts his tormented soul on "Pillows of feathers", and after he free his sensations in wings of colored feathers that fly towards new horizons, colorful perceptions of lightness that take flight of his creativity in the "Feathers flying ". His paintings are part of private collections in Italy and abroad.

Dr. Verónica Valadez LÓPEZ
(México)

Originally from San Francisco del Rincón, Guanajuato, Mexico. Bachelor of Communication Sciences and Master of Education. Journalist for 25 years at Diario A.M; creator and editor of the magazine "Amigos"; winner on two occasions of the "Golden Sun" by the National Circle of Journalists. Announcer and Speaker. Honorable Mention and Finalist of the Contest the 64th International Poetry and Narrative Contest 2019 of Junín, Buenos Aires, Argentina; participant of the Anthologies "Letras por el mundo 2019" and "Autores Selectos 2019" in Argentina, winner of the 2nd. Place of the Poetry Contest in Venado, Argentina, recognition in the "Poetry of the Pilar Contest", Spain. Distinction as "Teacher-Writer" by the H. Ayuntamiento de San Francisco del Rincón. Representative of Mexico in the V International Poetry Festival of Madrid 2019 and participant of the International Anthology "De thousand aromas", Winner of the 1st Place of Poetry, in the International Short Story and Poetry Competition of Peru 2020. Appointment as Sunflower Woman Ambassador by the Spanish Association Absorvaex, Member of the Union of Writers of the World Nations Kazakhstan, Doctor Honoris Causa by International Forum Creativity and Humanity of Morocco and Mil Mentes por México, and Member of the World Literature Academic.

HUMMINGBIRD

Flapping like hummingbird wings
I vibrate with delicate aromas of the soul
I motivate my dance of gods in your belly of madness
And I dance to the sound of your steps manifesting sweetness.

As the hummingbird absorbed your honeys
You are a flower that causes my thirst to love you
I suck every detail from you

I drink you, breathe you and stir my waters until you are exhausted.

I am legendary in your adventures and seas
And hummingbird that appears as a ray of sunlight on your body
I slide down your waist while I drink
And I take care of you like a virginal and new path.

I offer you my colors
I fill you with my flavors
I am a hummingbird, that among your skies I rise
And hummingbird ... that I go crazy on your flights.

WRITE POETRY

Write poetry, not just to rhyme the soul
Write poetry to feel and vibrate
Write beautiful words to let out the best of you.
Let go of the expression, let it flow
Memories, loves, passions and angers
Let words do for you what you cannot make come true,
let your expression lead you to create new worlds
New sensations and forbidden themes.

Add charm to your smile, turn it into Mona Lisa
Or make it the Great Wall of China just by expressing it in words.
Vibrate in the power of creation, vibrate with illusion
May your words be the song of the bird that trills
May your emotion be the caress that animates
And that love is manifested through your words.
Laugh, cry, sing, dream ... write poetry,
And you will know what it is to live in complete harmony.

Viacheslav Kupriyanov (Russia)

Viacheslav Kupriyanov studied in the High Navy School in Leningrad, graduated in 1967 from the Moscow Foreign Languages Institute (1967). Freelance writer, a member of the Russian & Serbian Writers Unions. He has published several collections of his own poetry and prose. He is a principal strategist of contemporary poets of free verse in Russia. Prize of Poetry International in Gonnesa (Italia), 1986; European Literature Prize, 1988, Yugoslavia. "Branko-Radicevic-Prize", 2006, Serbia. Bunin-Prize, 2010, Russia; "Mayakovsky-Prize", 2011, Moscow. "Poet of the Year 2012", Russia. Prize "European Atlas of Poetry" 2017, Respublika Serbska. Yugra-prizes, Khanty-Mansijsk, Russia, 2018; Naji Naaman literary prizes, 2018 (Japan/Libanon).). Last Russian book – "Controversies" ("Protivorechiya"), BSG-press, 2019.

RUSSIA'S DREAM

Russia sleeps in cold dew
and dreams
that it is America:
its chatterers are congressmen
its loafers are the unemployed
its hooligans are gangsters
its drunkards are drug addicts
its profiteers are businessmen
its Russians are Blacks
and it must fly to the Moon

Russia awakens in cold sweat
everything appears to be in place
chatterers are chatterers
loafers are loafers

hooligans are hooligans
Russians are Russians
only it must land
in the right place

and Russia again falls asleep
and stirs a Russian idea –
that America sleeps and dreams
that it is Russia

Translated from Russian by Dasha Nisula (USA, West Michigan Uni)

HUMAN LOVE

The terrible attraction
to strangers

The fear like a burden
of how to be
with your loved one

O the solemn certainly
of plants!

Their love
they have entrusted
to the insects
the birds
and the wind

Translated from Russian by Steve Holland

Vesna Mundishevska-Veljanovska
(North Macedonia)

Vesna Mundishevska-Veljanovska (born in 1973 in Bitola) is a member of the Macedonian Writers' Association, Macedonian Science Society – Bitola and Bitola's Literary Circle. She is the author of 13 books of poetry, two books of critical-essay texts, co-author of a book of poems for children and the author and co-author of 6 vocational books for teachers. Her poetry has been translated into many languages. She is represented in anthologies. She has won the award for the unpublished debut book of poetry (Literary Youth of Macedonia, 1994) for the book "In a dream – dream", the "Karamanov" award (Radovish, 2007) for the book "Vibrations of the Spirit", the award of the Macedonian Writers' Association for the best poem at the international "Linden Festival" (Skopje, 2016), first prize and jubilee plaque at the international Slavic translation competition (Russia, 2017), Macedonian Science Society's award for scientific and educational contribution in 2018, the award "Branuvanja" for the best poem at the Festival "Struga Literary Encounters" (Struga, 2019), the award "Literary Circle" for unpublished book of literary rewies (Bitola, 2020) and other awards. She is editor of the Journal of Culture – Literature, Drama, Film and Publishing – "Sovremeni dijalozi"/ "Contemporary Dialogues" (Macedonian Science Society), a member of the Macedonian Science Society' Ethics Committee, and was the editor of the literary journal "Rast"/ "Growth", editor-in-chief of the Journal "Contemporary Dialogues", editor and editor-in-chief of the bulletins "Plima", "Izrek" and "Razgledi", and editor of more then thirty poetry books and collections. She was president of the Literature and Culture Association "Razvitok" – Bitola and of the Literary Youth of Macedonia – Bitola, as well as secretary of the Writers' Association "Bitola's Literary Circle". She has performed at numerous literary events. She has become Ambassador of Peace in Cercle Universel Des Ambassadeurs De La Paix – Suisse/France since 2016.

VIRTUAL REALITY

In canoes, galleys and boats
people without vision
crisscross the glazed arches.

They are proudly pounding
on transparent floors
selling
(in)visible democracy,
(un)conditional freedom,
uh…,
open-mindness,
no-mindness,
mindness,
mind,
but…
stOP
!
Shhhhhhhh!

A finger
twisted and pointed
in parallel repetition
of undefined geometry
of round(ed) collision
of annular species and fence walls,
vibrates a new vision…
……….and………………………..
what if we were just decorative fish
in the aquarium
of some another dimension?

Vesna Andrejić Mišković (Croatia)

Vesna Andrejić Mišković was born on July 10, 1964. in Kruševac, Serbia. She grew up and was educated in Trstenik,(a small town on the banks of the West Morava), and lived for 38 years in Slavonski Brod, Croatia. She now works as a caregiver for the elderly and infirm in Karlsruhe, Germany. Behind it, three independent collections of reflective poetry have been published. She has also published her works in over 220 international and joint collections and anthologies. Some of her poems have been translated into nine foreign languages. In addition to writing poetry, Vesna also writes prose but a short form-haiku. She has won several valuable awards in Serbia, Croatia, Italia and around the world.

THE SECRET OF RIPE APPLES

And so the moment came
when among the snowflakes
stray ripe apples
from lonely years,
and barely holding on
for frozen clouds
keep the secret
of hidden dreams.

Watching them
I wanted to skip
a vault full of doubts
but she must have slipped
clutching a dry branch

thinking that there
is salvation in her.

She released all the birds
from the cages
and sang a lullaby
a grain of sand
making my eye itch,
and these restless hair
taught the east wind
to make thin strings
musical instruments
on the horizon.

I outgrow my stature now
all suspension bridges
and touching with ease
heavenly lat,
I pick apples
among the snowflakes
stacking them in a basket
of intertwined dreams.

Biting loose soil
(like Antigone)
I acknowledge
the universe and myself,
that I became myself
one of the apples
which may be (not) damaged
fell out of the lap
of unrequited love.

Wansoo Kim (South Korea)

Wansoo Kim achieved Ph. D. in English Literature from the graduate school of Hanguk University of Foreign Studies. He was a lecturer at Hanguk University of Foreign Studies and an adjunct professor at Incheon Junior College for about 20 years.
He has published 7 poetry books, one novel, and one book of essays. One poetry book, "Duel among a middle-aged fox, a wild dog and a deer" was a bestseller in 2012, one page from the book of Letters for Teenagers was put in textbooks of middle school (2011) and high school (2014) in South Korea, and four books (Easy-to-read English Bible stories, Old Testament (2017), New Testament (2018) and Teenagers, I Support your Dream) were bestsellers. He was granted a Rookie award for poetry at the magazine of Monthly Literature Space in South Korea, and the World Peace Literature Prize for Poetry Research and Recitation, presented in New York City at the 5th World Congress of Poets (2004). He published poetry books, "Prescription of Civilization" and "Flowers of Thankfulness" in America (2019), received Geum-Chan Hwang Poetry Literature Prize in Korea (2019) and International Indian Award (literature) from WEWU (World English Writer's Union) (2019). He published "Heart of God" in America (2020).

Children of Talebans

Teenagers
That even the blood of all desires is dried
By a whip of scary hunger every day
Hang all the hope of their life in Talebans' hands
Hung on the bait of free bread and free study.

Talebans light
A fire of hostility
In the heart of innocent children
With the brutal video
That Westerners killed Muslims.

They also light a fire of proud martyrdom in the children's heart
That a suicide bombing to aim at Westerners
Is the glorious way
To receive the eternal Heaven as a gift.

The children
Load the technique to make a bomb jacket and to kill people
In their heart blazing with hostility and martyrdom
And hurl all their life.

Even this moment a lot of children
With bombs wrapped around all their body as a band of glory
At a single motion
Burn their bud bright with jewels of their dream
And fly away reduced to ashes.

Classroom of Elementary School in Iraq

Sparkling eyes,
Which sit gathering
In the classroom
That has few desks and chairs,
Plant seeds of hope
In their hearts.

They write the teacher's words
In their hearts
Without the blackboard,
Books, and notebooks.

The booming of missiles
That often comes into hearing

Shakes the seeds of their dream to the roots
Tearing the childlike innocence of their heart.

During breaktime
Or when school is over,
Children, playing with the abandoned weapons like toys,
Are mortally wounded
In the sprout of their bright and untainted soul,
Or the whole blueprint of their life
Flies away in pieces.

Politics : I'll kneel

From now on,
However hard and painful I am,
I won't draw the rainbow about you
Nor will I raise the voice of complaint and resentment.

From now on,
I won't turn my back nor will I avoid your eye
Like the couple in whom the dregs of disappointment and anger
Has been piled up for many years.

From now on,
Even though you do hateful or evil deeds,

I'll become a mother with a sickly child,
Hug you shedding tears
Instead of a cane
And fold my hands falling to my knees
Worrying about your future.

Wang Mengren (China)

Wang Mengren is a famous poet and calligrapher in contemporary China, and he was born in 1959 in Fugou County, Henan Province, China. He is a member of Chinese Writers' Association, of Chinese Calligraphers' Association, a committee member of Henan Provincial Literary Federation, director of Henan Provincial Writers' Association and Henan Provincial Calligraphers' Association, vice president and secretary general of Henan Provincial Prose-Poetry Society, honorary lifetime president of Zhoukou Municipal Calligraphers' Association, and part-time professor of Zhoukou Normal College. His works have been carried on professional magazines such as People's Literature, People's Daily, Poetry Periodical, The Star Poetry, etc. He has won a special gold prize at the 2nd "New Demeanor Cup" Love Poetry Competition hosted by Poetry Monthly; the title of "excellent writer of prose-poetry in contemporary China" in 2007, Boundless Grassland literary prizes in 2013 and 2015, Poetry Monthly annual poetry (prose-poetry) prizes in 2013 and 2014, the Heavenly Horse Prize at the 11th Chinese Prose-Poetry Competition in 2017, the 4th annual prize (prose-poetry) of the Shandong Poets in 2018, and the 18th Lebanon International Literature Prize. He has published Literary Writings in My Humble Abode (in 9 volumes), The Writing of the Plain, and The Singer of the Plain, etc. Some of his poems have been translated into English, Italian, German, French, Spanish, Tamil, Japanese, Korean, Greek, and Russian, etc.

Translated by Zhang Zhizhong

Self Portrait

To insert the last daubing and dying
Into the splash of ink and wash of the silk scroll of Song Dynasty
For me to gaze closely

The red leaf of autumn
Before snow falling in south China
To solitarily wash out the mien of youth

The beauty of fair hills and rills
Slowly sinks into the dexterous hands
Her painting brush
Only bows its slim shadow to classics
Only communicate mutual agreement
With lights on fishing boat and riverside maple trees

A masterpiece to be handed down from generation to generation
Is a stretch of heavy shadow
Like a flame upon another flame of life fire
After a grand spectacle
To return to the soul gradually

She is so novel and so sober
She is so penetrating and so safe and sound.

Solitary Angling on the River

The wind from south Fujian Province
Must have checked the elegant white of a rolling blossom
The rain of south China
Seems to be ready for a thick layer of moonlight
Partitioned by hangover of the preexistence
Looking at me
To sing a love song of the old version

An eyeful of the ink and wash chapping lines
Is a writing brush made of goat's hair which has been fragrant
Looking at the tranquil river
Dangling
Yearning
As well as wandering light and clouds which are full.

Wendy Mary Lister (UK)

Wendy Mary Lister's work has appeared in various Magazine and literary journals; Tips for Writers uk; Reach Poetry uk; PoetCrit literary journal India; Bridge-In-Making India; Enchanting verses and a Poetry journal in Albania, plus varied magazines in India. She has also interviewed and published reviews of established Poet / author K.K. Stivastava Poet/author. She has an avid interest in the arts and varied culture, heritage. She is English; presently living in the city of Glasgow, Scotland for the last 7 years.

Moments Before It Closes—

I come here,
just as Mondays breeze lifts,
under the vein of morning's
complexion

I look outside where
the sun slopes upwards,
and sprightly air
passes-by:
air checking-out the gap
in the window

A voice half-loops;
A type of thought between
silent vitality in sleep
and moveable navigation
as I wake
A moment hardly noticed,

before it eases-off, noting the tick
on the clock,
the coming back to
life—

Another day begins,
another day,
another daydream
Invites itself towards everything:
Life to come

Daylight shapes the wait,
against the opening sky,
where I imagine myself beyond
slanting trees

Living In Glasgow—

This city it doesn't sleep, it's colossal.
Its echo searches new identity;
I was once a rose, an ancient fossil.
A slave to passion-contemptuously

I am a dying-star, halfway to dust.
Sometimes I can infectiously chortle;
Yet, today-it's a case of do or bust—
Yesterday weary, a vicious circle

I go everywhere, I go nowhere —why.
I am sad, I am light, I'm in-between;
I've fragility of a butterfly,
I would love the eyes of a peregrine

If a teary eye can wash away pain,
A rested heart can breath new life again

Xi Ke (China)

Xi Ke, a famous poet in contemporary China, was born as Yang Weizhou in 1962 from a family of Chongxin ancestry in Gansu Province of China. He is a member of the Chinese Writers Association. He began to write poetry in the 1980s and went to Shenzhen to host the "Wandering Poets Poetry Exhibition" in the 1990s. In 2012, he was invited to Israel to attend the 32nd World Poets' Congress. His works have been published in a variety of journals, and his published poetry collections include The Bend of Ruihe River, The Bronze Pot, Old Forts, The Wind Bell, Some Days of Mine and Me, No Need to Say Goodbye to This Life, The Collection of Xi Ke Poems, Village Past (Chinese-English), etc., besides his prose collections The Valley, My Life Has Nothing to Do with You, I Still Live. Some of his poems have been translated into English, French, German, Russian, Arabic, Spanish, Japanese, Dutch, Ukrainian, Albanian and Korean, etc. He now lives in Xi'an.

The Last Nation in History

I bathe in the luster that is approaching the uncrowned king
Following the procedure of absolute notarization to recall
The scenes from this event and the historic riots
How did I get the infamy of adultery?
Honestly, I'm the kind of person brave enough to die for honor
You had infusion when you were a kid, right?
The medicine seeped into your bones
I turned around and looked in the direction where I came
History itself repeats itself, but the reactions are not the same
I was attending the funeral of the last elder and finished
The gruesome task of burying his remains in the grave
Let him be left alone in some glory

Dressing as casually as before
But his eyes remain firm and maintain an awe-inspiring demeanor

I feel indignant from the inside
The cab drivers tell shameless jokes
Taking the whole thing as a laughing stock and laughing loudly
Newspaper says golf pro had an affair with stage star
Married women and young men are often rumored to be in love
It's a great pity that precious time was wasted on slutty women
The number of bachelors is increasing
They indulge in lovemaking between lads and lasses
Flowers and chocolates taking turn
A place to stay with no family
Money will be extracted by the landlady who is more vicious than the stepmother
The group gathered in front of the seaside tavern mocking blatantly
I can't even remember the exact time
Anyway, it's after 5 AM, right?
I remember kids still play with dogs (breed unknown)
I suggest they go behind the dunes and do that shit

Slow down time!
It's time to leave, the nostalgic, fondly remembered Queen's family
In the next few days, I have to find out the whereabouts of all those who are still alive
In fact, who am I really?
Let XXX equal my real name and address
God is of Jewish origin
The heir of the loong comes from the Yellow River Basin
...
Literature, News, Posters ... Multiplexes and more
The car drivers look through the day's newspaper
My favorite book in my life is "One Thousand and One Nights"
Really, the bodies of stowaways were found on the beach again (Genders unknown)
I was ready to be released from that air of death
I walk with my arm holding the other's arm
Where to go? No answer
Anyway, we walked past the hillock full of stones and fires

There, the ruins of the city back then
Still cradled in the silent arms of time, sleeping soundly.
Immersed in the dream of green fields and new pastures
We both continued to hold arms
Through the People's Square and other places
Recalling desperately the pure and great music
I am familiar with Mozart's Twelfth Mass
And AAA and other first-class musical works
Not that kind of religious song
Eclipsing all the sounds of nature

The crowd calls out, the last cry
Sing it again, sing it again
In the midst of all the noise
I saw the face of a horse
A novel substance composed of bones and flesh different from horses
What a kind life it is
Knives and guns should be used to catch and kill whales
Lies should be believed when facing crocodile
The roster draws a new form on the snow
Ancient folk ballads of the East
Depicting the ocean under a clear sky
That horse went to the end of the city
I watched the stout figure shrinking in the distance

Translated by Brent O. Yan

Yuleisy Cruz Lezcano (Cuba –Italy)

Yuleisy Cruz Lezcano was born in Cuba.
Published works:
"Pensieri trasognati per un sogno", 2013; "Fra distruzione e rinascita: la vita" , 2014; "Diario di una ipocrita", 2014; "Vita su un ponte di legno", 2014; "Cuori Attorno a una favola", 2014; "Tracce di semi sonori con i colori della vita", 2014; "Sensi da sfogliare", 2014; "Piccoli fermioni d'amore", 2015; "Due amanti noi", 2015; "Credibili incertezze, 2016"; "Frammenti di sole e nebbia sull'Appennino, 2016"; "Soffio di anime erranti", 2017; Upcoming publications "Fotogrammi di confine" with the editing house 'Laura Capone' and "Inventario di cose perdute" with the editing house 'Leonida Edizioni'; "Tristano e Isotta. La storia si ripete" 2018 – SwanBook Edizioni; Demamah il signore del deserto – Demamah: el señor del desierto; 2019 – Monetti Editore.

Travel

Exists, they say,
a train that goes to Tozeur,
a train like a lightning
fallen onto a spike,
full of aromas,
of past flavors,
of forgotten steps
along the path of violets.
There is another train
and I ride alone,
pushed by the hand of a bird
in the blue transparency
from the sky.
Exists a journey in the mystery,
where each step is paid
with the wounds,

stuck to the mind.
Exists a trip of slow hours
used in readings and contemplations.
There is a body's trip,
through the emotions
of deep eyes
and of impulsive breaths.
We travel, we travel alive
in the red twilights
hidden in our veins.
Sometimes we travel
with full hands
of seeds with roots
that grow upwards;
sometimes we have to bend the knees
against the asphalt
to pray for a need,
that more than a dream,
It is a requirement,
That explodes in our world.

(Free Fall)

Given the heaven of Falls,
I want to fall,
Rain over your face,
Lifted from eyelashes
of a group of Dreams,
Dancers with Rhythm
Over your eyes
of few common places
and laughter of cravings.

Yordanka Getsova (Bulgaria)

Yordanka Getsova was born in Bulgaria. She grew up in Veliko Tyrnovo, where she studied mathematics in secondary school. In 1991 she graduated as a Landscape architect from the University of Forestry in Sofia. Since 1991 she has been working as a teacher in vocational secondary education at the School of Architecture, Construction and Geodesy in Plovdiv.
Ever since she was a child, she has had a profound interest in poetry and arts.
Yordanka Getsova is an author of one poetry book titled "Symbiosis" – 2011. By now her second book titled "Life without substitutes" is ready for print.
Yordanka's poetry was published in periodical press, almanacs with poetry by teachers-poets and lyric almanacs. Her poems have been translated and printed in Polish in the almanacs of Grupa artystyczna KaMPe in London.
Yordanka Getsova is a prizewinner of poetry competitions.
Yordanka is a member of the Society of Writers in Plovdiv.

Enlightenment

Who lives in blindness won't forgive
the miracles I tell.
If only did they listen to the rain,
dictating gently to the roadway
Sip of life – a dancing water spring –
coming from so far away glaciers.
The solid ground is conquered by the will
of fragile sprout of flower.
In the veins of oaks' leaves
the sun embroiders all day summer
lace of heavenly calligraphy –
the one who sees can read
the script of their destiny

and chooses to bear a cross for life.
I stand in wicked time for magic
And keep a grain of faith
in handful soil –
so no one steels it.

Hourglass

Staring at the grains
so steadily falling
I think: there's no need
to keep them in hand.
A newer kind of gravity I forge
to pledge for love.
So close I keep
your heart to mine,
while
with bare hands
for me you move the mountains.
I sew your shirt, by breath –
the summer breath,
what if the chestnuts
crash in the pavement…
How do I love? – can't tell –
brushing off snow
sprinkled in my hair.
Don't clear the passage to sunset –
I light up the dawn!
Sharp saved tear cuts my eyelid –
a speck of sand peeks from inside.

Translated into English by Savina Getsova

**Dr. Zejnepe Alili – Rexhepi
(North Macedonia)**

Dr. Zejnepe Alili – Rexhepi born on 16th janary 1973 in Tetovo, where she finished her primary school and gymnasium high school. In 1997 she finished her studies Albanian language and literature in Philological faculty at "St. Ciril & Methody" University in Skopje. In 2008 she assessed successfully the theme of the magistrate: "The woman's figure on the Sterjo Spasse's novel", at the Philological Faculty – Department of Philological Faculty University of Pristina, and gets the title – Magistrate of Philological Science, December 2009, she enroled the doctorate at the University "St.Cirili & Methody", in Skopje, on the theme: "The woman's characteristics on the characters of Migjeni & G. Flober's work" and successfully defended the Doctorate Dissertation on 14th June 2010.
She published poetical and scientics-literature works:
Peng loti (poetry), "Konica", Tetovo, 1998; Ëndërr shtegtuese (poetry), "Flaka", Skopje, 2000; Ujëvara e syrit (poezi), "Ars", Tetovo, 2007; Ëndërr shtegtuese (poetry, II edition), Tringa-desing, Tetovo, 2007; The woman's Figure at Sterjo Spasse's work (literature study), "Ars", Tetovo, 2009; Under Eros' power (poetry), "Ars", Tetovo, 2011; The woman at Migjeni and Flober (liter stu.), "Ars", Tetovo, 2011; Poetics of the narrative literature (stud. and analyse), Arbëria Desing, Tetovo, 2014.

More than nonchalance

Scattered hair after the rain..., half drunk
As a dreamer you come.

Under the forelock your sharp eyesight appears
As an emerald conjure,
Beyond observes the hard life
That carries as relic, rooms with solitude of centuries.
Silence speaks for the weather turbulence

Like the apostles in pictures confined.

Everytime the wind ruins your dream,
You snuggle in my soul
That accepts you very friendly!

Again you remain a foolhardy hermit,
Mum as mystery
Nonchalant in my sadness.

You run away where there is no fiery sight,
In slush of pain the silence turned you.

Woman's intuition

Suddenly you came as a star fallen from the sky,
The time when the season was rasp
In reel of dreams you glimmered.

Heaven and hell as in the journey of Dante
You recalled the memories, but not the longing,
In the soul meanders forworn eidolon
In parting, like the sudden arrival.

Nor does the world fall in oblivion without you
With pain that does not stop just now,
Again autumn, again storm!.

How much I would like this autumn was in parting,
There is lamentation and expectancy everywhere,
In fighting arena the dream hangs up...
Among her: a Man or a God?!

© Rajashree Mohapatra (India) Reflection "50 x 30", 2021
Rajashree Mohapatra is poet and painter. She devotes her time in painting. Being a Deploma in Fine Arts she has deeply studied the traditional paintings as a source of history. For her , painting is a mode of creative expression and can communicate souls and can play an important role in making of the society. Most of her paintings can be found on the cover page of prestigious Anthologies.